PENGUIN BOOKS

THE WEDDING GUESTS

Meredith Goldstein writes for the *Boston Globe* and is the author of its hugely popular advice column 'Love Letters', where she dishes out pearls of wisdom to the lovelorn. She was born in New Jersey and now lives in Massachusetts.

The Wedding Guests

MEREDITH GOLDSTEIN

PENGUIN BOOKS

PENGUIN BOOKS

Published by the Penguin Group
Penguin Books Ltd, 80 Strand, London WC2R ORL, England
Penguin Group (USA) Inc., 375 Hudson Street, New York, New York 10014, USA
Penguin Group (Canada), 90 Eglinton Avenue East, Suite 700, Toronto, Ontario, Canada M4P 2Y3
(a division of Pearson Penguin Canada Inc.)
Penguin Ireland, 25 St Stephen's Green, Dublin 2, Ireland (a division of Penguin Books Ltd)
Penguin Group (Australia), 250 Camberwell Road, Camberwell, Victoria 3124, Australia
(a division of Pearson Australia Group Pty Ltd)
Penguin Books India Pvt Ltd, 11 Community Centre, Panchsheel Park, New Delhi – 110 017, India
Penguin Group (NZ), 67 Apollo Drive, Rosedale, Auckland 0632, New Zealand
(a division of Pearson New Zealand Ltd)
Penguin Books (South Africa) (Pty) Ltd, Block D, Rosebank Office Park, 181 Jan Smuts Avenue,
Parktown North, Gauteng 2193, South Africa

Penguin Books Ltd, Registered Offices: 80 Strand, London WC2R ORL, England

www.penguin.com

First published in the USA as *The Singles* by Plume,
a member of Penguin Group (USA) Inc. 2012
First published in Great Britain as *The Wedding Guests* in Penguin Books 2012

001

Set in 12.75/16 pt Garamond MT Std
Typeset by Palimpsest Book Production Limited, Falkirk, Stirlingshire
Printed in Great Britain by Clays Ltd, St Ives plc

ISBN: 978-0-241-96036-3

www.greenpenguin.co.uk

Penguin Books is committed to a sustainable
future for our business, our readers and our planet.
This book is made from Forest Stewardship
Council™ certified paper.

ALWAYS LEARNING

PEARSON

For Lorraine Goldstein, the bookworm

The Wedding Guests

Twenty-nine-year-old bride-to-be Beth Eleanor Evans, a slender, freckled, strawberry blonde whom people called Bee because of her initials, stood in front of the whiteboard she'd purchased that day at the Target off Route 103.

The board was the type of accessory one might find in a university lecture hall or on the wall of an executive meeting room at the Hampton Inn. But at her parents' house on this steamy late-September Thursday in historic Ellicott City, Maryland, Bee used the dry-erase board to put the finishing touches on the plans for her wedding, the most expensive celebration the Tower Gardens Country Club would host this fall.

Bee had spent more than an hour decorating the board's surface with an array of circles, squares, names, and numbers. The result of her work looked like a football play or a math equation left for Matt Damon's character in *Good Will Hunting*. But the design represented a seating chart, Bee's last remaining task before her extended family would arrive for her wedding, which was now less than forty-eight hours away.

Bee tucked a loose curl behind her right ear and leaned forward anxiously. The board showed thirty circles, each containing a number. Extending from each circle like spokes on a wheel were blue lines that held the names of coupled guests.

'Cousin Wesley and wife Katie,' said one blue spoke. 'Mr Barocas from Dad's work with wife, Yvonne,' read another. 'Jimmy Fee and date.' 'Mr and Mrs Rodman (neighbors).' 'Ed and Elaine Ryan (accountants).' 'Dr Weihong Zheng and husband (pediatrician).'

In the top right-hand corner of the board was a list of names written in bright red ink and all-capital letters: 'HANNAH MARTIN, ROB NUTLEY, NANCY MACGOWAN, VICKI CLIFFORD, JOE EVANS.'

Above the names, in the same crimson print, Bee had written the word 'SINGLES.'

They were the only guests to RSVP for Bee's nuptials without using their plus-one invites, and now they were the only names Bee hadn't yet placed on her seating chart.

It would have been acceptable in a recession for Bee to invite singles to the wedding alone, but Bee wanted every guest to have the option of bringing a companion. Still the singles had chosen to come alone, and Bee just couldn't understand it.

When she was single, Bee resented brides who didn't give her a plus-one invite simply because she didn't have a serious boyfriend. Bee vowed that when she got married, she'd send plus-ones to everyone. No one would have to be alone.

Almost everyone on the invite list had taken Bee up on her offer. Except for the singles, who, in Bee's opinion, were adrift not only on her dry-erase board but also in life.

Two of the singles were conflict prone. Another two had a history of embarrassing Bee in public. Another was a woman Bee didn't know at all, a friend of the groom's family who had a reputation as a shut-in.

Bee's wedding planner, who had become famous for planning the extravagant wedding of an ex-president's daughter, had told Bee after examining her invite list, 'No matter who you invite, there will be singles.

'You must expect an odd number,' the planner had said during their first meeting. 'No matter what you plan to do, the singles always skew.'

Bee smoothed her eyebrows with the back of her right hand, her favorite nervous habit, and studied the circles and spokes, which reminded her of the puzzles she decoded on the LSATs years ago. There were five unseated guests, each of whom needed to be placed at a table. But each guest had a specific set of requirements, making it impossible to seat them at most tables. For instance, one single couldn't be seated anywhere near her ex-boyfriend. Another single was often offensive and couldn't be trusted around uptight adults – including Bee's own family.

As Bee began scrambling the names and tables in her mind, she heard her mother enter the room behind her.

'Still with those five?' Bee's mother, Donna Evans, said, letting out a dramatic sigh as she joined Bee at the dining-room table.

Donna wore a gray tank top that said 'breathe' across the chest, the lowercase *b* and final *e* falling in line with her protruding nipples. Her matching yoga pants were cropped just below the knee. Donna's artificially blonde curls, highlighted to the exact shade of her daughter's, were pulled back into a tight bun.

'Just write them into the empty seats and be done with it,' Donna said, as Bee stared at her helplessly, her hands limp at her waist. 'Honey, these people are going to spend half the night on the dance floor anyway.'

Donna let out a frustrated harrumph, and then pushed past her daughter so she could get a better look at the list of singles.

After squinting at the names for less than a minute, Donna grabbed a marker off the table and began to scribble on the board. She wrote Vicki Clifford's and Rob Nutley's names on the empty spoke next to the groom's brothers and cousins. Next she printed Hannah Martin's name in tiny letters above the circle representing the table occupied by Bee's law-school friends and their spouses.

'We'll add an extra chair,' Donna said, before Bee could protest that the table was already full. 'The caterers can fit nine seats at a table for eight.'

Then, moving to the other side of the board, Donna wrote the names of the last two singles, Joe Evans and Nancy MacGowan, at the table with Bee's father's law partners and their wives.

Bee's dad, Richard Evans, bellowed from the next room. 'I swear – if you're both standing in front of that board in another five minutes, I'm going to take it outside and put it in the Dumpster and everyone at this wedding will seat themselves.'

Bee turned away from the dry-erase board in defeat. 'Fine,' she said to her mother, who had already returned the marker and about-faced, her sneakers squeaking on the hardwood floor as she made her way to the kitchen.

'Mom,' Bee called after her.

'What?'

'I'm hungry,' Bee said almost too quietly for her mother to hear.

'Have something light,' Donna responded sharply from the next room. 'No sodium. That dress has absolutely no give, honey.'

Bee turned around and took one last look at the names at the top of the whiteboard, glad that she had Matt and would never again find herself without a date. She wondered, briefly and hopefully, if her singles would ever change their circumstances – if Hannah, Rob, Nancy, Vicki, and Joe would ever become easy-to-place spokes on a seating-chart wheel.

Bee scowled as her thoughts returned to swallowing another salt-free meal. She reached forward and firmly wiped the singles list clean.

Hannah

'Can I be honest with you?' Dawn asked Hannah in a loud whisper with a cigarette close to its ashy death in her right hand, a pack of bobby pins in her left.

Hannah knew by now that this wasn't a real question.

After spending several consecutive days with Bee's precocious matron of honor, Hannah had learned that Dawn began most of her sentences by asking theatrically, in an almost-shouted whisper, 'Can I be honest with you?'

Rarely did the question correspond to the sentence that followed. Rarely did Dawn have any interest in honesty.

'It's nothing bad,' Dawn continued, taking in Hannah's cautious eyes and drawing out the word 'bad' as if it had two syllables. 'It's just that I think you might want to consider putting on some more makeup before everything gets going today. All the other girls and I wear liner.' Dawn opened her eyes wide to illustrate. 'I notice that you don't wear any eyeliner. I don't know if you can tell, but the rest of us – our eyes just pop. They pop in pictures. You have beautiful blue eyes, honey. I just don't want you to get lost in the photos.'

Hannah's nose was at least two feet from Dawn's mouth, but she was still overcome by Dawn's potent breath, which smelled of nicotine and Caesar salad. Hannah winced as Dawn released another puff, a nauseating blend of Parmesan and Parliaments.

Hannah wasn't used to people smoking in her presence. Most of her friends had quit years ago when New York City approved its smoking ban. She knew a few summer smokers, friends who lit up on Brooklyn roof decks and patios, but it was too uncomfortable to smoke outside in the city after November.

Quality time with so many southerners during Bee's wedding weekend reminded Hannah how lucky she was to live in a city that had chosen to ostracize smokers in just about every way possible. All of Bee's soon-to-be in-laws from Raleigh and Durham were shameless chain smokers. Some of them even worked for Philip Morris.

Hannah was somewhat surprised that a perfectionist

such as Dawn wasn't worried that her dress might end up smelling of smoke. But, Hannah supposed, if everything smelled like nicotine, it didn't really matter. It was a universal perfume, and only Hannah seemed to be bothered by its scent.

Dawn took a last drag from her depleted cigarette, prompting Hannah to lean back in anticipation of the smoky aftermath. Even in this expansive tower, with its high ceiling, Dawn's fumes seemed omnipresent, revealing themselves in the form of baby clouds under the bright ceiling lights.

There were two large, connected rooms on the top floor of the country club tower where Hannah, Dawn, and the rest of Bee's bridal party were readying themselves before the main event. The ceremony would take place outdoors, on the lawn, beside a white tent that was already set up for the reception. There was a plan B, in case of rain – a shorter ceremony in the club's dining room – but it wouldn't be necessary. It was a beautiful September day – still warm enough to go without a jacket.

The historic, brown-brick castle where the bridal party now primped was the oldest part of the country club, a members-only Annapolis institution that sat alongside Chesapeake Bay, on more than one hundred acres of open space for golfing, skeet shooting, and whatever else wealthy people like to do on weekends. To Hannah, the neo-Gothic tower from which the Tower Gardens Country Club took its name looked as if it had been transported straight out of a fairy tale. Its tall cylindrical shape, sterile exterior, stained glass windows, and the view of the well-trimmed green below, where guests would soon be milling about, made Hannah feel like Rapunzel, which was appropriate, she thought to herself, because she was just as trapped. If this were a movie, Hannah thought, unable to shut off her casting-director's brain, the locked-up bridesmaid version of her would be played by an imperfect yet likeable up-and-comer. Or better yet, an A-lister, but someone known for a good scowl. 'Kristen Stewart,' Hannah had whispered to herself when she first peered out the window from her tower prison. Emily Blunt, she'd then decided, acknowledging that at twenty-nine she was probably too old to be played by anyone in a *Twilight* movie.

Dawn, as matron of honor, would be played by Reese Witherspoon. That was a no-brainer. Dawn's cherubic face was framed by a bouncy blonde bob. She had a southern accent and sounded especially shrill when giving orders. Hannah wondered for a moment whether

Reese Witherspoon would be open to smoking on screen.

Casting with an imaginary budget was Hannah's favorite addiction. In real life she only had experience with indie films that paid the leads less than two hundred thousand dollars. The conservative budgets forced Hannah to get creative and to hunt for new talent, but she longed for the chance to cast a film that allowed her to hire the celebrities she'd developed crushes on over the years.

She was so close to getting one of those gigs. Hannah had been checking her phone obsessively for much of the morning, hoping she would hear something, anything, from Natalie Portman's agent, who today held Hannah's professional fate in her hands.

Hannah had spent weeks lobbying for the actress to take a role in an independent film that made up for its low budget with, in Hannah's opinion, an Oscar-worthy script. If Natalie signed on to the film, Hannah's career would undoubtedly change. The movie – and Hannah – would get national attention. New investors would throw the director some much-needed cash. Natalie Portman could turn this movie into a *Rachel Getting Married*, a cheap, good film with big returns.

And there was reason to believe Natalie would say

yes. Her agent had been optimistic; Natalie had read the script and enjoyed it. The actress liked that the project would be directed by a woman. Natalie had even called the dialogue 'enchanting' in an e-mail that her agent had forwarded to Hannah. But there was the matter of scheduling.

'She's booked for four solid months, to film that sequel,' the agent's young assistant had explained two days before Hannah hopped the Acela to Baltimore to get to Bee's wedding. The agent's assistant, who had fielded all of Hannah's pestering phone calls, had become her spy, sending her quick text messages whenever she overheard her boss talking about the project.

'I only need her for twenty days,' Hannah had pleaded with the assistant, as if she had any say in the matter. 'She has to have twenty nonworking days during that shoot. I mean, her character is on another planet for half of the movie, right? Isn't there any downtime?'

Hannah resented the mediocre, big-budget superhero movie that was not only getting a sequel but ruining her own small, quality film.

'Listen, she really wants to do it, and I know they're trying to work something out,' the assistant had said.

'When do you think I'll get a definite answer?' was

Hannah's reply, as she balled up four pairs of underwear and tucked them into the side pocket of her suitcase for the wedding weekend.

'You won't get a final answer until next week, but I'll probably know something on Saturday. There's this big agency party at my boss's house on Saturday, and if Natalie is doing this film, my boss will be bragging about it to everyone. I suppose I could text you if I hear anything.'

'Oh, my God, thank you! I'm going to a wedding on Saturday, and if I've cast Natalie Portman in a film, I want to be able to tell all my friends. And maybe an ex-boyfriend or two.'

'I completely understand,' the assistant had said, sounding almost too empathetic.

It was now late Saturday afternoon and no one had texted. Not even Hannah's best friend, Vicki, who had promised to check in as soon as she arrived in Annapolis.

Bee's wedding planner, whom Hannah decided would be played in her imaginary big-budget wedding movie by Bonnie Hunt from *Jerry Maguire* and *Cheaper by the Dozen*, made it clear to Bee and her bridesmaids that once they were inside the tower with their dresses on, they would have to stay put until the wedding began.

The larger of the tower penthouse's two rooms had a television, a Wedgwood blue velvet furniture set, and a sizable bathroom with two full-length mirrors, so there was no acceptable reason to leave, the wedding planner had said, with her eyes on Hannah as if she could read her mind.

The planner explained that when the clock struck five and the guests had found their seats, each woman would walk down the spiral staircase, exit the tower, take the arm of a groomsman — or the father of the bride, in Bee's case — and make her way straight down the aisle, which was actually a meandering stone path as historic and well-manicured as the rest of the grounds.

The wedding wouldn't start for another hour, but Dawn was already lining up her cosmetics on top of the end table in the larger of the two rooms. Her methodical arrangement reminded Hannah of the way the metal tools were displayed in a dentist's office. Dawn organized her collection of beauty products by size — the skinny eyeliner pencil next to a tube of mascara next to a box of blush next to a tray of eye shadow.

Hannah wondered whether she might be able to postpone getting tweezed and painted for another half hour or so. Her dress was on, but she hoped to hold off being made up like a prom queen for as long as possible. She walked over to one of the tower's windows and rubbed the back of her neck so aggressively that she felt the chain of pearls dig into her skin. She tugged at the clear strap of her bra, which pressed uncomfortably against the back of her neck. It was the most complex piece of lingerie she'd ever worn – a padded support system that had to be special ordered for the occasion by all the bridesmaids. Hannah had watched the other women slip into their special bras without help but had been unable to figure out how to put the bra on by herself. It wound up being a two-woman job; Bee and Dawn had surrounded Hannah to fasten her into the contraption, which crisscrossed her lower back twice and fastened with a sharp-cornered metal clip just above the axis of her spine.

'Does it have to be this tight?' Hannah had whined to Bee after the brassiere had been secured.

Dawn had answered before Bee could respond. 'Any looser and you'll fall out of your dress, honey,' she'd said sternly, peering at Hannah's breasts disapprovingly. 'You're already going to be spilling over.'

17

Hannah had already called Rob twice, from her temporary prison in the tower, hoping he might calm her down about the bra, her impending walk down the aisle, and Natalie Portman, whom Hannah assumed was less likely to give her good news with each passing hour. Rob Nutley was supposed to be at this wedding. He'd RSVP'd, and had told Bee that he'd happily attend, and now, living up to everyone's expectations of him as the reckless and irresponsible one, he was a no-show. Hannah had been counting on Rob to get her through the weekend, but now there would be no one but Vicki, who, these days, wasn't much of a source of support to anyone.

Still clutching her BlackBerry as she stared out the window, Hannah looked down and saw a missed call. Rob.

She selected 'call back' and watched as Rob's number lit up for the third time that day. Her stomach flipped when she heard him pick up, already laughing into the receiver.

'Don't laugh. I need you,' Hannah whispered loudly, prompting Dawn to throw her a judgmental glance from the couch. 'Please. There are women here who are trying to assault me with eyeliner. Isn't there any way you can just hop a flight now, at the last minute? You'd be here before the end of the reception. I'll split the cost, whatever it is.'

'I do love it when you beg, but no, my dear, I can't leave Austin.' Rob paused and added more thoughtfully, 'It's not the money. There's just something off about Liz today. I can't leave her alone in the house.'

'Fine. Maybe I'll call you later,' Hannah said, hanging up before he could respond. Her posture sank as she abandoned hope that Rob might change his mind.

Hannah walked from the window back to Dawn, who had just covered herself with powder that was two shades darker than her face. Hannah sat down beside her and nervously stroked the buttons on her Black-Berry, peering down at it every few seconds to check for missed calls from Rob or Natalie Portman's agent's assistant.

Out of the corner of her eye, Hannah could see Bee in the adjoining room, smoothing the lines of her gown, which was still on a hanger. It was a fitted, strap-less, ivory dress with a scalloped-pattern bodice that reminded Hannah of a mermaid and a small train that opened up like a fan. Bee had explained to Hannah months ago that she'd hoped to wear her mother's wedding dress, a simple chiffon A-line gown that had been preserved in a garment bag in Donna's closet for almost three decades, but when she tried it on, she couldn't zip it up. Donna had always been a size 4, and although Bee struggled to maintain that size during her college days, she was now content with being a size 6.

Now Bee wore nothing but white lace underwear, a strapless bra, and control-top pantyhose that shrunk her silhouette by about an inch. The waist of the nylons extended past her belly button like a bodysuit. Her hair was twisted into a bun made of braids, which to Hannah looked dreadfully uncomfortable and inappropriately severe.

Hannah adored Bee's strawberry locks, especially when they were loose at her shoulders, tousled and light. She never understood why brides always wore their hair in complicated, tightly pinned patterns. It reminded Hannah of the way the dead look at wakes – overly made up and unrecognizable to the people who knew them best.

Bee was surrounded by the two other bridesmaids, Jackie and Lisa, who, like Hannah, were already in their long black gowns, with their hair ironed straight. They were discussing the best way to get Bee into her wedding dress without scuffing it or endangering her princess coiffure.

'Maybe she should step into it,' Lisa, the passive bridesmaid, suggested.

'No,' Jackie, the stern bridesmaid, answered aggressively. 'If she steps in, she runs the risk of stepping on it or getting it dirty. It should go over her head.'

'The woman who sold it to me told me to step into it,' Bee said thoughtfully. 'And these floors look perfectly clean to me. But . . . maybe Jackie's right. Let's go over my head, just slowly.'

When Bee had asked for help getting into her dress, a task that would require the aid of two people, Hannah opted to stay with Dawn, whom Hannah assumed would want her own lady-in-waiting during the dressing process.

Dawn's gown was not like the other bridesmaids' dresses. It was similar in that it was a black halter with an empire waist and plunging neckline, but unlike Hannah's uniform, Dawn's dress had an ornate bow at the waist and a small satin train in back. Hannah had never seen a matron of honor dressed differently from the other bridesmaids. She wondered if it was a southern wedding tradition or a new fad. With nothing to do but chitchat, she dared to ask Dawn about her attire.

'I didn't realize the matron of honor wore a different

dress. Is that how they do it down south? I've never seen that before.'

'Where I grew up,' Dawn said slowly, emphasizing her Reese Witherspoon drawl, 'maids of honor were encouraged to distinguish themselves.'

'Where did you grow up?' Hannah demanded, unable to control the tension in her voice.

'In Roanoke,' Dawn answered sharply.

'Where's that?' Hannah asked, instantly regretting the question, which was bound to be interpreted as an insult.

'In Virginia. Just about two hours from Richmond. Did you miss geography class, honey?'

Dawn flashed one of her debutante smiles.

'I'm bad with geography,' Hannah said, attempting to recover quickly by using the meekest and most feminine voice she could muster. Hannah looked at her phone again, first to make sure that she hadn't missed a text about Natalie Portman, and then to check the time. There was less than a half hour before the wedding. She exhaled exhaustively and let her eyes float up to meet Dawn's. 'And, Dawn, I – I'm also bad with makeup, so if you want to put eyeliner on me, feel free. You're the professional.'

'I'm not just a professional, honey. I'm the best,' Dawn said, adjusting her tan girdle, which stretched from midthigh to the complicated halter bra, which didn't seem to be bothering her at all. All she wore over it was a T-shirt that said 'Lady Tar Heel.'

'When I get done with you,' Dawn continued, 'Tom is going to be on his knees, begging you for forgiveness.'

Hannah winced at the sound of Tom's name. She cracked a few of her knuckles.

'I don't want Tom on his knees,' Hannah said unconvincingly, her voice suddenly shaking. 'I don't want him back. I really don't care what he thinks. Bee is making too big a deal of this whole thing.'

It was only a partial lie. When Hannah fantasized about Bee's wedding, where she'd see Tom for the first time since their breakup two and a half years ago, she didn't see herself reuniting with him romantically, at least not instantly.

Hannah had longed for Tom's return for the first year or so after their breakup, but that yearning had evolved into a series of revenge-and-rejection fantasies that began to seem almost plausible once it became clear that they would see each other at Bee's wedding. Hannah would be all dressed up, confident, and surrounded by their shared friends, who missed them as a couple.

Hannah liked to imagine that Tom would spot her from across the room during Bee's reception and would be drawn to her much like he'd been when he'd met her during his junior year of college.

Tom would notice that she'd stopped highlighting her hair, which turned out to be a pretty chocolate color that finally matched her eyebrows. He would also see that she'd lost the twenty-two pounds she'd gained after graduation, which Hannah had determined was the real reason Tom had left her, despite his many claims otherwise. Tom would be disarmed by Hannah's new confidence, intimated by her posture. He would discover that she'd stopped biting her nails, his least favorite of her many bad habits. He would hear from Bee, or maybe Vicki, that Hannah had been hired by a reputable casting office that handled national commercials and real grown-up films. No more low-budget theater. No more finding actors to star in hospital videos about diabetes care.

Tom had told Hannah shortly before their breakup that taking those corporate casting jobs made her a sell-out, that there was no point in casting projects that weren't even meant to entertain. 'You're not really happy,' he'd said to her during the four-day fight that resulted in the end of their relationship. 'You said it yourself. This is mindless work.'

But years later those terrible jobs had paid off. The

young directors whose first gigs were in bad theater, directing touring productions of *Scooby Doo: The Musical*, the ones who got their first paychecks producing sexual-harassment-training videos for big companies, were now directing real films. They remembered Hannah and hired her out of loyalty, just as they'd promised they would when they'd met her in her early twenties.

That's how Hannah had found this new gig, the one she hoped would be a starring vehicle for Natalie Portman. The director of the film had worked with Hannah four years ago on a regional, nonunion car commercial. Now she was directing a film with a six-million-dollar budget.

Tom had been wrong; those awful jobs put Hannah exactly where she'd hoped to be in her late twenties. It was Rob who had been right. He was the one who had sent e-mail pep talks telling Hannah to stay in New York and stick it out. He'd even sent her a funny note after seeing her first national television commercial with SAG actors.

'Perfect casting for the tampon commercial,' his brief e-mail had said. 'I really believe that this woman is afraid of leaks. I am frightened for her. Really. Congrats.'

In Hannah's fantasy of Bee's wedding, she and Tom wouldn't speak during the reception. They would glance at each other from across the room. They would make it clear that each had taken notice of the other. But there would be no contact until after the wedding was over, when Tom would come knocking on Hannah's hotel-room door, begging for a reconciliation. He would take back everything he'd said to her on the night he'd moved out, when he'd told her that he didn't think she was capable of ever being someone's wife. He would tell her that he'd been wrong to leave New York and that he no longer believed it was so important to live close to his family in Boston. He would say that New England felt too small and puritanical and that he missed dining with Hannah in pretentious restaurants in the East Village and going to off-off-Broadway theater productions that starred her actor friends, despite the fact that Tom had complained about those outings when he'd lived with her.

Tom would tell her that the worst night of her life – the night he left – had also been the worst night of his, and that after his sister rushed down from Boston to load up her car with his belongings and move him up north, he almost instantly realized that he'd lost his anchor in life and his best friend. He would tell Hannah that he thought about her every day, especially before he fell asleep at night.

In this fantasy, Tom would be played by Paul Rudd, Hannah decided. Paul Rudd was about ten years older than Tom, but he still looked young enough to play a twentysomething. And the casting choice would appeal to all the women Hannah's age who had been *Clueless* fans, Hannah thought, totaling the imaginary box office returns.

After showing up at her hotel room, Tom, or Paul Rudd, depending on Hannah's version of the fantasy, would poke his head through her door once she opened it, tilting his face so that it would be easier for their lips to meet, but Hannah would put her hand on his chest to stop him.

'It's too late,' she, or maybe Emily Blunt or Kristen Stewart, would say in a flat tone.

'Don't say that,' Tom or Paul Rudd would respond, almost whimpering.

On a good day, Hannah could stop the fantasy there. She would give closure to the scene by imagining herself shutting her fictional hotel-room door in his face. Sometimes she would go so far as to invent a new boyfriend, who would be waiting for her on her fictional hotel-room bed. Strangely, in Hannah's fantasy the new boyfriend was also played by Paul Rudd. Hannah hadn't quite worked that one out yet.

Of course, sometimes it was difficult for Hannah to be good. Sometimes she didn't want to end the fantasy with a safe rejection of the college boyfriend who had left her behind. Sometimes, when she imagined this scene, she'd tack on an ending that had her pulling Tom through the door by his tie and making love to him on the hotel-room bed, groaning and grabbing pillows. Usually she'd imagine Tom as himself in those moments. She didn't see Paul Rudd as the kind of guy who'd groan or grab.

Hannah was satisfied with either fictional outcome, whether it was rejecting Tom or the cinematic lovemaking. Replaying one fantasy or the other in her mind had made it easier to fall asleep for the past few months. It had certainly made it easier to diet and exercise in preparation for the wedding.

Of course, even after losing weight and getting an overpriced haircut and manicure with the bridal party that morning, Hannah believed she looked horribly unpolished next to the camera-ready, radiant matron of honor. Dawn was technically just the wife of one of Bee's law-school buddies, but she was part of the pack that had become Bee's second family since college.

Bee was a lawyer now. And a southerner. The quiet, most studious member of Hannah's bunch at Syracuse

University had made good on her unspoken promise to her family that she become an attorney, like her father, and get married before she turned thirty. Bee's only surprising postcollege decision was choosing to marry Matt, who, unlike Bee's family, was boisterous and emotive.

Bee had fallen in love with Matt Fee during their first year of law school at the University of North Carolina at Chapel Hill. She hoped to be an estate planner. He would become the in-house attorney for his family's granite company as soon as he passed the bar. By marrying Matt and changing her name – which she planned to do – Bee would become Bee Fee. This didn't seem to bother her.

'Bee isn't my real name,' Bee had told Hannah, shortly after the engagement was announced. 'My name is Beth, if you remember correctly. It will be Beth Fee.'

'No one calls you Beth, Bee,' Hannah had responded dryly through the phone. 'Bee Fee? Who wants to hire a lawyer named Bee Fee? It sounds like "beefy." Can you please keep your maiden name?'

'I'm going to use it as my middle name. Beth Evans Fee. I'll still be Bee. Just Evans instead of Eleanor.'

'Ugh, Bee, it sounds so stupid. Bee Fee, Esq.'

'Hannah, will you please not ruin this?'

'Fine,' Hannah had said, muttering a last 'Bee Fee' to herself.

Bee had only mentioned her friend Dawn to Hannah a few times over the past year, which is why Hannah had been surprised to hear that the much younger spouse of one of Bee's law-school friends had earned matron of honor status so quickly.

Sensing Hannah's distrust of Dawn over the phone, Bee had tried to justify her new friend's quick promotion.

'This isn't just about who's my closest friend, Hannah. You know you're more important in my life, but I need someone who can help me with the maid of honor's duties, like the shopping and the showers. You hate this stuff – planning frilly parties. Dawn loves it. She lives for it.'

'I'm not offended, Bee. I don't need to be your maid of honor. I do hate this stuff – passionately. But what about Jackie? You've known her since you were born. Isn't she going to feel slighted?'

'Jackie hates this stuff too. At least she does now that she's single. I just couldn't bring myself to put her in charge of my wedding details. It seemed . . . insensitive to ask her to sit around planning someone else's big day after she had such a bad breakup. And you'll see – Dawn is good at this. It's her job.'

As Hannah soon learned, dresses, eyeliner, and cere-monial duties were actually Dawn's job. The twenty-three-year-old proud native of Roanoke was a professional pageant coach – meaning, she prepared young girls to compete in beauty pageants. Families who wanted their daughters to have an edge during the competition paid Dawn thousands of dollars for pageant tips and polishing lessons. Dawn taught the young women how to groom themselves and strut. She helped them choose the necessary outfits, from gowns to taste-ful-but-cleavage-baring bikinis. She worked with girls to develop a talent competition routine, even if they didn't have any talent. She quizzed them about their hopes and dreams, because at some point during every pageant they would be asked.

'Never mention your politics,' Dawn advised. 'Never mention world peace. You have to choose a real cause and stick with it. I recommend something that has to do with animals or military families, especially here in Virginia.'

Dawn had never been to college. She'd started her one-woman consulting business as soon as she was too old to compete in pageants herself. She was making enough money by the time she was twenty to buy a cream-colored Ford Expedition, which had a personal-ized license plate: 'TRUBUTY.'

'Can I be honest with you?' Dawn said to Hannah when the two first met at Bee's bachelorette party two months ago.

Bee and her bridesmaids had arrived one by one from their various East Coast hometowns and had gathered at the lobby bar at the Atlantic City Hilton, where they'd be spending the night. Hannah, who had been fixated on Dawn's profession ever since Bee had disclosed it over the phone, couldn't help but ask why pageant contestants needed professional help – from anyone besides a therapist.

'Pageant coaching is not what you'd think,' Dawn answered, pretending to ignore the tone of Hannah's question. 'You're with these girls from start to finish – I mean, for months and months. You're like their mother, I swear it. You're there for the concept planning. You're there for the shopping. You help with weight watching. You help with the heels and the hair. You do speech training. You're like a fairy godmother. And then, when they win, all they want to do is run into your arms.'

'So you're like a fairy godmother who demands weight loss?' Hannah asked, already tipsy from two glasses of Riesling, prompting Bee to throw her a warning glance from across the lounge table.

'I don't demand that anyone lose weight,' Dawn

responded calmly, just before taking a sip of her fluorescent martini. 'Most girls want to look their best. Some
girls don't need to lose weight before their big day. Some
do.'

Hannah accepted this answer with a nod and let her
eyes roam to the front door of the hotel lobby. She was
anxiously awaiting the arrival of Jackie, Bee's best friend
from high school in Maryland.

It wasn't that Hannah knew Jackie well. It was that at
first glance Dawn, the unknown matron of honor,
looked so blonde, so southern and painted with rouge
and eye shadow, that Hannah felt the need to see Jackie's
dark curls and pale skin.

The last time Hannah had seen Jackie was at Bee's
twenty-fifth birthday party a few years before. She and
Jackie had spent much of the night making fun of everyone in the bar. Hannah honestly enjoyed Jackie, at least
while drunk. She would cast Julia Stiles as Jackie because,
even though the actress was blonde, she shared Jackie's
wry smile and husky voice.

Bee and Jackie had known each other since they were
babies. They shared a bunk at summer camp in Maine
for six consecutive years and played tennis as a pair
through high school. They went to the prom with twin
brothers, Chris and Ed Shanahan, and were each other's

first phone call when they lost their virginity during their freshman years of college.

But they'd grown distant as they moved closer to their thirtieth birthdays, which is why Jackie had been passed over as maid of honor. Jackie's longtime boyfriend, Kevin, had committed several over-the-top betrayals before leaving her last year. Since the split, Jackie had been aloof and occasionally mean to friends – namely Bee – who were happy in love.

At the bar in Atlantic City, on the night of the bachelorette party, Bee told the story of Jackie and Kevin so that all the other bridesmaids knew what to expect from her oldest, dearest, and somewhat estranged friend, who had yet to arrive.

Jackie, Bee explained as the women leaned in over their cocktails, had majored in finance in college and now investigated corporate fraud. Her firm, which had office space in a high-rise in New York's Financial District, was hired by big company executives to find out which of their employees were misusing corporate credit cards. Jackie had saved her clients millions by finding the businessmen who had used their company-sponsored American Express accounts to pay for personal car repairs and steak dinners. She'd once caught an exec using his card to withdraw thousands of dollars in cash advances, which he used to pay his kid's thirty-thousand-dollar private-school tuition.

Kevin had been Jackie's boyfriend in college and had moved with her to New York. The relationship was blissful and she'd assumed they'd get married – until she discovered that Kevin had not only been cheating on her with one of her work acquaintances, but that he'd opened a credit card in Jackie's name without her knowledge.

According to Bee, Jackie was still paying off the twenty-six-thousand-dollar debt that Kevin had racked up paying off old debts from college, buying himself toys he didn't need, and taking the other woman on secret lunches.

Jackie had discovered Kevin's fraud in the most basic way, when a credit card company – one she often dealt with during work investigations – called to inform her that she was two months late on her payments. She explained that she didn't have a credit card with that company, that there must be some mistake. The representative read off the last four digits of her social security number and date of birth as confirmation and then gave her the details of her ballooning balance. Jackie assumed she was the victim of identity theft until the credit card agent began to read a list of what was purchased with the card – the Xbox that now sat on her living-room floor and the bright green, supposedly aerodynamic running shoes that Kevin had brought home the month before.

When Jackie confronted Kevin about the call, he told her that he'd developed a secret spending habit because he was depressed. He promised he would seek professional help and assured her that all his bad behavior was the result of a chemical imbalance, which ran in his family.

After Kevin's sixth therapy session, he'd come home in a rush, explained to Jackie that she was an enabler, and told her that he needed to move out for the sake of his own mental health. He promised to make payments on the card after he left, but he never did. He'd never even bothered having his mail forwarded. Jackie had taken responsibility for the rest of the bill without trying to contact him. She'd rationalized that she deserved to pay the price of overlooking the one crime she was trained to catch.

A year after the breakup, Jackie was more reserved and cynical than she'd ever been, according to Bee, who delivered Jackie's tale to Hannah and the other bridesmaids at the hotel bar as if it were a haunted mystery. She whispered dramatically, her eyes wide. Hannah imagined Bee holding a flashlight under her chin.

Bee explained that when she asked Jackie to be a bridesmaid, her old friend accepted, but only after a long pause. Bee admitted that she often wondered whether the credit card and cheating disaster had left Jackie incapable of celebrating anyone else's happiness.

'Maybe it just takes longer than a few months to get over that kind of loss and betrayal,' Hannah had snapped defensively in Bee's direction after hearing Jackie's sad tale at the hotel bar. 'Being left without warning . . . It can ruin you,' Hannah continued, perhaps revealing too much about herself to Bee's other bridesmaids, who were all married or about to be.

Hannah had imagined that she and Jackie would cling to each other during the bachelorette weekend and the Annapolis wedding. They'd be the only New Yorkers and single women in the pack. But it was clear after just a few hours in Atlantic City that Jackie wanted no part of Hannah's camaraderie and that she had little interest in bridesmaid duties in general. Beyond that, Jackie already had a new boyfriend. When the fraud detector finally joined the other women at the hotel bar, she explained that she was dating someone new – an ear, nose, and throat doctor named Will. He'd be her date to the wedding. When Bee asked excitedly if it was serious, Jackie just shrugged.

It was hours after the bachelorette party dinner, when Bee was fall-down drunk at a place called the Smile Club and the still-energetic Dawn demanded that the group stay out for just one more hour, that Hannah looked to Jackie for support, a voice of reason to lead the group back to the hotel so the drooling bride could vomit and get some sleep.

But before Hannah could solicit Jackie's second opinion so they could defy Dawn as a twosome, the fraud detector announced that she had a headache and would be heading back to the hotel room early. 'But you guys,' she said, not making eye contact with Hannah, who stared at her in disbelief, 'you stay out and have a good time.'

Hannah threw her head back, furious at the unspoken betrayal. Without Jackie's dissent, Dawn was able to lead the weary group to two more bars, where she flirted with men in baseball caps, leaving Hannah responsible for the overintoxicated Bee, who could only murmur phrases like 'Do you think Matt and I are gonna get divorced?' and 'Do you think he'll cheat on me?'

Hannah tried to reason with Dawn, who had as much energy at 11:00 p.m. as she'd had five hours earlier, when the group started drinking.

'Dawn,' Hannah said, trying to be as polite as possible, 'I think Bee's going to get sick. I think we should take her back to the hotel.'

'Baby,' Dawn said, clapping twice in front of Bee's wilting face, 'you've got to boot and rally!'

'Can I be honest with you?' Dawn yelled, this time directing her commentary to Hannah. 'This is one of Bee's last nights of freedom. She's not going to be happy if she wakes up and finds out that she was in bed by midnight.'

It was another eighty minutes before Dawn allowed the group to return to the hotel. And that was only because Bee had vomited on herself at the bar – booting without showing any signs of rallying.

Dawn had sprinted out of the club to find a cab as soon as Bee became a spectacle. Lisa, the shy bridesmaid, had run behind her, as Dawn yelled over her back to Hannah, 'Good luck! She's all yours!'

It had taken Hannah twenty minutes to clean up Bee's mess and get her out of the bar. Once they were outside, Hannah held Bee's waist and rubbed her back as she helped the bride-to-be vomit into an Atlantic City storm drain. When Hannah was confident that Bee had emptied her stomach, she flagged down a cab and helped Bee get in.

The driver banged his head against the back of his seat when he saw Bee's queasy face in his rearview mirror. 'She better not puke,' he said. 'If you puke, it's two hundred dollars extra.'

'She won't,' Hannah said, as Bee swallowed her saliva and grimaced.

Bee barely made it through the ride. She vomited between Hannah's feet as soon as they stepped out of the cab and then leaned in so Hannah could give her a hug.

Hannah held her tight, ignoring the mess between her shoes, and then led Bee slowly through the hotel lobby, which was more crowded after midnight than Hannah would have expected, even for a casino town. Not wanting to lose sight of the sweater Bee had been wearing, which was cashmere and probably expensive, Hannah kept the vomit-soaked cardigan balled up in her left hand. She used her right hand to clutch Bee's s right elbow, first steadying her and then leading her past the front desk and toward the elevator.

After a few steps, Bee's tube top fell down.

It was probably loose, Hannah assumed, because Bee had lost weight in preparation for the wedding. Hannah clenched her teeth as the spectators gasped. Bee had gone braless for the night, and with the tube top around her stomach, all was revealed. Three college-age men in the hotel lobby gawked at the topless woman in front of them.

'Holy shit,' one said, grinning.

The second young man, who wore a Rutgers sweat-shirt, even took out his cell phone and held it up to Bee so he could take a picture. Hannah stopped short and stared him down.

'I swear to God, if you take a picture of her, I will take that phone and shove it straight up your asshole,' Hannah said, happy to unleash some anger, which was really meant for the bullying Dawn and the abandoning Jackie. The young man lowered his phone and looked down, sufficiently scolded. His friends were bent over, drunk and laughing.

Bee looked down at her naked top half and giggled along with the men. 'I'm naked, Hannah.'

'I know, Bee,' Hannah responded, gently.

'My nipples,' Bee said when she was almost to the elevator.

'There are two of them,' Hannah answered. 'Two nipples. Both accounted for.'

They rode up on the elevator to the eleventh floor with two suited men who looked like they were on a business trip. Hannah tried for a second time to lift Bee's tube top so that it covered her breasts, but it fell down again almost immediately.

'Nice night,' Hannah said to the men, with a half grin, giving up.

'Yes,' said the taller of the two men without taking his eyes off the breasts in front of him. 'Not too chilly.' Then both men looked at their feet, their faces red.

When Hannah got back to the room and swung open the door, with one hand still clutching Bee by the elbow, Dawn and Lisa were already in pajamas, seated together on one of the beds, watching David Letterman. Hannah angrily walked the still half-naked Bee through the room and led her straight into the bathroom. She slammed the door behind them.

After a few minutes of sitting on the edge of the tub as she held Bee's head over the toilet, Hannah heard Lisa, the law-school bridesmaid who had been quiet for most of the night, tap lightly on the door. 'Do you need anything, Hannah? We picked up boxes of cookies and chips on the way back and there are still a few left. There's also some soda and water.'

'No,' Hannah snapped, almost instantly regretting her tone. She was angry at Dawn and Jackie, not the meek Lisa, who Hannah guessed was probably a nice person. Lisa was passive and useless – probably a terrible lawyer

– but nice, nevertheless. Hannah decided she'd be played by Katie Holmes.

Hannah waited until Bee heaved two more times and then helped her into the tub. She removed what was left of Bee's clothing, tossing an expensive pair of jeans and white underwear to the other side of the toilet, and then ran the water, which came out ice cold. Bee howled.

'Just stay put,' Hannah said. 'It's going to warm up in two seconds.'

'You don't have to do this,' Bee said. She was sobering up now. Her eyes had become less glassy. She stared at Hannah thoughtfully.

'Sure I do,' Hannah said, sitting on the bathroom floor, her back against the wall. 'You did this for me.'

'I did?' Bee asked, confused.

'Twice. You did this for me sophomore year at Matt Dorfman's apartment, when I puked on my own lap – and I think my vomit was grosser than this, if that's possible – and you did it again a few years ago after Tom and I broke up.'

'I don't remember you puking after Tom left.' Bee hiccuped.

'I was puking emotionally,' Hannah said softly, remembering that night. 'I called you after Tom and his sister left with all his stuff, and you drove all the way from your parents' house in Maryland. You cleaned my apartment while I cried and watched an entire season of *Lost*, and you stayed with me for a week until I was ready to sleep alone.'

Bee smirked, rubbing her arms with the warm water.

'Of course I did,' she said proudly, swallowing a belch. 'Can I have toothpaste?'

'Sure,' Hannah said, reaching across the sink for Bee's cosmetics case and grabbing the small tube of Colgate.

'Hannah?' Bee asked, as she squeezed a dollop of green onto her finger and then stuck it in her mouth. 'Do you think Matt is a good guy? I mean, do you think we'll be happy?'

Hannah tilted her head and smiled reassuringly. 'Bee, he's not your dad. You're not your mom. This is a totally different marriage. It's yours, not theirs.'

By the time the process was over and Bee was in fresh pajamas, it was 2:00 a.m. and the other bridesmaids were asleep, breathing heavily. Jackie and Dawn had fanned out like angels over the two full beds, while Lisa slept awkwardly on the floor in front of the television. Hannah saw that the room's one roll-out cot had been opened and was left vacant; Lisa had most likely reserved it for the vomiting bride-to-be. I will be nicer to Katie Holmes, Hannah thought as she watched

Lisa try to fall asleep without blankets on the hotel carpet.

Hannah helped Bee lie down on top of the small cot and then lowered herself to the floor next to Lisa, who briefly opened her eyes long enough for Hannah to say, 'I'm sorry I yelled at you, Lisa. I was just up to my ass in puke.' Both bridesmaids smiled.

After a few minutes of shivering without bedding, they inched toward each other and spooned. Hannah thought about Tom for a moment, as she often did before she fell asleep. She allowed herself to imagine that it was him next to her instead of a bridesmaid she barely knew. Hannah tried to block out the silhouette of Lisa's feminine frame and pictured Tom's broad shoulders as she sighed in the dark and closed her eyes.

It was the next morning that Hannah decided to follow the meek-but-wise Lisa's lead. Dawn might be a selfish beauty pageant coach, but in the context of Bee's wedding, it was better to obey her than to defy her. Jackie might be a more understandable alpha – someone she might befriend in real life – but she offered no reward, no compensation for loyalty. Jackie just wanted to be left alone, which did Hannah no good.

Hannah also admitted to herself that as much as she despised Dawn in most ways, the pageant coach was strangely familiar to her. And that morning after the bachelorette party, as Hannah watched Dawn groom herself carefully before checking out of the hotel, Hannah realized why. Back in New York, Hannah was almost always surrounded by actors, attention-seeking pretty people she'd cast in commercials and movies. They weren't real friends.

Hannah knew that most of the actors who took her to restaurants and gave her free theater tickets were only interested in spending time with her because they wanted more work.

But Hannah had grown used to keeping these disingenuous actors close, especially since Tom had left. They always offered her something to do on the weekends.

At parties she would find the worst of them, the most wickedly adorable and judgmental actor, usually a gay man, and cling to him. It was her way of ensuring that she would be entertained throughout the night, and that she'd keep herself from becoming his target. In the context of Bee's wedding, Dawn was the closest thing to the meanest, most adorable gay man that Hannah could find. 'If I think of her as a drag queen, I kind of like her,' Hannah explained to Vicki on the phone after the bachelorette party weekend. 'As a gay man, she's almost lovable.'

'Everything you're telling me sounds moderately

homophobic. And this Dawn person sounds horrendous,' Vicki had responded. 'Keep me away from her in Annapolis. I won't be able to forget that she's a woman. And I certainly won't be able to forget that Bee is now best friends with a beauty queen.'

The beauty queen thing no longer bothered Hannah. If her goal was to devastate Tom by presenting herself as an ideal partner, someone who could be played by Emily Blunt, she needed professional help. She needed a pageant coach.

Now, at the country club in Annapolis, sitting like a puppy dog at Dawn's side, Hannah watched as the matron of honor opened up a second pastel-colored tackle box filled with even more makeup. On the side of the box was a bumper sticker that said 'MRV.'

'What does that stand for?' Hannah asked, pulling her hair back so that Dawn could get a better look at her face.

'Miss Roanoke Valley, which I was,' Dawn said proudly. 'And I was also first runner-up in the Miss Virginia pageant.'

'Wow,' Hannah said, surprised at herself for being legitimately impressed. 'Wasn't it weird? I mean, when you were a kid, did you want to do the pageant thing or did your mom make you?'

'Not that it's wrong,' Hannah added, softening the question. 'It just seems like a lot of pressure for a little kid.'

'Can I be honest with you? Honestly, I loved it. I was a natural. I know the media makes it look awful – the JonBenét incident didn't help – but really it's about self-esteem and womanhood. It's about loving yourself.'

'I see,' Hannah said, her voice soft. 'Dawn,' she continued, changing the subject, 'I want to look good, and I trust you, but I don't want to look like a southern belle. I can't pull that off. Please don't make me look . . . you know . . . over the top.'

Dawn rolled her eyes. 'What does that even mean?'

'I think that means no baby blue eye shadow. And maybe no body glitter. I want to look good – but not like I'm at a cotillion. I want to look like me, just better.'

Dawn grinned. 'Cotillion makeup is usually very subtle, just so you know. Body glitter was designed for go-go dancers and prostitutes. I don't own it, and I don't condone it. Okay, hon?'

Hannah let out a deep sigh and nodded. The reality of the wedding had set in, and Hannah was already exhausted. Tom was probably already in town, maybe even on his way to the country club. He was with his date, a guidance counselor named Jaime.

'Honey, are you okay?' Dawn asked, suddenly looking more genuine than Hannah thought possible.

'I do want him back,' Hannah said, surprising herself as she lost control, tears suddenly soaking her still-liner-free eyes.

'Sweetie,' Dawn responded, pulling Hannah to her chest. 'Sweetie, you'll get him back in a snap. You're gorgeous.'

Vicki

'You play?'

'Hmm?' Vicki looked up to see a teenage boy pointing at the case strapped to her back.

'Sorry. I was just wondering about your instrument. What kind is it?'

'It's just a basic Takamine acoustic. Nothing special,' Vicki responded with a shrug and a half smile.

'Are you in a band?' the boy continued.

'No. It's just a hobby. I just like to play before bed. I sing myself to sleep.'

'Cool,' the boy muttered, and then he went off to join his parents, who argued quietly by the historic hotel's front door.

Vicki had come up with a few canned answers to the guitar question because inevitably someone would ask.

It was usually a man or younger woman who inquired. Women Vicki's age and older rarely took interest in the guitar case. At most they'd scowl, as if they'd decided that Vicki was far too old to be carrying an instrument on her back.

Vicki imagined that traveling with a guitar case was something like being pregnant. Strangers felt entitled to pass judgment or know more. Instead of 'How far along are you?' it was 'Are you in a band?' or 'What do you play?' You were just supposed to answer.

Vicki's shoulders tensed as she watched the hotel clerk swipe her credit card for incidentals. It pained her to stay here. The Robert Johnson House was a beautifully restored brick building that, according to the plaque on the wall, was home to the Johnson family in the 1700s. It was probably an ideal place to experience Maryland's capital as a tourist, just steps away from the waterfront, but it was a huge waste of money for Vicki, who had thousands of unused Marriott points from her work travels. It was Hannah who had demanded they stay here.

'I'm a bridesmaid. I have to stay with the wedding party,' Hannah had explained to Vicki on the phone. 'We can get a room at the Robert Johnson House or the Governor Calvert House. The Robert Johnson House looks smaller and is probably cheaper. Honestly, Vicki, both places look beautiful, at least on their websites. I mean, aren't you sick of Marriotts anyway?'

'Not really,' Vicki answered honestly. 'I like chain hotels. They feel like home. There's no guarantee that some old Annapolis inn will even have cable.'

Now that Vicki was there, she could see that she'd jumped to unfair conclusions about what the tiny inn would offer. The Robert Johnson House, which sat next to its sister hotel, the Governor Calvert House, on historic, cobblestoned State Circle, had been updated with flat-screen televisions that looked primed for HBO. Vicki squinted to identify the glow of a Coke machine in the distance. She sighed, relieved. Maybe she could convince Hannah to return to the room early, buy bags of M&M's, and watch *Saturday Night Live*.

Once Vicki had her room key in hand, she grabbed the handle of her small suitcase and wheeled it past the front desk, eager to enjoy her last hour or so of freedom before the wedding. But before she made it out of the lobby, she was interrupted again.

'Do you play?' asked the man behind her.

'Yes,' she said sharply, whipping around to face him. She softened quickly, surprised at how easily his face disarmed her. He had full cheeks and gray hair that belied his childlike smile. He was in his forties or fifties, younger than her parents but not by much.

'You're a musician? Do you have a gig? At one of the bars downtown?' the man asked, hopefully.

'No, it's just a hobby. I'm here for a wedding.'

'Oh great,' the man responded, adding a shaky laugh. 'Let me guess – the Evans-Fee wedding?'

Vicki's shoulders tensed again, causing the guitar case to inch up her back.

'Yeah. Bee's my close friend from college.'

The man laughed nervously again. He cleared his throat. 'I'm Bee's uncle, Joe.'

'Oh. I think Bee's mentioned you. I'm Vicki. I was Bee's roommate at Syracuse in our freshman year. We've been friends ever since.'

The man stared as if she'd said something offensive. His smile wilted. He was silent, barely breathing, his body stiff like electronic equipment that had run out of batteries. Vicki waited, but his face didn't change. His eyes were the only part of him that moved. They took in her facial features one by one until they stopped at her lips.

'Okay, then, I'll see you at the party,' Vicki said, awkwardly about-facing and continuing down the hallway that led to the rooms. 'Weird,' she whispered to herself as she picked up her pace.

It was probably nothing, Vicki thought as she fiddled at the door with the old-fashioned metal key. Hannah was right. Maybe she did always jump to the conclusion that everyone was out to get her. Maybe people were uncomfortable around her because she'd done something to make them uncomfortable. Maybe Bee's uncle was just tired. Or maybe he was having a stroke.

As soon as she was safe in her hotel room, Vicki threw down her luggage so she could finally remove the heavy guitar case from her back. She set it down carefully on one of the room's two double beds. She chose the bed closer to the window, out of respect for Hannah's small bladder. Vicki had learned during their many weekend road trips in college that Hannah was happiest when she was given the bed closest to the toilet.

Vicki leaned over the guitar case and unlocked both latches so she could inspect what was inside, which was not a guitar at all.

Instead of an instrument, the case held a lamp, which Vicki removed delicately, keeping it level as if it were a bowl of scalding soup. She brought it to the wall outlet next to the bed and set it down on the floor. She then plugged it in and sat crossed-legged in front of it. Once the lamp had warmed up, Vicki leaned over it so its invisible rays shined up at her face. Then she reached over for the remote control on the nearby end table.

Vicki's therapist had told her not to do this, that watching television was a bad idea – especially while she was having quality time with the lamp. Dr Howard couldn't say for sure that the light and sound coming from the screen negated the effectiveness of the lamp, but they certainly didn't help the lamp do its job.

'Television is part of the problem, not the solution,' Dr Howard had said in his central New York accent, which was a blend of Midwestern *o*'s and New York City *a*'s. 'You do this all day and all night. This is depression. No more reality shows. No more cop shows. No more shows, period.'

With that in mind, Vicki quickly turned off the hotel television before she could even see what was on. She'd actually grown used to living a mostly TV-free life since she'd started seeing Dr Howard a year ago. He was the one who had encouraged her to buy the seasonal affective disorder lamp.

Ironically, the only time she felt drawn to the remote

control was when she was with sitting with the SAD lamp. It was so boring, staring at a lamp for a full hour each day. It wasn't easy during lamp time for Vicki to practice cognitive behavioral therapy, Dr Howard's prescription for ignoring all the things that upset her.

Vicki had purchased the lamp about six months ago for two hundred and fifty dollars, from an online medical-supply company recommended by Dr Howard. There was no guarantee that the light would change Vicki's life, Dr Howard had explained, but it was worth a try and seemed to be much safer than upping her dosage of antidepressants for the third time.

The lamp came with its own case, which was light enough and easy to carry – perfect for Vicki's frequent business trips. The only problem was that the case was emblazoned with the lamp's brand name. 'SAD-Lite,' it said, in thick black letters.

People either knew what Vicki was carrying or they'd ask, which was worse.

'What's a SAD-Lite?' one of Vicki's colleagues had inquired during her first road trip with the lamp.

'It's a thing . . . for my laptop,' Vicki had responded, unprepared for the question. 'It hooks up to my laptop. For wireless.'

The man frowned suspiciously.

'Is it one of those depression lamps?' he asked, ignoring her answer. 'My wife's brother has one.'

'No, I said it was for my computer.'

'Hmm,' the man grunted in disbelief.

Just before her second road trip with the lamp, Vicki remembered the guitar case in her spare room. She'd bought the instrument during a day trip to Ithaca when she was still with her college boyfriend Rich. He'd been in a band and told her that if she learned to play, she could join them on a song or two, as if that were an attractive offer. She could barely keep a straight face when she watched Rich's band perform its rock covers and six original songs, three of which were about taking a woman's virginity.

Vicki had told Rich, as she shelled out fifty dollars for the old instrument, that she would use the guitar to start a rival band with Hannah so they could finally make use of their long list of fake band names. But she and Hannah always had better things to do, and the Takamine had gone untouched for years.

But it now served a greater purpose. The guitar case turned out to be an appropriately sized, inconspicuous vessel for the lamp. So far none of her coworkers had demanded to see the instrument. They never asked her why she brought it on the road. As far as they were concerned, she was simply committed to her new hobby.

If only her coworkers knew that she didn't even know how to hold a guitar. If only they knew that that the thing inside the case had been purchased to prevent her from spiraling into an emotional abyss.

Vicki had told Hannah about the SAD lamp when they spoke on the phone a few weeks before the wedding, just so there were no surprises. Hannah had called to find out whether Vicki wanted to share a hotel room on the night of the wedding instead of sleeping in separate, expensive quarters.

Vicki didn't need to split the cost of anything. Unlike Hannah, whose New York City rent devoured her income, Vicki saved most of what she earned. She made a respectable corporate salary, which in Rochester made her rich. And because she was always traveling for work, she hardly spent any of her own money. Meals and cars were always expensed. Her utility bills were low because she was rarely home.

She decided quickly that she would share the room with Hannah and pay for it herself, just so her broke friend didn't have to worry about it. Hannah had already paid too much for Bee's high-end bridesmaid's dress and the fifty-two-dollar bra that, Hannah had explained, was a wedding requirement.

Vicki did have some anxiety about sharing a hotel

room with another human – she was too used to traveling alone – but her fears were tempered by her desire
to see Hannah, a real friend, who made her laugh, unlike
her acquaintances in Rochester.

There were probably a few interesting twenty- and
thirtysomethings at Vicki's office, but she would most
likely never meet them. As an interior designer for
Walton's, a national supermarket chain known for its
upscale prepared-food section, she spent 90 percent of
her time on the road, visiting stores around central New
York and Pennsylvania to make sure that the bakery
signs were placed an appropriate distance from the ceiling and that the walls in the new stores had been painted
the right shade of yellow.

She only spoke to a few people a day, usually to give
them orders about moldings or wallpaper. She was out
of practice with real conversation. That's probably why
she'd been so awkward during the phone call with
Hannah about the SAD-Lite.

'I have to tell you,' Vicki had said, when she firmed
up plans with Hannah a few weeks before, 'I'll be bringing a lamp.'

'Like, a heat lamp?' Hannah asked, confused.

'A depression lamp. A seasonal affective disorder
lamp.'

'You have seasonal affective disorder?' Hannah asked skeptically. 'You seemed fine during all those years up in Syracuse. It snowed for two years straight and you were pretty content, if I remember correctly.'

'Who knows? Jesus, Hannah, I have no idea what I have.' Vicki responded with a frustrated laugh. 'I have something. I just don't know what it is.'

There was a pause. Vicki waited, desperate to know what Hannah now thought of her once-normal friend.

'Can I try the lamp too?' Hannah finally asked, playfully.

Vicki smiled into the phone, relieved that Hannah was still making jokes. 'Sure.'

'Is this about Rich?'

'No!' Vicki barked. 'No. God, no. Not everybody wants to get back together with their college boyfriend, Hannah.'

'Fine, then,' Hannah snapped. 'Is this – could this be because you spend all day in grocery stores? Because that would be my guess,' Hannah asked, more seriously.

'No,' Vicki answered too quickly.

'Well . . .' she continued, after taking a moment to think. 'Maybe it is. I don't know. I just know that this lamp is supposed to help me not want to jump off a bridge.'

'Okay,' Hannah said slowly. 'Wow. A lamp.'

'Yeah.'

'Can you get a tan from it?'

'You're an idiot.'

Hannah moved on, telling Vicki all about Bee's brides-maids, who sounded truly awful from Hannah's description of the bachelorette party in Atlantic City. Then Hannah brought up the subject of Tom, whom she would be seeing for the first time since he moved out almost three years ago.

'I'm freaking out,' Hannah admitted. 'Just the idea that he'll be there with some woman. I don't know if I can take it.'

This was one of the reasons Vicki missed living near Hannah. Hannah wasn't at all ashamed that she was still pining for a guy she hadn't dated in years. Vicki always felt the need to look strong, or at the very least to keep her misery to herself, but Hannah was never private about her emotions. She shared, even when it was inappropriate. She could have been a great actress, Vicki thought as she listened to Hannah's jealous spiral.

'Supposedly he lives with her,' Hannah shout-whispered. 'Supposedly she moved in with him after, like, two months. Supposedly she's totally normal, nothing special. Bee googled her and apparently she looks . . .

64

regular. Not a supermodel or anything. But maybe Bee is just lying to me to keep me sane. She's probably perfect.'

'Have *you* googled her?' Vicki asked, afraid of the answer.

'I can't,' Hannah said sheepishly. 'Bee won't tell me her last name. I tried googling "Tom Keating" and "Jaime" and "guidance counselor," but nothing came up.'

'That's probably for the best, Hannah. In this case, the Internet is not your friend.'

Vicki had spoken to Hannah a few times after that, to confirm the details of their trip. Hannah would arrive three days ahead of Vicki to do bridesmaid duties. She would stay with the other bridesmaids in a hotel suite in the Governor Calvert House until the night of the wedding, when she'd switch over to share the room next door at the Robert Johnson House with Vicki.

Now, with just two hours until the ceremony, Vicki guessed that Hannah was already at the country club waiting for guests to arrive. With the lamp still on and the remote control back in its place by the bed, Vicki reached over to her purse and pulled out a paperback book, *My Sweet Audrina*.

Vicki had not told anyone – not even Dr Howard –

that when her depression became unbearable about a year ago, she began buying V. C. Andrews's books at the Barnes & Noble down the street from her apartment complex. She didn't think Dr Howard would object to her reading smut; it was just that she was too embarrassed to tell him about it.

They were the same steamy novels Vicki had read as a kid, after finding her mother's secret stash in her family's basement closet. There had been about twenty-five of the books in her mother's collection back then, some by Andrews, others by authors of a similar bent. When Vicki found the paperbacks as a thirteen-year-old, she'd been mesmerized. It was grown-up erotica. She couldn't believe the way the authors discussed sex so vividly, the way they described organs with unsubtle euphemisms and explained the dramatic, life-changing ecstasy that was sexual intercourse.

It was because of those books that Vicki was supremely disappointed when she finally had sex for the first time as a senior in high school.

V. C. Andrews had led her to believe that a woman could quite literally feel a man's orgasm. She remembered reading phrases like 'she felt him come inside of her,' and had assumed that penises were something like fire hydrants. Once levers were released, they would spray with force. She imagined that whatever came out of penises at the point of ecstasy coated the inside of a woman's vagina with something soft and nice, like movie-popcorn butter. Vicki couldn't wait to feel it.

And there was always clawing. In V. C. Andrews's world, people always clawed during sex, marking each other's bodies with scratches and bruises. It was never about violence. It was about uncontrollable passion. Sometimes the sex involved incest. Vicki would never admit it, but she'd liked those scenes best. It was taboo on top of taboo. Sibling rape. Cousin love. Beautiful twins who slept with the same man.

When Vicki eventually had real seventeen-year-old sex with the boy she dated through graduation – who was not at all related to her – she was somewhat shocked by the lack of sparks, scars, and hydrant geysers. There was nothing except for a little bit of pain and a sloppy rhythm. She had to be told when it was over.

Vicki's sexual relationship with Rich at Syracuse had been no help. They adored each other and managed to stay in a committed relationship during their last two years of college, but Rich did not believe in the passionate lovemaking described in V. C. Andrews's books.

Once Vicki tried to claw at Rich, simply to see if she could work him into a frenzy worthy of *Flowers in the*

Attic, but Rich instantly objected to the aggressive behavior.

'Ow! Vicki, what the hell are you doing?' Rich yelled when Vicki dug her nails into his back, imagining she was Cathy in *Petals on the Wind*, one of her favorites.

'I was excited,' Vicki responded, embarrassed.

'Fine, but don't hurt me.'

And there was never a geyser when he had an orgasm, even after they stopped using condoms. Sometimes she felt squishy, but it only made her want to shower.

Vicki had assumed that her rediscovery of V. C. Andrews would be a short-term phase, but within a month she'd bought more than twenty books. She now had a stash much like her mother's and found herself rereading each book more than once, sometimes skimming through them to find the sex scenes. She'd even considered buying a Kindle, just so it would be easier to bring more than one book on the road.

Vicki flipped the paperback open to a dog-eared page. She smiled, knowing full well that she was just a few paragraphs away from a sweet and confused heroine consummating her love with claws and enjoying a fire hydrant on blast.

It was an hour later, and time for Vicki to slip into her formal wear, when she finally took a good look at the hotel-room walls. She could identify the color: mocha wash. White stone for the trim. Ivory moon for the ceiling. Walton's used ivory moon for its back offices. She wondered dully what the Robert Johnson House decorators had chosen for the bathroom as she walked in to fix her hair.

When she was presentable, she glanced longingly at *My Sweet Audrina*, lying on the bed, and then stuck it firmly in her purse. She walked into the hallway, closing the door behind her, and then swore, realizing that she'd left her room key inside. She dumped the contents of her purse onto the floor, just to make sure. No key. She'd have to get another one downstairs when she returned for the night. She took a few unbalanced steps toward the lobby in her sharp black heels and heard a vaguely familiar male voice call to her from behind.

Rob

$\mathcal{R}$ob opened the Ziploc bag and removed one of the small white pills.

He wasn't sure how this one would go down with alcohol, but he figured the worst possible side effect would be nausea, and it seemed worth the risk.

Hannah's phone calls from the wedding had made him anxious, and he suspected that the white pill might help.

He placed the small oval on his tongue and took a sip of the Belgian beer he'd bought earlier that night at the specialty market down the street. The beer tasted like Bud Light, which was ridiculous because it cost three times as much.

Rob glanced at his phone, which was where he'd left it, on top of his poorly assembled IKEA coffee table. All of Rob's furniture was one missing screw away from breaking. Rob didn't like reading directions, so he put things together by guessing. He often finished such projects only to find that he hadn't used all the nails and hinges that came in the box. The end table next to his bed had just broken the week before under the weight of three heavy books. The two bookshelves in his living room swayed whenever he added to his library. He was careful moving around in his apartment, knowing that at any moment it could all fall down.

Rob had received so many phone calls today that he was beginning to hear phantom rings. He found himself checking and rechecking the phone. He considered turning it off but didn't want to. To be honest with himself, he'd admit that he was desperate to see the small screen turn bright green and show Hannah's number one more time. He didn't necessarily want to answer her calls, but he wanted her to keep reaching out.

That was Rob's thing, Hannah had always said, wanting to be wanted.

This was the most Rob had thought about Hannah in years. Almost a decade had passed since his three years at Syracuse, and when he was busy with his real life in Austin, it usually felt as if he'd invented the memories from that time in his life or, better yet, that he'd seen them on a television show and adopted them as his own.

It seemed inconceivable that he'd once lived in central New York and failed out of school. Only his second life seemed real.

Most people didn't even know that Rob had attended Syracuse. To his friends in Austin, he was the guy who worked for the University of Texas library, a job that allowed him to get a degree for free. He was the guy who easily managed a good grade point average and graduated with recommendations from three of his English professors. In a few months, he'd start applying to grad schools. He freelanced, writing book reviews for the local alternative weekly.

Up until now his only tangible proof that Syracuse had ever happened were student loan bills and occasional calls and e-mails from Hannah, who would update him about his old friends, namely Bee, Vicki, and Hannah's ex-boyfriend Tom, who had been Rob's closest male companion back at school.

He was always happy to hear about them, but this was the first time he'd longed to see them. There was something about the idea of Bee getting married and Hannah's panicked voice that made Rob desperate to see Hannah's face, watch Bee walk down the aisle, and then drink beers with Vicki after everyone else had fallen asleep.

He was shocked by how giddy he felt when Hannah began contacting him yesterday afternoon, at the start of what would be a weekend of events celebrating Bee's nuptials.

The first frantic phone call had come in a few hours before Bee's rehearsal dinner. It was from a 917 area code, a number he didn't know.

'This is Rob,' he'd said, giving his standard greeting.

'When do you get in? Tell me it's today,' said the female voice, rushed and slurred.

'Who is this?'

'It's Hannah. Rob, it's me.'

'Don't yell at me,' he said, letting out his throaty laugh. 'We haven't spoken on the phone in, what, a year?'

'First of all, it's been a few months at the most,' Hannah said, quickly doubting her answer.

'Maybe a year,' she admitted. 'Second of all, why is my number not programmed into your phone? That's how you're supposed to know it's me. My name is supposed to pop up on the little screen. Why didn't my name pop up?'

'I don't keep any numbers in my phone.'

'Then how do you know who's calling you?'

'I answer the phone and the person on the other end of the line tells me who they are.'

'Jesus, Rob.'

'If you remember, Han, we didn't even have cell phones in college, and we managed just fine.'

'You know,' Hannah said, suddenly thoughtful, 'I was just thinking about that the other day. I didn't even get my first cell phone until I moved to New York. How did we ever find each other back then?'

'Messenger pigeon, if I remember correctly. Actually, I think I blew into a conch shell and you came running.'

Hannah was silent, trying to come up with a comeback. After her pause went on for too long, they both broke down, giggling.

'Tell me you're getting here soon, because I'm losing my mind.'

Rob released a heavy sigh and braced himself, his hand pressing against his kitchen counter. 'I'm not coming,' he admitted stiffly.

'What?' Hannah yelled. 'What? What do you mean you're not coming? You RSVP'd yes! You e-mailed me three months ago to tell me that you were coming. Bee thinks you're coming. You're on the seating chart. Bee sat you next to Vicki.'

'Some things came up. I didn't get a flight. It's a long story.'

'Jesus, Rob. This is so – ugh! This is so 2001. You

can't still be selfish and irresponsible like this. You can't skip a wedding after you've told people you're coming. The food costs money. People take these things seriously.'

Rob rolled his eyes, now aggravated. 'Bee won't even notice, and we both know she has plenty of money.'

'You know very well that Bee will notice. You know that she'll look for you, of all people,' Hannah said, giving Rob an extra sting.

'Hannah, I'm sorry. It's not happening. I'm in Texas.'

He heard her mutter something to herself, but he couldn't make out the words. 'Rob,' she finally said, making his name sound as heavy as a bowling ball, 'this isn't fair.'

'These people are crazy,' Hannah continued, now whispering as if she'd been kidnapped and her captors were in the next room. 'Everybody's on drugs – like, mood drugs. Bee's mom has been a vegetable. I swear I haven't seen her once without a drink in her hands. And the best man? It's this guy named Jimmy Fee, and he's so stupidly attractive that every time he walks into a room Bee's mom looks like she wants to drop her pants. And I can't say I blame her. Thank God he has a girlfriend.'

Rob laughed silently.

'So Donna's drinking, eh? How does she look?'

'Bee's mom? I don't know. She looks like a mom. Listen, I need you. Please find a flight. I can't do this alone.'

'You'll survive. Just take pictures – especially if they're making you wear something low cut.'

'They're making me wear a pearl necklace. I don't think I can do this.'

Rob considered all the lewd jokes he could make about pearl necklaces, but he refrained. He could hear the tension in Hannah's voice and decided it would be best to bring the conversation to an end as quickly as possible.

'Do you know what a pageant coach does, Rob?' Hannah rambled in her panicked whisper. 'I bet you don't. Just guess.'

'Easy there,' Rob said, ignoring the question. 'Just hang in there and we'll talk soon. You can call me if there's an emergency. Just take a deep breath and try not to take everything so seriously. It will be over in less than forty-eight hours.'

'Fine,' Hannah had said softly. He imagined her pout.

'Keep your head up, kid,' he'd said, just before pressing the 'end' button too quickly for her to respond.

Rob had looked down at the blank phone screen and

impulsively saved her number, with her name, making her the only official contact in his address book.

He'd gone on to picture her crouched in the corner of a hotel room, or maybe at a hair salon, making calls to him covertly, desperate for his companionship. He imagined what it might be like to be there in Annapolis, at her side, whispering words in her ear that would crack her up, just like he'd done in college.

Although the more he thought about it, Rob had to admit that despite all the times he'd made Hannah laugh uncontrollably, he'd never really been a source of comfort for her. Their secret, passive-aggressive affair, which had lasted the better part of their junior year – Rob's last year at Syracuse – had made Hannah miserable and forced her to lie to her close friends. Rob was never respectful, showing up at her apartment for attention sometimes as late as three in the morning, but she would always open the door and let him in.

There was never 'all-the-way sex,' as Hannah called it. Never penetration.

There was usually what Hannah called 'everything but,' which meant an hour or so of feverish petting and then three hours of talking.

They never told anyone about their late-night dates. Hannah said it would hurt Bee too much. Bee – who had harbored a crush on Rob since meeting him in their dorm freshman year – was lovely, of course, and Rob had to admit she was conventionally better looking than Hannah or any of the other women he'd fooled around with while at Syracuse, but she was too wholesome and easily awestruck by his antics. She looked at him like he was James Dean, and he could never live up to whatever it was she saw. Rob tried to explain all this to Hannah one night, in bed, after she asked him matter-of-factly why he wouldn't pursue Bee.

'I find it odd that you're asking me that after what we just did,' Rob said, after a pause, rubbing the back of Hannah's neck as she nestled her head in his armpit.

'Come on, Rob. I'm just curious. She's really attractive and she's the nicest person we know.'

'That's part of the problem,' Rob said. 'She's like a doll. I'd feel like a dirty old man, touching her.'

'Rob, first of all, you can't be a twenty-year-old dirty old man. Second, Bee has slept with more people than I have.'

'Is that true? How many people has she slept with? How many people have *you* slept with?'

'She's slept with five, and I've slept with two.'

'Two? Only two?'

'Only two.'

'You've got to get out more, Hannah.' Rob was silent for a moment before murmuring, 'So I'd be lucky number three?'

'In your dreams,' Hannah had muttered back as she lifted herself from his chest and turned to face her bedroom wall, which she'd painted mint green to mark the start of the spring semester. The color reminded Rob of toothpaste. He missed the dark purple from the fall. He couldn't understand why she and Vicki made a big production of repainting their bedrooms every six months. Hannah had explained that Vicki, a future interior decorator, believed that they should start each semester with a new color scheme, but it didn't make sense to Rob. Paint was expensive and the fumes in their apartment never quite dissipated. The smell of lingering chemicals made him feel like he was losing brain cells, especially during the spring, when Syracuse was buried in snow and all of Hannah's windows were sealed tight.

Rob had enjoyed his late-night visits to Hannah's room, the physical intimacy and the hours of chitchat, but he'd chosen to end the secret routine shortly after her walls went the way of Crest and Colgate. By mid-February of their second semester, Rob could foresee how the year would end, with him dropping out of school and moving to Austin. He had tentative plans to stay there for a few months, until he could figure out what he wanted to do next. He'd decided it would be best to separate from Hannah sooner rather than later. He'd been spending too many nights with her, and it was becoming more of a relationship than a tryst. So on the final Thursday of the month, on a weeknight he almost always spent at Hannah's, he just didn't show up.

By March, Rob had replaced Hannah with Alexis, a girl in his anthropology class. She was from Long Island and had a nose ring. Alexis didn't talk much and was only interested in all-the-way sex.

Hannah realized soon enough that she'd been passed over. She met Alexis at one of Rob's band's gigs and pretended not to be offended. Hannah became cold to Rob but she never confronted him. That didn't surprise him. There had been an implicit agreement about their routine, that it was something they'd never speak of outside her apartment.

It wasn't until the day they'd all packed up to go to home for the summer that Rob showed up at Hannah and Vicki's apartment for the last time and told Hannah, in front of her bedroom walls, which were already chipping thanks to this semester's cheap paint job, that he wouldn't be returning to school in the fall. She responded by yelling about his grades and his future, but her shaking hands and quivering lip suggested there was more to it than that.

They'd spent one more weekend together as friends. Tom, Rob's only real male friend at the time, was new to the group and had invited them all to his parents' summer house on Cape Cod. It was supposed to be a send-off for Rob, but Hannah had barely acknowledged him. Bee had also kept Rob at a distance during the trip and seemed to be consoling Hannah, like she might have known about the affair the whole time.

Later that summer, after he was settled into a studio apartment in Austin, he received a letter from Hannah. It had been written on a computer, probably so she could spell-check it, he thought. He hoped it was an apology for her coldness but wasn't surprised to find that it was a list of accusations. Most of her sentences started with the phrase 'I feel like' and ended with a word like 'intimacy' or 'accountability.' The note didn't ask for anything specific; it was just an airing of grievances. Rob never responded.

Hannah called him the following Christmas, to catch up. She made no mention of the note. Instead she asked about life in Austin and offered him updates about the group. She admitted that she and Tom had started dating and was relieved when Rob congratulated her instead of getting angry. Since then she'd called him about once a year and had sent occasional e-mails. She'd told him all about her career in New York, and he'd watched clips of her casting projects on YouTube.

The only time he'd called Hannah had been a few years ago, after he heard from Bee that Tom had left Hannah to move closer to his family in Boston. Bee had explained that Hannah was devastated. And it had devastated Rob that Hannah was so miserable to lose Tom.

Tom Keating was a buddy whom Hannah had dubbed the 'prep-school boner' after meeting him for the first time. But soon enough Hannah welcomed Tom to the group, inviting him to their movie nights and on day trips with Vicki, Rich, and Bee.

After Rob dropped out of school and moved back to Texas, Tom almost effortlessly took his place in Hannah's life, first asking her to a movie, then stopping by for late-night talks – and then late-night 'everything but.' He even managed to become her boyfriend by October of their senior year, which meant he'd become lucky number three.

Tom actually called Rob to ask for his blessing, as if

Hannah were his property. The call would have infuriated Hannah, had she known about it.

'Do whatever you want, Tom,' Rob had said, trying his best to sound unaffected.

Rob had just finished moving into his first apartment in Austin and, covered in sweat, surrounded by boxes, he quickly lit up a cigarette. 'Hannah wasn't even my girlfriend.'

'I know, man, but she really liked you. And I know you cared about her. She told me that. She said you guys might have been serious had it not been for Bee's crush on you and your failing out of school and all.'

This news flustered Rob, who was shocked to hear that Hannah had not only been serious about him but had disclosed her feelings about him to Tom.

'Well, that's flattering, Tom,' Rob said, patronizingly. 'I'm glad Hannah enjoyed our quality time together, but, really, I'm in Texas. Go get laid. Do whatever you need to do.'

'It's not about getting laid, Rob. I really like her.'

'Tom, I'm kidding. Really, you have my blessing.'

When Rob got off the phone that day, he picked up one of the books he'd just unpacked, a coffee-stained copy of John Sayles's *Los Gusanos,* and chucked it against the wall.

Hannah and Tom wound up dating happily during their senior year and stayed together after graduation, when Tom offered to follow Hannah to New York City. From what Hannah had told Rob in her occasional e-mail dispatches, the twosome had lived in Queens for three years and then moved to Brooklyn. Tom had found a satisfactory job at a political-consulting firm near City Hall. All was well until he decided he was sick of the city and wanted to live in Boston near his family. He hoped to run for office in his hometown someday and needed to start a life in Massachusetts.

Hannah had no interest in leaving New York, unless it was for Los Angeles. So that was that.

Rob didn't know many details about the split, whether Hannah had begged Tom to stay or if there was a chance they'd reunite. Rob's awkward call to Hannah after hearing about the breakup had been brief. Hannah had other friends to lean on. He was all the way in Texas, mostly out of touch and uninformed.

Rob had not seen Hannah in person since that trip to Cape Cod. These phone calls reminded him that Hannah was quick witted and capable of making him laugh, something he rarely did these days.

And now that he was taking time to think about it, Hannah had always been a very good friend to him, even before they began a physical relationship. She'd always helped him with school, forcing him to study for tests that they both knew he'd sleep through. She spent her late nights quizzing him about his parents, the father he never met and the mother who had spent much of his teenage years traveling with her boyfriend.

Hannah had even cleaned Rob's apartment once, on the weekend when he had the flu and couldn't get out of bed. She was on her hands and knees in his bathroom, swearing that unless she killed the germs he'd get sick all over again.

He never returned those favors. In fact, it was he who had driven her Ford Tempo into a pole on her twentieth birthday, shortly after calling her predictable for wanting to go home early. He later argued, to their mutual friends, that Hannah should never have let him drive after four beers and that allowing him to do so was also predictable.

He'd never asked her about her family, never made it comfortable for her to talk about her feelings, even when he knew she was desperate to share.

In Rob's mind Hannah had always expected too much of him and had set herself up to be irrationally disappointed when he behaved like himself. It was unfair. Rob had never pretended to be anything he wasn't. Even now he was just a guy who sent nice e-mails and said funny things on the phone. He wasn't a guy who actually showed up for her when it mattered.

When Rob first received the 'save the date' card for Bee's wedding—the one that showed Bee and her husband-to-be standing in an apple orchard — he was actually charmed. It was the closest he'd ever come to being a proud parent.

In the picture Bee wore a puffy vest over a long-sleeved T-shirt and jeans. She looked blonder than he remembered and even prettier. Her cheeks were rosy and her smile was genuine. She looked confident. It was a Bee he'd never seen.

Behind her, with his arms around her waist, was Matt Fee, the lucky guy. Rob had heard from Hannah in an e-mail that Matt was a lawyer, but in this picture he looked more like a football star. He had wavy hair that was just a shade or two darker than Bee's and arms that were about three times the width of Rob's.

The picture showed Bee and Matt posed behind two bushels of apples. The text over the image said, 'We've picked each other!'

Rob would have expected an apple-picking pun on a 'save the date' postcard to make him angry or at the very least annoyed, but, much to his surprise, the card pleased him. Bee deserved this. She was introverted and kind, and she should have someone who'd treat her well. She'd had a rough go of finding a partner in college, no thanks to her long-term crush on him and her tendency to be Hannah's quiet sidekick.

Bee was beautiful, but most of the young men at school treated her like a purebred dog. She seemed too wholesome and refined to play with. And it was clear, whether Bee wanted it to be or not, that dating her meant marrying her, or at the very least being true to her. Most men in college weren't ready for that responsibility. Rob wasn't surprised that it wasn't until law school that Bee found a man who, like Matt, was ready to be loyal.

When Rob first saw the 'save the date' card he examined it closely, as if it were his patriarchal duty to approve of what he saw. This older Bee had put on some weight, which was a good thing. In college he'd always suspected she was starving herself – often surviving on Snack-Well's cookies and low-fat yogurt – to become as small as her mother, a naturally petite woman who, according to Bee, was addicted to yoga and spinning classes. This older, more mature Bee on the 'save the date' card looked content. And Matt, with his tree-trunk masculine torso and five o'clock shadow, seemed like the kind of man who could provide for someone, a stable fellow whose closet was lined with pleated khaki pants and baseball caps.

Rob usually didn't like guys in caps, but he was happy Bee would be marrying one. He'd been so comforted by the idea of Bee in a good relationship that he'd decided to go to the wedding, despite the distance and the insufficient funds in his bank account. When the actual invitation arrived, he'd immediately checked off the 'yes' box and RSVP'd. It was the first time in his life he'd remembered to RSVP for anything.

But that was where his uncharacteristic enthusiasm for someone else's happiness had ended. Weeks went by and he hadn't bought a plane ticket. At first, it was the cost. He went online and saw that tickets from Texas to Baltimore were about six hundred dollars and included several annoying stopovers. He'd e-mailed Hannah, 'I'm waiting for a price drop. Don't worry about it.'

Rob's job in the library at UT paid well enough, but he'd been living from paycheck to paycheck since his ex-girlfriend Lucy Barber had moved out. When Lucy moved in with him, two years ago, she'd agreed to pay half the rent, which was only fair. For the first time in his life, Rob was able to pay off some of his Syracuse debt and save some money.

But Lucy only lasted six months as a live-in girlfriend. Their failure to live together successfully wasn't a shock to either of them; even before Lucy moved in Rob knew that she was unreliable and that she abused prescription medication. But Rob was smitten with her and willing to take the risk. He'd never been the stable one in their dizzying relationship and it made him feel good about himself to keep someone else on track.

Unfortunately, he was too much like her to balance her. Within weeks of moving in, he was dipping into the never-ending supply of pills prescribed by the doctors who believed medication was the answer to her mood swings.

Lucy had left more than a year ago – and had promptly moved in with her much older ex-boyfriend – but she'd been nice enough to leave behind her twenty-four-hundred-dollar Pottery Barn couch and three Ziploc bags packed with pills, the ones she knew he liked.

He knew her departure had been for the best, but Rob still missed Lucy terribly, specifically the sex, which was easier with her than it had been with anyone else. It was simply sex, rather than a reward for making promises he couldn't keep. There was never emotional negotiation.

He acknowledged to himself – and to Lucy just before she took the last of her belongings – that their split was his rightful comeuppance. He deserved to be on the other side of this type of breakup, just once. It was a valuable life experience, he'd rationalized.

After Lucy, Rob slept with a few women, mostly friends of friends, but more recently he'd refrained from the process of sexual courtship altogether. He'd gone without intercourse for months, the longest gap since he lost his virginity. The lull was because of Liz, not that he blamed her.

Shortly after Lucy packed up the last of her wardrobe and returned the key, Rob, on a whim, rescued a mutt from a local shelter. He didn't know why he'd done it. He'd never owned a pet.

It was a Tuesday afternoon. He was driving home from the grocery store and passed the same animal shelter he drove by at least twice a day on his way to and from the university. Inexplicably he made a U-turn and pulled his car into the shelter's driveway.

He left two hours later with a mutt that was part golden retriever and part something else, maybe German shepherd. He named her Liz after Liz Phair because one of her songs was playing on the local college radio station as he drove home from the shelter.

Liz, the dog, was already five years old when Rob first met her. There were younger, cuter dogs, but Liz's sad eyes drew him in. He was Charlie Brown and she was the tiny, wilting Christmas tree. Rob figured that if he didn't take Liz home, she'd probably be put down.

Liz's first incident occurred about a month after Rob adopted her. The dog got up from her favorite lounging spot in Rob's tiny living room and suddenly took off, as if she were on a greyhound track. She ran straight into the television set, which tipped over, making a thud so loud Rob worried it would fall through the floor. The wooden table on which the television had been perched, another haphazardly constructed IKEA item that was missing two of four necessary screws, fell to pieces seconds later.

Seemingly unaware of the damage she'd just caused, Liz began stepping backward, almost moonwalking, until her tail beat against the back wall. Then she fell on her side, moaning and twitching. Her eyes bulged, glassy and full of fear.

Petrified, Rob sprung off the couch and attempted to pin down Liz's legs.

'Come on, baby. Come on, baby,' Rob repeated to the dog. He assumed she was dying.

But after about a minute and a half, Liz relaxed and blinked. She looked spent and confused, as did her owner. Slowly she used her hind legs to prop herself up. She leaned into Rob for support to help her get on all fours.

Rob lifted Liz and walked to the couch. He stroked her hair and kissed the back of her ears.

'It's going to be okay, babe,' he said without conviction, his voice trembling.

He lifted her again and set her down on the couch next to him. He waited until she closed her eyes and began breathing heavily in sleep before he went into the kitchen to dial the number on the 'Pet 911' magnet the vet had given him when he had first adopted her.

Rob angrily dialed the 1-800 number, which forced him to hunt for the digits that corresponded to the letters *p*, *e*, and *t*.

A man answered the phone.

'Well, sir, you can bring her in, but it's about one in the morning, and we see dogs in order of the severity of their emergency,' the hotline man said. 'If she's no longer having a seizure and she's asleep, I'd recommend waiting until tomorrow.'

Rob made an appointment with the animal hospital for the next day and returned to the couch, where Liz still snoozed, her smooth canine torso expanding and contracting with each breath.

He stayed up watching her, the television still on the floor, until he fell asleep by her side.

When they went to the hospital in the morning, she was diagnosed quickly. It was canine epilepsy. A common disorder.

'I didn't know dogs got epilepsy,' Rob said to the vet, a short, round, middle-aged woman with thinning hair.

'Why wouldn't they?' she answered, too sharply for his fragile state.

Showing no sympathy, the doctor laid it out for him in simple terms. Liz's condition could be temporarily controlled with medicine, which would cost about seventy-five dollars a month. Eventually, though, the attacks would become more frequent and the dog would have to be put down.

'How much time does she have?' Rob asked, whispering, as if he didn't want Liz to hear.

'She could live one, maybe even two years before the attacks become too frequent to manage and too painful for the pet,' the doctor said. 'It's an expensive commitment, and she's well past her salad days. If you choose to put her down now, we can accommodate that request.'

Rob, who sat across from the vet in a fabric chair

covered in dog hair, looked down silently at Liz, who was back on her feet and pressing her head against his leg lovingly.

'Sir,' the doctor said in a softer voice, 'maybe you should take a few days and think about it.'

That night in bed, with Liz at his feet, he did the math. Twelve hundred dollars a year in meds and blood tests, plus the dog food. Plus the three hundred dollars he no longer had coming in from Lucy for rent.

'Fuck it,' he said out loud, causing Liz to lift her head and look at him woozily.

The next day Rob picked up a prescription for the pills, which he mixed with the dog's dry food, as recommended. The vet's pharmacist also advised Rob to consider finding a home with more open space. The safest place for a dog to have a seizure would be on a soft lawn where there would be room to twitch and run from side to side without bumping into anything sharp.

That's when Rob found the place he'd been living in for about eight months now. It was a smaller house that rented for eight hundred dollars a month. Less for more and in a less-desirable neighborhood – but unlike the old apartment it sat on a half-acre backyard.

'It's for Liz. So she can have her seizures,' Rob had told Ben, one of his closer friends in Austin, who occasionally stopped by for beers, when he wasn't with his wife or touring with his band.

'How romantic,' Ben had said.

When Rob thought about going to Bee's wedding, he'd considered Liz and what he would do with her for an entire weekend. He could ask his brother to come down to Austin to watch her. Jeremy lived in Dallas and was always looking for a way to escape from his family.

But just as he'd never booked a ticket to Maryland, he'd never called his brother. It was for the best, Rob thought. He didn't trust Jeremy not to bail on the dog for a night out with his old friends from college.

Rob shook his head and reached for his phone. He was right to have stayed in Austin. But maybe he should call Hannah back, just to give her another pep talk and to find out about everyone else from school. He picked up the phone, scrolled to the only name programmed into it, and dialed just one more time.

he ride from Baltimore to Annapolis felt longer than it should.

Only about thirty miles separated the Maryland cities, but warm weather, even in September, scrambled traffic patterns. Phil found himself idling in each of the towns along the route, listening intently to the radio traffic reports. Glen Burnie. Severn. Parole, which he imagined as a town inhabited by ex-cons. Phil had probably been to some of these towns for high school basketball tournaments, but the intervening years had erased all memory of them.

Since moving to Baltimore after college, Phil hadn't left the city much. He was a twenty-minute drive from his childhood home, where his mother still lived, with a Newfoundland puppy, which had replaced her last Newfoundland, which had replaced the one before it.

Phil's condo, which he bought almost seven years ago, on his thirty-second birthday, was a short walk from his job at Camden Yards, though he never traveled to the ballpark by foot. His hometown felt less safe to him than New York, Philly, or any of the other cities he'd visited for games. Phil's stature didn't help matters. Being six foot six and broad shouldered came in handy at the ballpark, where he was in charge of security, but on the street Phil believed his height and lumberjack's build made him a target. People assumed he was a tough guy, which he wasn't.

Phil now spotted signs for Annapolis, which meant he'd be on time for the wedding. It was probably a good thing, even though Phil would have gladly skipped the ceremony and arrived just in time for the reception. He was only going to this wedding because his mother couldn't. Technically, he wasn't even invited to the wedding. It was his mom, Nancy MacGowan, who was a dear friend of the groom's mother. The now-sixty-something women had been inseparable when they lived in the same town, back when Phil was a teenager and the groom's family, the Fees, spent two years living in the Baltimore suburbs so they could expand their family business from North Carolina to Maryland and Virginia. All these years later the women did the best they could to see each other as often as possible, which wasn't much.

Nancy had been giddy about attending the wedding. Not only was she excited to see her old friend Barb and Barb's son, Matt, for whom she'd babysat when he was a boy, but she'd been planning her attire for the occasion for months. Rarely was there an excuse for her to leave town, let alone wear a dress and talk to strangers.

It was luck that Matt happened to fall for a woman whose family was from Maryland. If this wedding hadn't been local, Nancy would have never RSVP'd to say she'd attend.

But two days ago, a cold came on. A cold or a stomach virus, Phil suspected. It was an illness she didn't want to describe, which meant diarrhea might be involved. Phil figured she would have rallied from anything besides that.

'Nothing worse than being sick when it's still warm out,' Nancy told Phil on the phone, and Phil agreed.

'Do you want me to come down there on Saturday?' Phil asked his mother, thinking, selfishly, that it would be nice to do some free laundry and see the dog.

'I can take care of myself,' responded Nancy. 'But, Philly, honey, you'll have to go to Annapolis for that wedding and sit in my seat. Barb told me the plates cost almost two hundred dollars apiece, and I won't be wasting her money. I'm going to call Barb and tell her you'll be representing the family.'

Phil could not believe it.

'Jesus, Mom,' he bellowed. 'You gotta be kidding me. I don't even know these people.'

'Watch your mouth,' Nancy snapped.

And with that Phil knew there was no getting around it. One of his precious weekend days off from the ballpark would be spent celebrating the nuptials of two people he didn't even know.

Even though the ride had felt unbearably slow, and Phil had assumed he'd be one of those people who walk in midceremony, he was soon riding along the sparkling bay in the direction of the Tower Gardens Country Club, with ten minutes to spare. Phil got out of the car and took a deep breath, smelling his surroundings. It was a perfect almost-autumn day. It was his favorite time of year at Camden Yards: the spring games were too chilly, the summer games too steamy. Phil looked forward all season to two perfect weeks at the end of September.

It was also the most joyous time of year for the staff because it represented the end of a long run. Unless the Orioles made the playoffs, which hadn't happened since the late nineties, the final night of the season would be right around the last day of the month. Comfortable weather meant a light at the end of the tunnel.

Just past the parking lot, Phil saw what he estimated to be a crowd of two hundred or more people in formal wear, looking for a place in rows of white seats. The women stepped quickly as their heels sank through the damp soil beneath them. Most of the men wore black suits. The women wore short black getups or silky pastel or floral dresses and metallic sandals, which seemed to be a trend this year, based on what he'd seen at the ballpark.

Phil hated to admit that the place was beautiful. If he wasn't set on getting married in a church, he'd do it at a spot like this, he thought. The club looked like the kind of place where a nineteenth-century naval officer would get married or play golf. The lawn looked as shiny as Astro-turf and was protected by a row of well-groomed shrubs. Squinting, he could make out a line of sailboats just beyond a wooden fence marking the border of the property.

A teenage boy greeted him as he made his way to the seating area. 'Friend of the bride or groom?'

'Neither,' Phil replied, instantly regretting the joke. 'Groom. Sorry, man. Groom. My mom's a friend of the groom's mom.'

'That's my aunt, Barb.'

'Right. Barb. I haven't seen her since I was a kid. Great lady,' Phil said awkwardly, as the young boy pointed him in the direction of one of the last empty seats on the groom's side of the lawn.

Phil noticed that the bride's side was at least a quarter emptier than the groom's, which made him feel bad for her. Barb's family, a rowdy bunch that seemed already drunk and lively as they waited for the ceremony to start, made the bride's small clan appear uptight and depressive.

Just before taking his seat, Phil opted to change camps and walked briskly to one of the empty seats on the bride's side, just to help even out the look of things. He chose an entirely free row, hoping he wouldn't have to sit next to anyone, just in case he smelled.

Phil was an impeccably clean guy who showered twice a day, before and after games, but because of the hectic summer baseball schedule, he'd not been organized about maintaining his wardrobe. He was fanatical about cleaning his ballpark uniforms and his go-to khaki pants from the big-and-tall store, but he'd lost track of some his off-season attire and formal wear. When Nancy told Phil about the wedding, just two days ago, he reluctantly jotted down the details, the time and place, and hung up the phone to begin the search for his one fancy ensemble, which had been missing somewhere in his bedroom since his nephew's christening in July.

After an hour of looking under the bed and in laundry piles, Phil had found the crumpled gray jacket and pants in a bag that he'd put together to bring to the dry cleaner, which, of course, he never did.

A few minutes in the dryer had done the trick – his suit was crease free. Unfortunately, though, Phil couldn't get rid of the odor. Even though almost two months had gone by, the suit still smelled like the buffalo wings he'd devoured after the christening. The scent made him hungry and slightly nauseated.

Phil wondered if the couple sitting in front of him could smell him. He wanted to apologize to them and to explain why he stunk like wings, but he kept his eyes on the wedding program in his lap. He'd never attended a wedding where every name in the program was unfamiliar. Usually when he went to weddings, he was in the program. He'd been a groomsman twelve times – for most of his college ball teammates – and a best man twice.

Phil ran his fingers over the name of the groom and tried to remember when he last saw Matt Fee. Phil had few memories of Barb's family, even though they were so important to his mother. He wondered if he'd blocked them out.

Now that he was older, he realized that Barb was probably his mother's only outlet for adult communication during his father's last years. Phil was just a kid when his father was diagnosed with the disease that eventually killed him, something that his brother explained to strangers as 'not quite Parkinson's, not quite Lou Gehrig's.'

The disease was not quite anything, from what Phil could remember. It was a dark fog that took over his father's brain and robbed him of his ability to write, walk, and, eventually, breathe.

At first Nancy, Phil, and Phil's brother, Mickey, assumed that the often-grumpy and wisecracking patriarch of their family was simply depressed. Frank had become increasingly reserved and quiet, but they attributed it to the loss of his own mother, who had died the previous year.

Eventually Nancy confronted Frank about his prolonged gloom. His answer was frightening. 'I think I'm not well,' was all he'd told her, as a tear rolled down his right cheek.

Within a week, they were at the hospital for scans and consults. Within a month, there was a diagnosis.

'It's called frontotemporal dementia,' Nancy told her sons, who sat on the family's floral couch with their heads down. Frank was there too. He was in his favorite leather reclining chair, staring out the window.

The progression of the disease was actually rather slow, which Phil secretly resented. If Frank had died quickly, if he'd lost his capacities within a year, Nancy wouldn't have lost her forties tending to a sick man who went from being angry to vegetative over the course of six very long years. It seemed like it would go on forever, and Nancy kept him by her side for as long as she could.

That was Phil's most significant memory of Nancy's friend Barb Fee – what she said to his mother the night she realized she would have to put her husband into a home.

Phil was on his way from his bedroom to his living room to watch television, when he overheard Barb and Nancy whispering. He listened, hidden in the shadows of the hallway.

'You can't take care of him anymore,' Barb had said softly. 'You've been an angel. You've done him right. But this is beyond you and it's bad for the boys. It's time to bring him to a rehab facility, Nancy.'

'No,' Nancy had said unconvincingly. 'Not yet.'

'You're going to do it, and I'll help you.'

Phil heard his mother let out a sob. Usually she cried inaudibly, her eyes welling with tears as she spoke clearly. But this was a real release punctuated with whimpers and hiccups.

Nancy heaved as she tried to take a breath. Phil squatted as quietly as he could and hugged his knees with his arms as he tried to keep himself from letting out his own sobs. He knew that his tears weren't about his father, who snored loudly in the bedroom next to his. It had been more than a year since he'd accepted the fact that he'd lost the dad he'd known as a kid. But he mourned for his mother, Nancy the saint. Life should have been easier for her, but she'd been saddled with an unfortunate circumstance. And soon Phil would leave her to go to college. And Barb, who had quickly become Nancy's best friend, had plans to move back to Raleigh. Phil's mom would be alone.

That night, after he heard Barb shut the front door behind her, Phil silently pledged his devotion to his mom, whom he now realized could have dropped his father at a nursing home years ago. Alone in his room, he cried for her. He promised himself that he would be her partner from then on, no matter what. He would drive home from college as often as he could. He wouldn't leave Maryland as long as she lived there.

And that's why he was here in Annapolis, stuck with a bunch of strangers on a country club's lawn. Phil would give her whatever she needed.

Nancy had shared the wedding details with Phil in one rambling sentence. Barb's son Matt had met the bride at law school in Raleigh. She was from Ellicott City, Maryland, only about twenty minutes from where Phil had grown up. She was rich. Her dad was a lawyer too.

Fascinating, Phil had thought sarcastically, as his mother continued with the background.

Phil never understood people like Matt Fee who had jobs at law firms and banks and companies, how they could wake up every day and go to work without slipping into depression. Phil loved his job, despite how the world perceived it. He worked security at a ballpark, but as the boss of the operation it wasn't like all he did was kick people out or tell them not to smoke. It was difficult to explain to strangers, but his profession was far more complicated than that.

As head of security, Phil oversaw a staff of 130 people who were responsible for up to forty-five thousand baseball fans over the course of four emotional hours. The job took great concentration and coordination, and the profession became more complicated every year. On some nights Phil took charge of the welfare of a specific high-profile player, usually someone like Alex Rodriguez, to make sure he could get around without getting mobbed by fans or enemies. Phil had also been assigned to watch over celebrity baseball fans at least a dozen times. Last season, when the Red Sox were in town, a few famous actors from Boston showed up with their entourages at the last minute, asking to watch from the owners' box. The Orioles front office was happy to comply, thrilled about the publicity. Phil sat with the famous Bostonians to make sure no one got hassled on their way in and out. Phil loved to tell the story, about how one of the A-list actors didn't eat anything for the entire game, even though the owners had sent up rows of dogs and wings.

'And that's why I'm not famous,' Phil would tell his friends, patting his stomach. 'I like not having an eating disorder.'

Some nights Phil would take it upon himself to stand in the ballpark's family section to make sure no one got drunk and raised a middle finger around the kids.

And something unexpected would always happen during games, something that made his job feel more like psychology or anthropology.

For instance, just last month he got a call that a fan had seen some pervert jerking off in the big bathroom near Gate H. He did what he was supposed to do – call the cops immediately – but then ran down to the bathroom to peek through the cracks between the stalls to see if the guy looked dangerous.

When Phil got to the bathroom and looked through the crack, he saw that it wasn't some old Peeping Tom or pervert masturbating in the stall – it was actually a kid, a teenage boy feverishly playing with himself in front of the toilet.

Phil rolled his eyes and walked to the bathroom door, where three police offers were ready to pounce.

'Officers,' Phil said, half-smiling. 'I'm sorry I called you out for this. It's a kid. It's not a pedophile or criminal or anything.'

'Sir,' one man in uniform responded, 'we got an indecent exposure call and we're going to have to check it out.'

'Guys, guys, look, I know you're just doing your job, but why don't you let me talk to him. If anything seems weird, I'll bring him out to talk to you. But for Christ's sake, if the police yell at him for snapping his carrot, his dick probably won't work for the rest of his life.'

The policemen softened. One actually smiled.

'Thank you,' Phil said, walking back to the stall.

He knocked quietly on the door. 'Hey kid, open up.'

Silence.

A nervous, cracking voice finally said, 'Is there a problem?'

'Kid, open up,' Phil said, louder.

About a minute later, the red-faced kid, who looked even younger now that he was out of the stall and standing up straight, glared defiantly at Phil, who towered over him by more than a foot and a half.

'What's wrong? I didn't do anything wrong.' The boy's voice was trembling. Phil worried that the kid was going to cry right there in front of him.

'Kid,' Phil said softly, now noticing that other men in the bathroom were staring. 'Kid, come with me.'

They walked to the corner of the bathroom. Phil leaned in so he could make better eye contact.

The kid was now crying. Tears streamed down his cheeks as his face became a beet.

'Listen. Calm down. It's okay. Look, you can't jerk off in a public bathroom. We all do it, but if someone can see you, like, in a place like this, where there are big spaces between the doors, someone's going to think you're a creep and call the police, like they did today.'

'Someone called the police?' The boy was shaking, wide eyed.

'Someone thought they saw an old man jerking off in the bathroom. They thought you were a pervert. Look, there's nothing wrong with jerking off, but you have to do it at home.'

'I do,' the kid whined, wiping his eyes. Phil hovered over the boy so that the men at the urinals couldn't see his tears. Now Phil looked like the creep, he thought to himself, mildly amused.

'I always do it in private,' the kid continued in a rush. 'But I'm on vacation with my mom and dad and my sister and we're all in one hotel room, and it's been four days and this is the first time I've been alone and I just had to do it.'

Phil couldn't believe this. He wiped his forehead as the kid continued.

'My sister brought her friend Hayley, and I'm sleeping on the floor next to her and –'

'Kid,' Phil said, not wanting to hear any more. 'You don't have to tell me this stuff. You're not in trouble and I get it. But you can't jerk off here. Just don't do it again. Now go find your parents and watch some baseball.'

Usually the real work came after the games were over. Phil's job required him to stay late at the ballpark and fill out a log of everyone the guards had kicked out during the night, adding a special note about those who had been arrested. His favorite part was writing the 'reason for expulsion.'

'Fan peed over railing.' 'Tampa Bay fan spit on young child in Orioles hat.' 'Male Blue Jays fan made unwanted sexual advance toward Orioles fan.' Only when he wrote this stuff down did he realize how ridiculous people get when they drink.

Phil never thought he'd still be working at the ballpark in his late thirties, but what started as a summer job during college had become a career. He'd worked his way up the company ladder and now sat at meetings with people in the Orioles front office. The players knew him by name. Some called him Mr MacGowan.

His favorite part of the job used to be chatting with those players. Ten years ago he was in awe of them. Now, though, he was at least a decade older than the stars and wise enough to see that most of them were punks who didn't realize how lucky they were to get millions a year for doing what they love.

These days his favorite part of the job was managing a crop of college kids who worked part-time security, just like he had in school. He liked being a cool boss. He let them leave early and sent them home when they looked hung over. He gave them nicknames like Shrek and Seatbelt.

The baseball schedule was inhuman of course. It was almost impossible for Phil to see anyone besides his mother from April through September, and that had sent at least a few women running in the other direction. Women always told Phil they understood baseball – the fact that there are 162 games in a season and that half of those games are home – but they would always act surprised and betrayed come spring, when Phil could no longer make plans for Saturday nights. They were angry, as if he hadn't warned them.

And now, as he settled into his white folding chair, which under his weight sunk into the perfect Annapolis lawn, the smell of his suit thankfully muted by the more powerful scent of the salt water nearby, Phil looked around, suddenly taking notice of how things looked at a formal event outside the ballpark. Everyone seemed to be paired off or in groups. He sat alone, with an empty chair on either side of him, feeling more unattached than he had in a very long time.

His phone buzzed on the side of his leg as he contemplated his solitude. Phil gratefully pulled it from his pocket until he realized, with a sinking feeling, that it was his bookie.

Joe

Joe was well aware that he was not wanted at his niece's wedding, at least not by Donna, his sister-in-law, who was a hateful, Botoxed shrew, in Joe's opinion.

He only saw his brother, Richard, about once a year at the most and always at Richard's Maryland home, a stodgy brick four-bedroom not far from Ellicott City's historic main street, which Donna thought was the most interesting place on the planet.

Donna had never allowed Richard to visit Joe in Vegas, even though Joe had invited him at least twenty times over the years. Joe and Richard had never been close, but he longed to show off his accomplishments in Vegas, specifically his thriving restaurant-supply business, which he knew would fascinate his older brother. Donna never let the kids go either. Like a tourist, Donna called Joe's hometown 'Sin City,' as if it were populated only by prostitutes and drug-addicted gamblers. If only she could see the number of wholesome and annoyingly loud families that inhabited the casinos these days. They'd basically taken over one of Joe's biggest clients, the New York-New York, thanks to the hotel's roller coaster and miniature Coney Island-themed arcade.

Things had been going so well at Joe's company that he hadn't been to visit Richard in almost three years. To be honest, it wasn't just that work was busy. There was no reason to go to Maryland these days. Bee, Joe's favorite niece, was a grown-up now and lived down in Raleigh with her fiancé. Bee's brother, Eric, had wisely vacated Maryland to go to college in New York City and spent most of his summer vacations traveling through Europe on Richard's dime. Joe couldn't bring himself to visit Richard if it was only going to be the three adults.

Donna usually began her attack shortly after Joe arrived, only giving him minutes to unwind before she asked him pointed questions about his daughter, as if it was Joe's fault that his ex had chosen to live twenty-five hundred miles away from where he could earn a decent living to support their child.

Joe's ex, Rachel, was a teacher. She and their daughter,

Cynthia, lived in Maine, near Rachel's family. Joe's child support paid for most of their expenses, which is why living in Nevada, where he had a steady income, seemed to be the obvious priority, at least in his mind. Joe was many things, but he was not a deadbeat dad. He gave them plenty. When Donna accused him of being an absentee father, he always responded, 'Can't teachers work anywhere? Why the hell does Rachel live up in Maine? It's a choice!' That usually ended the conversation. Dinners were finished in silence.

Joe had suffered through a phone conversation with Donna about a week ago. She'd called him, demanding to know where he planned on staying during the wedding weekend.

'You can't stay here,' Donna had said, not very politely. He could picture her in her designer sweats, always over-exercising. Her life was a series of downward dogs and extra miles. She'd saddled her daughter, Bee, with a complex about her looks and weight, which is why he'd always tried to build her back up with compliments when he'd visited during her teenage years.

Hearing Donna's voice made him regret RSVP'ing at all. 'I wasn't going to stay with you,' Joe had answered defensively.

'We have Matt's parents in the guest room – Matt is

Bee's fiancé – and we have my parents in Bee's room. We don't have any extra beds.'

'I reserved a room at one of the inns, Donna, and I know who Matt is. You don't have to tell me who my niece is marrying.'

'Fine, then. And, Joe, I'm just reminding you that the wedding is black tie.'

Joe grunted. 'Donna, it says "black tie optional." I have a nice suit. It'll be fine.'

'Just make sure you look presentable.'

Joe resented Donna's reminder – as if he'd ever looked less than presentable in her presence. He might be a man who had married and divorced too young, lived in 'Sin City,' and had a daughter he barely saw, but he could certainly dress himself. In fact, dressing himself had always been one of his special skills. Joe's brother, Richard, was like their father – a man whose wardrobe consisted mainly of nondescript brown pants and ill-fitting suit shirts. But Joe had always costumed himself like a catalogue model. He was something of a clotheshorse, with a walk-in closet lined with well-tailored suits and stylish shoes. He fit right in on the Vegas strip, but whenever he visited family on the East Coast, he realized that most people – the kind of people who lived in the suburbs and had desk jobs – were comfortable dressing as if they worked in a bank.

Women loved Joe's fashion sense, which was convenient, because Joe loved women. Joe usually preferred to hit on out-of-towners, and on any given day there were thousands to choose from.

His small company serviced about forty-two gambling-district restaurants, most of which were in hotels. He spent the majority of his afternoons visiting with restaurant managers about supplies, and would usually stay for a free meal, which he'd eat using the silverware he'd ordered specifically for the establishment.

After his work was over for the day, he'd wander out to one of the hotel bars, where he'd talk up a pack of single women on a bridesmaid getaway or, come spring, students on break.

About once every two months he'd fly to Reno. That's where most of his new business came from. Almost a dozen new restaurants that popped up during the recent housing boom had signed with his company, desperate for high-end sets of forks, knives, and metal chopsticks.

Joe's business partner was a friend from college who'd given him a sales job when Joe realized he'd have to pay child support to his pregnant ex. Joe was good at convincing people to buy things and wound up making his friend more money than either of them thought possible. Within a year, his friend made him partner.

Joe loved the work, except for the trips to Reno, which he believed was the real Sin City. He always felt depressed as soon as he got there. It was like the worst parts of Vegas, with no bright spots. Old ladies blowing their retirement at slots. Drunken bachelor parties with no bachelorettes. Unattractive couples fighting over money.

But last year in Reno, he'd met her: Victoria. A thirty-year-old graduate student who went by Vicki. She had short black hair and looked like a part-Asian Tinker Bell. She'd been sitting at the Japanese steakhouse bar, sipping white wine and staring at a martial arts film from the 1970s that played on a loop on one of the restaurant's flat-screen monitors. Her eyes were glassy. Not drunk but tired. He approached her without his usual confidence and asked her timidly if he could pay for her next drink.

'No thanks, I'm fine,' she'd responded, in a raspy voice that surprised him.

'What if I told you I wouldn't really be paying for it?' Joe had countered.

The woman shot him a confused look.

'This restaurant is one of my clients. I'm its supplier. When I'm here, I get my meals comped. We can just put your drink on my check.'

He held his hands up in surrender. 'No strings attached. You just look like you could use a free drink.'

The woman smiled tentatively. 'Well . . . if you're not really paying for it . . . Okay. Thank you.'

After four more drinks, she agreed to accompany him back to his room. She seemed amused by her decision, shaking her head and flashing a weak grin as she took off her clothes by his bed as he watched.

'I've never done this before,' she'd said, 'although I'm sure that's what everyone says.'

'No, I believe you,' Joe had responded. 'I do this all of the time,' he'd then said, surprising himself.

The woman, Vicki, now naked, had shrugged and smiled at him, her eyelids half-covering her pupils. 'Thanks for your honesty.'

The sex had been unimaginative and depressing. Vicki seemed defeated, as if she were having intercourse to avoid doing something else.

Still there was depth to it all, in Joe's mind at least. He decided that she needed someone like him, that there was a reason she'd chosen to have an uncharacteristic night of intimacy with him rather than going back to her room and watching television. He wanted to know more about her and to see her again. But he never thought to ask her for her last name. She was gone by the time he woke up.

He ran down to the Japanese restaurant the next day to see if he could get her name or room number from the bartender, but Joe was reminded that he'd comped Vicki's drinks. There was no record of her at the bar.

Joe was supposed to leave for Vegas that evening, but he postponed his flight by a day on the off chance that he might see her again. He waited at the bar one more time, hoping that she would return, looking for him. She didn't. At about two o'clock he wandered back to his room, hopeless and dejected. There was no way to reach her. He couldn't even remember where Vicki said she had studied. He considered asking the hotel's security to go through its tapes so he could at least get a visual. But they'd never agree to it. He'd sound like a predator.

He figured that if she wanted to see him, she could always contact the restaurant and ask the bartender who had paid for her wine. He held out hope that she would. But months went gone by and she didn't. Vicki was a ghost.

In reality Joe had a girlfriend now. He hadn't when

he'd met Vicki, but about four months ago he met Sarah and had been seeing her regularly ever since. She was a concierge at the Wynn. She'd studied hotel management at Cornell and was on track to make her way up to the front office. She was thirty-one, a pretty redhead from a good family. But Joe figured that, because of their age difference, their relationship was most likely temporary. Recently – as in a week before Bee's wedding – she'd turned to him and asked whether he was opposed to more children. He didn't have an answer.

'Let's table this until I get back from Maryland,' Joe had told her, kissing her forehead.

He'd considered bringing Sarah to the wedding, but he didn't want to send the wrong message to her about his level of commitment. Now in his midforties, he wasn't sure that he could remain in a relationship with someone so interested in starting a family. And, frankly, he didn't want Sarah to go to Maryland and see how his brother's family treated him. Around Sarah, Joe was the grown-up. But in Maryland, around Richard and Donna, Joe was a screwup. He was Peter Pan. Joe didn't want anyone from his Vegas world to see how he looked through his brother's and sister-in-law's eyes.

After parking his rental car in the small lot behind the quiet inn, Joe waited in line to get his key. The small brick building disoriented him. He was used to big lights and sleek, flashy hotel interiors. This place was the definition of nautical quaint, with brown leather chairs and prints of waves and ships hanging from exposed-brick and wooden walls. In front of him were a few businessmen, a couple who looked familiar – maybe his own second cousins – and a woman at the front of the line who had a guitar case strapped to her back. As she walked away from the wooden desk, her key in hand, Joe couldn't stop himself jumping out of line to bother her. He was a sucker for women and instruments, especially when they wore leather jackets. They made him think of Lita Ford – a poster of her had hung in his childhood bedroom.

Joe took a few quick steps, following the woman as she moved to the elevator.

He yelled at her backside, 'Do you play?'

The young woman whipped around, almost knocking Joe in the face with the guitar case. Usually musicians are more careful with their instruments, he thought.

'Yes,' she said, forcing a thin smile.

Joe felt his palms become damp. This woman was beautiful, he thought. And her hair, while shoulder length, was just like Vicki's had been, wispy and jet black. Unlike Vicki, whose hair matched her dark Asian eyes and muted olive skin color, this woman's complexion reminded him of Snow White's. Her opaque, messy bob fell against almost translucent ivory skin. She didn't wear makeup, and her lips looked cold and purple. Joe quickly shamed himself by wondering what this woman might look like if she cut her hair to Tinker Bell length, so she better resembled Vicki from Reno. This woman was as close as he could get to the real thing. He pictured what she would look like naked and wondered if she would mind if he called her Vicki. He concentrated on remaining calm and trying not to turn red.

Joe took a deep breath and asked if she had a gig nearby. Maybe he could sneak out of the wedding early to see it.

'No, it's just a hobby,' the woman explained. 'I'm here for a wedding.'

Joe relaxed, now sure that he wouldn't have to let her out of his sight. He introduced himself as Bee's uncle, Joe, and suddenly regretted that he made himself sound so old.

'I'm Vicki,' she said, and then she continued – but Joe could no longer hear.

It had been more than possible for Joe to skip this

wedding. In fact, Donna had probably expected that he would blow it off to avoid the East Coast and his family responsibilities at all costs. And yet he'd purchased a ticket, booked a rental car, and reserved a hotel room with months to spare, as soon as he'd received the invitation. He assumed his uncharacteristic enthusiasm about the wedding had something to do with his love for Bee, who had always been so smitten with him when she was a child. But perhaps there was a cosmic reason for him to be here. And perhaps there was more to his decision not to bring Sarah than a simple avoidance of commitment. Joe was a spiritual person. Not superstitious, but a believer in karma and fortuitousness. Maybe there was a greater purpose to all this, he thought, rubbing his moist hands on the side of his pants.

His head pounded. He looked down, quickly surveying what he was wearing and what Vicki – this new Vicki – might think of it. Tailored gray pants. A weathered white T-shirt under a blazer. It was fine. He looked up, suddenly aware that it must be time for him to respond to whatever this Vicki had been saying, but by the time he raised his eyes all he saw was the bulky shape of the guitar case moving along ahead of him. Just as he jerked forward, she turned the corner and disappeared.

Hannah

*H*annah was made up now, eyeliner on, staring out the window onto the country club's lawn. She squinted to identify every ant-sized person with dark hair, to see if it was Tom. One dark-haired ant was a maybe. But looking closer she noticed that the man's shoulders were too broad and his stride too short to be Tom. Her stomach settled with a mixture of disappointment and relief as she observed the now-unfamiliar man take a seat with the groom's family. The agony would continue.

With only twenty minutes to spare before the start of Bee and Matt's afternoon wedding ceremony, most of the guests had arrived at the Tower Gardens Country Club, where they now circled the rows of white seats like vultures in formal wear. They paused in pairs to have quiet conversations about whether it would be more comfortable to sit up front, close to the makeshift altar where it would be easier to hear the vows, or in the back, where they'd have better access to the bathrooms.

While the guests meandered around the chairs, young men in maroon jackets hurried about the patio between the lawn and the reception tent. They arranged wine-glasses on tables and brought out trays of ice for the cocktail reception, which would keep the guests busy between the 'I do's' and the real party, which wasn't scheduled to begin until forty-five minutes after the vows.

From the window where Hannah stood, in the citadel above the Tower Gardens club, the guests looked like tiny dancers, stick-figure twosomes who appeared to be taking part in a grand waltz before settling in seats. Their movements were similar and circular. Hannah imagined that at any moment she would hear music and see them curtsy and bow.

She propped herself up on her toes, with her nose almost touching the glass, to get a better look. She squinted intensely, pretending she was a sharpshooter, her eyes darting between the shapes on the lawn.

Despite their reduced size, Hannah could identify some of their faces. She saw the two guys who had lived in the apartment above Bee during their junior year.

They were holding the arm of similar-looking women, presumably their wives. There was Bee's dad, Richard, who seemed to be having a discussion with the pastor on the edge of the property. Hannah also spied a few members of Bee's and Matt's extended family who had been at the rehearsal dinner the night before.

Hannah wiped her fingers over the glass where her nervous breath had created a small, circular patch of fog. She self-consciously rubbed her chest, which was mostly bare. The black material of her bridesmaid's dress dipped low, revealing more cleavage than she was used to. The complicated bra, which pushed her cleavage toward her collarbone, only made the ensemble more revealing.

Hannah continued to stare down at the grounds below and dug her short nails, which had been manicured and painted for the first time since college, into the windowsill. The old wood was soft. Her tiny nails made a dent as she pressed, causing a few chips of brown paint and red nail polish to fall to the perfectly clean hardwood floor. She put her fingers in her mouth and wondered if she was giving herself lead poisoning. She closed her eyes and imagined the chips of paint traveling from her tongue to her head, where they would kill her brain cells and put her out of her misery.

'Hannah,' she heard Dawn order sharply behind her.

Hannah whipped around to see Dawn standing about two feet away, beckoning with her pointer finger. 'Can I speak to you for a second over here? Just a second, hon. Over here.'

Hannah moved slowly in her new shoes as she walked to Dawn. The entire wedding party was dressed and ready now. Jackie and Lisa still stood by Bee, smoothing the back of her train and validating her with compliments about her makeup, hair, and tiny waist. Hannah knew that's what Bee needed. She did look gorgeous, but she was probably still insecure, undoubtedly worried about how she'd look in front of her mother. Hannah was relieved that Bee would now be based in Raleigh, closer to Matt's family, who showered her with warmth.

'What's up?' Hannah asked Dawn unsteadily, her eyes shifting in anticipation of whatever scolding the matron of honor was going to deliver. Dawn's eyes were tight, her lips pursed. With no warning, she grabbed both of Hannah's pinky fingers, one with each hand.

'Stop that right now,' Dawn barked in a whisper.

'Stop what?' Hannah asked, stunned.

'Look what you're doing,' Dawn continued more quietly, turning Hannah's palms face down so the she could see the tops of her nails, which had been painted red on Dawn's orders. Hannah saw that her hands had become a mess of chipped polish. Thanks to the color, it looked like her largest digits were bleeding.

Dawn dropped Hannah's hands and lifted her face by her chin. She moved in close so they were eye to eye, close enough for a kiss. On any other day, Dawn was at least two inches shorter than Hannah, but in the stiltlike heels the maid of honor had chosen to wear to compensate for her long dress train, she towered over Hannah by at least an inch.

'Can I be honest with you?' Dawn whispered, her fingers still clutching Hannah's chin, her tone sweet but severe. Hannah didn't answer. Her eyes were wide, her face flushed. She simply nodded in agreement.

Dawn responded by saying nothing. She stared into Hannah's eyes, surveying Hannah's frown, her own eyes growing kinder and more sympathetic the longer she looked.

'What? What are you looking at?' Hannah asked nervously. Her words ran together as she moved her head back and forth, trying to free her face from Dawn's grip.

'I'm sorry about the nails,' Hannah continued quickly. 'I didn't even know I was doing it. I'm not used to nail polish. No one will be able to see. I'll hide my hands in the pictures, I swear.'

'It's not the nails, baby,' Dawn interrupted, dropping her hand from Hannah's chin and grabbing her by the pinkies again, this time squeezing them with force. 'I'm upset, baby, because you're stressing everybody out. Bee is going to have to walk down the aisle in just a few more minutes, and you're in the corner of the room, alone, looking out the window like you're some sort of deranged serial killer who's going to pull out a gun and start shooting the guests.'

Dawn moved to Hannah's side and leaned in so her mouth was at Hannah's ear. 'This is not about you right now,' Dawn whispered, her lips touching Hannah's earlobe. Hannah winced at the contact. Dawn continued unfazed. 'Can you stop thinking about yourself and focus on your friend? Can you focus on Bee right now, honey?'

Hannah's eyes moved to Bee, who, on the other side of the pristine penthouse, looked like a porcelain doll. Her eyes were closed now as Jackie and Lisa shuffled around her, bending over awkwardly to fluff the bottom of her dress. Bee's lips moved silently as she rehearsed lines, presumably the vows she'd written herself. Hannah could sense Bee's anticipation of the performance to come. She hated speaking in front of people. She'd struggled with it in law school, often calling Hannah for tips from the theater world. Hannah had always told her to pretend she was someone else. 'You're a lawyer. So just walk up to the podium and imagine that you're . . . Susan Dey from *LA Law*.'

'I wasn't allowed to watch *LA Law* when I was a kid, Hannah,' Bee had said, her voice cracking.

Hannah now placed her hands over her eyes and let out a long groan. 'Oh, god, I'm awful. She's over there, preparing to commit to someone for the rest of her life, and I'm not even paying attention. Just tell me what to do, Dawn. Am I supposed to go over there and fluff her skirt?'

'Hannah! Look at me!' Dawn ordered in her loud whisper, forcing Hannah to uncover her eyes and make eye contact with the maid of honor. Dawn's voice was softer but became almost vicious when she noticed that Hannah was beginning to cry.

'No. Absolutely not,' Dawn said quickly, using her pointer finger to wipe the first teardrops from Hannah's eyes before they made their way to her cheek. 'No tears. Tears are not an option right now. You have makeup on.' She took Hannah's hands and laced them in her own.

'Look at me.'

Hannah shut her eyes tight, holding back the moisture.

'Look at me!' Dawn hissed loud enough for Lisa to look over from Bee's corner of the room, puzzled and concerned.

Hannah silently obeyed. Her eyes popped open. She blinked fast to keep the tears at bay.

'I want you to take a long, deep breath in,' Dawn instructed authoritatively.

Both women inhaled, their eyes locked. 'Now out,' Dawn said, prompting them to exhale simultaneously.

Dawn let Hannah's hands drop limp at her sides.

'Honey,' Dawn said, 'you have to cut this out.'

'I'm sorry. I just keep looking for him down there. All this waiting – it's driving me crazy. I just want to see Tom and get it over with. I want to see him, feel miserable, go back to the hotel, and get on with my life. I'm sorry. I want to be here for Bee . . . but all I can think about is the fact that Tom is down on the lawn with some other woman. Some . . . guidance counselor. And when I'm not looking for him, I'm checking my stupid phone. And there's nothing. No messages. No Natalie Portman. No nothing.'

Dawn cocked her head to the side, not even asking why Hannah had mentioned Natalie Portman. Without warning, she shuffled away from Hannah and over to her makeup case. Hannah watched as Dawn opened the plastic tote and took out a small change purse from which she removed three white pills. Her heels clacked on the wood floor as she returned.

Dawn grabbed Hannah's right hand, delivering the pills to her palm. 'Put those pills in your mouth and wash them down,' Dawn instructed, nodding at a half-consumed glass of flat soda that Hannah had nursed earlier in the day.

Hannah chewed on her lip, eyeing the white tablets. 'What are they?'

Dawn flashed a smile. 'Two will calm you down, and the other will keep you nice and alert. I give these to my pageant girls before shows. They help with nerves. These are going to put you in a better mood.'

Hannah shook her head slowly. 'I don't know, Dawn. I don't want to fall asleep or get sick. I have a low tolerance for medication.'

'You won't get sick, honey,' Dawn said, grabbing the cup of soda and placing it in Hannah's free hand as she spoke. Their faces were so close that Hannah could see the small strip of adhesive that locked a pair of fake eyelashes to Dawn's lids.

'Can I be honest with you, Hannah?' Dawn continued as Hannah studied her face, so round and healthy, her teeth too white. 'You have to do this for Bee. These pills are going to get you through the ceremony with a genuine smile on your face. Bee should be focused on her wedding day, and right now she's worried about you.

'If you take those pills now,' Dawn continued in her signature loud whisper, 'you'll have a good three or four hours and then you can go straight up to your hotel room and fall asleep. You'll wake up in the morning perfectly rested.'

Hannah looked down at the pills, which were beginning to melt in her sweaty palm. 'And I need to take all three pills? Is that the recommended dose?'

'Honey, my girls take more than this and most of them are still in their teens and weigh less than a hundred pounds.'

'And what will happen after I take them? What do they do exactly?'

'Well, nothing very noticeable,' Dawn said, revealing her victory smile as she watched Hannah pop the pills into her mouth and take a quick shot from the soda cup. 'In about twenty minutes or so, you should feel calm, cool, and ready to walk down the runway. After a while the medicine wears off, and you'll just want a good nap.'

'You mean the aisle,' Hannah said, now grinning herself. 'You said "runway."'

'Whatever you want to call it, sweetie,' Dawn said, her tone still light.

'Thanks, Dawn,' Hannah said softly. Dawn gave Hannah a quick wink and then about-faced and walked toward Bee so she could make her own final inspection of the bridal gown.

Hannah stood where she was, sipping the rest of her soda as she watched Dawn tend to Bee, circling the dress to see it from all sides. Dawn then leaned in and whispered something that made Bee giggle. They gave each other a quick, formal hug, barely touching so that they wouldn't smudge each other's faces and gowns.

Hannah smiled at the sweetness of the uncomfortable embrace. She considered joining them, but she couldn't stop herself from indulging just one more time. First, she checked her phone. No Natalie. Then she walked over to the window to do one final search from above, eyeing the top of each head on the lawn below to see if she recognized Tom's hair, the black-licorice tuft that she used to run her fingers through as he fell asleep in her lap.

Hannah had never seen such dark hair on such a fair-skinned person before meeting Tom at Syracuse. It was even darker than Vicki's hair, which was inky against her white skin.

Tom's dramatic coloring was what he and Hannah first talked about on the night they finally acknowledged each other.

Tom had been a friend of Rob's – one of the few people Rob had deemed worthy of his attention during his three years at school. The two young men had met in a women's studies class that fulfilled the campus's 'cultural understanding' course requirement, which had been created just a few years before, shortly after swastikas were found painted on bathroom stalls in a few of the dorms.

Tom and Rob had taken to getting beers after their Wednesday afternoon women's studies 'discussion lab,' which Rob described to Hannah as 'twelve women in fur-lined boots talking about the potential for fourth-wave feminism.'

'Based on the forty-five minutes of unintelligible bullshit I hear each week, I fear for your gender,' Rob told Hannah during one of their illicit, late-night discussions. Rob had arrived shortly after eleven thirty, and they'd quickly agreed that they were both too tired for physical intimacy. Rob positioned himself so his head was on Hannah's chest, which put them in an uncharacteristically tender embrace. Hannah stroked the top of his head with her fingers and wondered for a split second if, with Bee's approval, she and Rob could be more than what they were.

Rob then snapped her out of the fantasy with talk of his new friend. 'You should really spend some more time with Tom though,' he said, thoughtfully. 'He said he'll probably come to the show on Friday.'

'I'm shocked that you like that guy,' Hannah responded, moving her fingers in light circles on his scalp. She stared at the ceiling, examining the mistakes in her fall-semester paint job, the small splashes of green that had found their way onto the light fixtures, probably because she and Vicki had been drinking while they decorated.

'I thought you said I should make more male friends.' Rob shifted away from her and moved so he was on his back, his hands behind his head.

'I know,' Hannah said, sighing and shivering as she let him go. 'There's just something about Tom that makes me feel weirdly defensive. I've barely talked to him the two times we've met, and I feel like he's staring at me, judging me.'

'I think you're being neurotic. He's a good guy,' Rob said. Within minutes, they were both asleep.

It was just a few days later that Hannah had her first real conversation with Tom. They were all at some forgettable house party, a bunch of acquaintances all connected by the band Ostrom and Madison, named for the off-campus intersection where Rob had been cited by a police officer for public urination in his freshman year. The classic rock-inspired group featured Rob on guitar, Vicki's then-boyfriend Rich on drums, Matt Dorfman on bass, and a musical theater major named Jared Novak doing lead vocals. No one ever called Jared Novak by just his first name. He was always Jared Novak, said quickly as if it was one word.

Despite Hannah's distaste for the band's music, she enjoyed watching Ostrom and Madison perform, especially when she was with Vicki. Hannah and Vicki, who had become fast friends during their freshman year, when they lived in the same dormitory as Rich, Rob, and Bee, would position themselves at shows in whatever dark corner they could find, belittling the music – specifically the always-gesticulating Jared Novak, whose stage presence was far more appropriate for dinner theater than a college rock act. Bee would usually stand beside them, laughing at their jokes. Sometimes she tried to get them to behave. 'Vicki,' she'd say, stifling her own giggles, 'you realize you're making fun of your own boyfriend.'

'I'm well aware of that,' Vicki would respond, grinning.

On this particular night, the evening of the forgettable house party, Vicki had stopped into Hannah's bedroom at the last minute to explain that she'd have to skip the festivities to stay home to comfort the girl who lived in the apartment above them who was having a pregnancy scare. Vicki had found her sobbing in the piles of snow on their shared front porch and offered to take her to the drugstore to get an over-the-counter test.

'Ugh,' Hannah said, already bundled up for the walk to meet Rob and the band. 'If you're not going, I'm not going. It's so frigid out there. I'd rather just order in from Alto Cinco and watch television.'

'No, Hannah, you have to go. Bee's parents are in town, so she can't go. I told Rich we'd be there, so one of us has to show up. And I've heard that Jared Novak is going to cover Queen. Go, and tell me everything.'

Hours later, after Hannah had made small talk with all the regular followers of Ostrom and Madison, she wondered if she could send a mental message to Vicki to explain what she was missing – which was Jared Novak wearing a bright orange, blue, and red striped coat that looked like it was left over from a musical production. Hannah imagined what Vicki might be doing just then, probably helping their neighbor interpret colors on a urine-covered stick.

As Jared Novak wailed the lyrics to Led Zeppelin's 'Fool in the Rain,' shifting back and forth like Robert Plant as he repeated the phrase 'light of the love that I found,' Hannah was surprised by Tom, who was suddenly at her side, looking casual, a red plastic cup of beer in each hand. He handed one to her, and she accepted.

'Hey there.'

'Hey.' She looked away from Tom and back to the band, concentrating on the music as much as she could without wincing.

Tom smiled, running his fingers through his mane. 'They sound good tonight, right?'

'Who?'

'The band.'

Hannah bit her lip and turned her head from Tom, the side of her face revealing her grin.

'What? You don't think they sound good?' Tom smirked.

'Rob sounds good. Rich sounds good, I guess,' Hannah said, nodding her head in the direction of the music. 'But Jared Novak?'

'You're not a fan of Jared Novak?'

Hannah paused so they could both hear a snippet of Jared Novak's vibrating wail.

'*Now my body is starting to quiver. And the palms of my hands getting wet,*' he whined.

'Lord. I don't want to think about Jared Novak quivering,' Hannah said, now laughing. 'Did you see him in *Joseph and the Amazing Technicolor Dreamcoat* freshman year?'

'Sadly, I did not.' Tom leaned against the wall and inched toward her so he could hear her better. Their shoulders touched.

'Well,' Hannah said, standing on her toes so she was speaking into Tom's ear, 'I saw it. It was glorious. And I'm pretty sure he stole that coat he's wearing tonight from the costume shop. It was red and orange and pink and violet and blue.'

Tom laughed as he cut her off. 'And ruby and olive and violet and fawn,' he continued.

'You got that joke. You know *Joseph* lyrics,' Hannah said, moving closer. 'Oh no, that means you're a theater geek.'

'No,' Tom said, still laughing. 'My sister is though. She's done *Joseph* twice. She did *Guys and Dolls* twice too. I know all the words to, like, five or six musicals.'

'You're a good brother.'

'I tell her that all the time,' Tom said, placing his hands in his pockets and all of his weight on one shoulder against the wall. 'Rob tells me you're a theater geek too. The real deal.'

'I guess,' Hannah said, her eyes shifting as she wondered how much Tom knew about the terms of her relationship with Rob. 'I am a theater major, it's true. But I'm not an actor. I want to be on the production end of things. Maybe producing. Or casting. I have a casting internship in New York City this summer.'

'Casting sounds interesting,' Tom said, now close enough that Hannah could smell his shampoo. 'My family likes to cast the fake movie of our lives. It's what we used to do in the car on long trips. We drove from Boston to Florida once. We cast ourselves, our friends, our friends' friends . . .'

'And who plays you?' Hannah asked, feeling her cheeks flush from the beer.

'You know, I can't remember who we said would play me. It changed every few years as I got older. My mom always wanted to be played by Susan Sarandon.'

'Who wouldn't want to be played by Susan Sarandon? Does she look like Susan Sarandon?'

'Not really,' Tom said, letting out a low chuckle. 'She's fair skinned, with straight hair – your typical Boston Irishwoman. More like Sissy Spacek. I look nothing like her. My dad and I are Black Irish, although I suppose he's gray Irish now.'

'Black Irish?' Hannah asked, puzzled.

'You've never heard of Black Irish? It's what they call the pale Irish-Catholic people like me with the jet-black hair. We're all over New England.'

'I don't know many Irish people at all, to be honest,' Hannah said, slurring from the beer. 'If I do, they don't talk about it much. My hometown is pretty Jewish actually. In seventh grade I went to, like, twenty bat mitzvahs. I didn't know that was unusual until I got to college.'

'You're Jewish? You don't look it. Not to stereotype. God, can I take that back? That sounded worse than I wanted it to.'

'No, it's okay. I wasn't born Jewish, but I was raised that way since I was a kid. My mom remarried someone Jewish. Martin is my dad's last name, but my mom is Kathy Feldman now.'

'Mazel tov,' Tom said awkwardly, not quite pronouncing it right. He was in front of Hannah now, his back to the band, hers against the wall.

'So,' he continued, seemingly unaware that he only left a few centimeters between their faces. 'How serious is it with you and Rob? He's failing out of school, you know.'

153

Hannah looked down and placed one hand on the back of her neck for a nervous rub. She stepped to the side so she could see the band again and put some distance between her and Tom. She bit her lip and kept her eyes on Jared Novak as she considered her response.

'Rob and I are not a couple. We're just friends,' she finally answered curtly.

'I didn't mean to pry,' Tom said, trying to step in front of her again, his eyes panicked. 'I'm sorry. I was just curious. Rob's great. He's a good friend. It's just – you seem pretty put together, and I can tell that you do a lot for him. He was telling me after class the other day that you're trying to help him get his grades up. That's . . . That's really great. But like you said, you're not even a couple. And he's kind of a mess. Do your friends even know you're sleeping with him?'

Hannah's jaw dropped. She looked away, shooting an angry glare at Rob, who leaned back oblivious, his guitar in his hands. His eyes were pained as he accompanied Jared Novak's cover of 'Don't Think Twice, It's All Right.'

'Jeez, Hannah, I'm sorry. I keep putting my foot in my mouth. This isn't any of my business. I'm – Rob is great. Forget I brought any of this up. I think I'm just drunk. Please don't listen to anything I say tonight.'

'I'm not sleeping with him,' Hannah said sharply, glancing back at Rob, whose eyes were now shut tight. He was probably trying to imagine that someone other than Jared Novak was singing what Hannah knew was his favorite Bob Dylan song.

'It's none of my business really,' Tom continued as he tried to step into Hannah's sight line. 'Please, forget I said any of this. I'm just jealous. I've had six beers. I shouldn't be opening my mouth.'

'Jealous?' Hannah asked, bringing her eyes back to Tom and feeling somewhat tipsy herself. She tried to prevent a smile, but her lips curled around the edges.

'Jealous,' Tom said, smiling back.

Hannah could remember charging into Vicki's room later that night, bubbling about the comment, dissecting its meaning.

'I think "jealous" means jealous,' Vicki had said, after a big yawn. She lay in bed, underneath three layers of flannel sheets and a down comforter. The duvet matched her walls, which were now the color of cinnamon. 'I think it means he wants to date you, which is something you should take him up on. He's nice. He's single. Bee isn't in love with him. And he doesn't show up at our door at two in the morning to ask you to give him a hand job.'

'Wow, Vicki. You know, Rob's our friend. And you know this is complicated.'

'You know I love Rob, but I don't like all this sneaking around. It's time to end it.'

Hannah groaned. 'You're just cranky because you've been talking about abortion all night.'

Vicki let out an exhausted giggle. 'Probably. Hey – was the band still playing when you left? Rich is supposed to come over when they're done, and I'm exhausted. If you think he's going to be a while, do you mind just leaving the back door open for him?'

'Well, let me put it this way – when I was leaving, Jared Novak had just started to perform a medley from *Cats*. I don't think you should wait up.'

'Very funny,' Vicki said, yawning again and turning to face the wall.

Now, almost eight years later, the memory of Tom's admitted jealousy was still swimming in Hannah's brain. She could already feel Dawn's pills working. Her shoulders had dropped, relaxed. Still at the window, she brought her hand to her torso, feeling for the edges of the underwire that was burrowing into her skin.

Suddenly her eyes were drawn to a black Q-tip-like dot on the lawn below. Next to the familiar black dot was a blonder dot, a poof of styled hair on top of a short, slender woman whom Hannah had identified as Tom's girlfriend, Jaime, the guidance counselor. Hannah's hands were suddenly moist. She turned from the window and walked to the opposite corner of the tower's top room, to find her bag. She took out her phone and sent a quick text message to Vicki, who she guessed was already finding her seat down below. 'He's here. With her,' the message said. Hannah stood back up quickly and felt her ankles quiver.

'Dawn,' Hannah yelled suddenly. She took a quick step backward, surprised by the volume of her own voice.

'What, sweetie?' Dawn said from the other side of the room.

'Nothing important,' Hannah said, smiling lucidly. 'I just wanted to say thank you and that you're very good at your job.'

Dawn grinned and walked over to Hannah's lookout. She touched the tip of Hannah's nose and smiled.

'I know, baby. You're feeling a bit better, aren't you?'

'Yes. Yes, I am,' Hannah said, confident and beaming, wiping a small line of sweat that she felt forming on her upper lip. 'Let's do this thing.'

Just then Bonnie Hunt, the wedding planner, walked briskly through the door.

'Ladies, it's time. Line up in your order. Bee, you stand right behind your maid of honor. And . . . excuse me, Hannah? You're Hannah?'

'Yes?'

'Do you need a tissue?'

'Why?'

'You're just sweating a little, over your lip. And you have something on your chest. Are those paint chips?'

Hannah looked down and saw that she'd wiped pieces of nail polish and paint from the window ledge across the top of her cleavage. 'Oh!' Hannah exclaimed, quickly shuffling to the corner to grab a napkin, which she used to dab her lip and clean her chest.

'Okay, then. Hurry up, everyone. Lisa's going to be first. Then Jackie. Then Hannah. Then Dawn. Then Bee. When you hear me say go, you can take off one by one. Remember to wait three full seconds between each step. Count one Mississippi, two Mississippi, three Mississippi. Your groomsman will be waiting for you at the bottom of the staircase. Bee, your dad is right at the bottom of the spiral stairs, behind the other guys. He'll grab you as soon as you make it onto the grass.'

In line Hannah squeezed her sweaty palms into fists. She arched her back and bent to the right of Jackie so she could see Bee, who stood as close to Dawn as possible.

'Bee!' Hannah said, too loud again.

Bee looked forward at Hannah, her smile tense. 'What, Hannah?'

'You look fucking amazing,' Hannah said gruffly, her hand on her chest with pride. 'Never listen to your mother. You're a fucking knockout.'

'Thank you,' Bee responded stiffly.

'Now!' commanded Bonnie Hunt. The march down the spiral staircase began, just as Hannah began to feel really, really dizzy.

Joe

*I*t had all happened so quickly. One minute she was a stranger and the next she was by his side, their shoulders touching. It had started when he left his hotel room, the door making a loud click behind him. It was then that he heard her voice. She was muttering profanities to herself. He'd only spoken to her for a few seconds in the lobby before he'd ruined things, but he knew it was Vicki. His heart had thudded loud in his chest. He hadn't expected to see her until he arrived at the wedding.

He turned to the right and there she was, standing just two rooms away, with both of her hands in her small purse as she mumbled expletives. 'Goddamn it,' she said.

She was oblivious to his presence. She quickly dropped to a squat and dumped the contents of her handbag onto the floor in front of her room. There wasn't much to see – lipstick, car keys, a cell phone, a paperback book. She grimaced and let out one more 'shit,' before collecting her belongings. Once she was upright again, she began striding toward the lobby.

'Hi,' Joe said, tentatively calling out to her. She whipped her head back in his direction.

'Hi?' Vicki answered as if it were a question, squinting to identify who she was talking to.

'It's Bee's uncle, Joe,' Joe said, with a half smile, his forehead tense. 'You know . . . from the lobby.' His fingers fumbled, causing him to drop the keys to his rental car. He bent carefully to pick them up, silently praying that his suit wouldn't rip. Vicki, having gathered her belongings, took two steps toward him and gave him a weak smile.

'I'm sorry. I don't have my glasses on. And I'm sorry for the foul language. I left my room key on my dresser,' she said, her right hand clutching the tiny purse covered in shiny black beads.

'They'll have another key at the front desk,' Joe said, shifting his weight as he heard his own voice crack. 'You can get one when you come back. I'd say you could get it now, but we should probably get over to the wedding. It starts in less than a half hour.'

Vicki was much taller than she'd been in the lobby,

Joe thought, shooting a resentful glance at her spiked shoes. He didn't like it when women did this – wore shoes that propped them up like stilt walkers. She was also dressed for a funeral, he thought, eying her shape-less black dress that hung like a sack and cut off just below the knee. Despite the warm weather, her legs were covered in black panty hose.

His eyes fell to her bag again. He eyed the paperback book that was sticking out of the top. He couldn't read the title but recognized the romance-novel typeface. His ex, Rachel, read those kinds of books. The words looked like cake icing, purple and swirly.

'Pleasure reading?' Joe asked as they walked toward the lobby with at least two feet between them. 'You're going to read during my niece's wedding?'

'Bee would expect nothing less from me,' Vicki said, allowing a quick smile. 'I'll try not to read through the vows.'

Joe laughed, maybe too loud, he thought. He kept himself a few feet behind her, suppressing the urge to reach over and hug her.

She didn't look like the original Vicki, not her face at least, but there was something similar about her default expression – a melancholy, detached pout – that allowed him to continue his fantasy.

Reno Vicki and Maryland Vicki had similar bodies: small and almost elfinlike. The sack dress didn't stop Joe from being able to make out Vicki's small frame and tiny breasts. She didn't appear to be athletic, just naturally thin – probably the kind of girl who ate candy for breakfast and smoked cigarettes during lunch, he thought.

Joe's girlfriend, Sarah, whom he suddenly remembered was waiting for him in Vegas, was the opposite of that type of girl. She was always working out, always running. Joe had started to resent Sarah's constant training for half marathons, the fact that she now spent every Sunday morning taking a long jog with one of her friends from boot camp, a program that required her to get up at 5:00 a.m. to do military-style exercises on the already-hot Nevada pavement. Her routine reminded him of Donna.

Joe eyed Vicki with his peripheral vision now that they were moving through the lobby side by side. Her shoulders were tense, her posture unyielding. She eyed the framed nautical prints on the walls and let out a sigh to fill the uncomfortable silence.

When they reached the front door, he saw her dig through her clutch once again, this time grabbing her car keys. Joe let out a small cough to remind her he was there and spoke up, his voice insecure.

'Why don't you drive over with me? We're going to the same place. I don't mind giving you a lift.'

Vicki stopped in front of the exit to look back at him. She squeezed the key already in her hand. 'Thanks,' she said, taking another step toward the sunlight. 'But I might want to leave early. And I'm giving my friend, one of the bridesmaids, a ride back. I need my car.'

'I'll leave whenever you want,' Joe said, almost pleading. 'You don't really want to have to navigate through Annapolis late at night, especially if you're going to have a few drinks. It's surprisingly dark once you get away from the cobblestone. I plan to stay sober and, really, I can head back to the hotel whenever.'

He'd said too much too fast, he thought. He was too desperate.

Vicki clutched her car keys and looked at the glass door as she pondered her options. She glanced up at the ceiling, biting her lip.

'Really,' Joe continued, 'it's no big deal. Whenever you and your bridesmaid friend are ready to get out of there, we'll leave.'

Vicki shrugged and tilted her head. 'I guess . . . I guess that's fine,' she said, looking in the direction of his face without making eye contact. 'I can always call a cab if I need to leave on my own.'

'Okay, then,' Joe said, grinning and using both hands to usher her toward the door. 'After you.'

She followed him to a gray sedan in the small parking lot down the street from the inns. He hit the unlock button on his key chain with force but heard nothing. They each pulled the door handle on their side of the car but the vehicle was still locked.

'I don't think this is your car,' Vicki said, staring at him accusingly.

'Shit. You know, you're right,' Joe said, laughing nervously. 'These rental cars all look the same. I think mine's a Mercury.'

Joe hit the red button on his key chain, which set off a loud siren just a few cars away. Vicki jumped at the noise, her eyes wide and angry.

'Sorry,' Joe yelled over the noise, quickly hitting the button again to silence the alarm. Her face was still sour. 'I should have warned you,' he said softly and apologetically. 'I just wanted to find the car. That's me over there. I'm the Sable.'

They walked to the other gray car and settled themselves in the front seats. Vicki buckled her seat belt and stared out the window. She turned her head so far to the right that Joe couldn't see either of her eyes, just her ear and the jet-black hair that almost covered tiny pendant earrings.

He started the car as quickly as he could, fearful she might jump out. 'Don't worry. We won't be late.' She remained silent and clutched the bag in her lap with both hands.

'So,' Joe said, his voice trembling, 'you're a guitar player by night. I know that much. But what's your day job?'

Vicki kept her eyes out the window as he spoke. He tried to identify her facial expression in the window reflection.

'Are you a lawyer like Bee?' he asked, trying again.

'No,' Vicki said flatly. 'I'm an interior designer for a grocery store chain.'

'Sounds exciting,' Joe said, relieved that she'd responded.

'Does it?' Vicki answered, turning toward him. Intimidated by her sudden attention, he looked back at the road and clutched the wheel. He took a deep breath before speaking again.

'It sounds like a good, solid job,' Joe said, his eyes focused on the SUV in front of them. 'Interior design sounds exciting to me. I know a few interior designers who do restaurants in Vegas. It's an interesting business, although I don't know what it's like to design a grocery store. Do you work for a specific chain?'

'I work for Walton's.'

Joe nodded. 'We don't have Walton's out in Vegas, but I remember them from my East Coast days. So, what does an interior designer for a grocery store do? Do you decide where they put the milk? Or do you pick out the wallpaper?'

'Walton's doesn't use wallpaper, except for the wall behind the customer-service desk,' Vicki said, allowing herself to relax more comfortably in the passenger's seat. 'Really, there's little creativity in the designing I do. Every Walton's looks the same, with a few exceptions. The bakery signs are identical in every store. The majority of the walls have to be buttercream yellow. I'm basically just a project manager. I travel to all the stores in my region and make sure everything looks right. I order repaints when things chip.'

Vicki let out a sigh, drained by the explanation.

Joe's eyes narrowed as he thought of a next move.

'You probably have a great apartment,' he said, peering to his right to see if she was still engaged in the conversation. 'I mean, the walls in your apartment don't have to be buttercream yellow, do they? I bet you get pretty creative at home.'

'I guess so,' Vicki said, nodding. 'Actually, my place is pretty beautiful. The cost of living is so low up in

Rochester that I was able to order some pretty high-end furniture, stuff I dreamed about in college. It's just that nobody sees it. No one really wants to come to Rochester, and I don't blame them.'

Joe grinned, picturing her lounging in silk pajamas on a velvet couch all alone. 'I'm sure it's beautiful,' he continued, now more confident that she was participating in the back-and-forth. 'Is there anything redeeming about Rochester? Honestly, I'm surprised you don't live in New York. I assumed you were a New Yorker when I saw you in that leather jacket in the lobby. And the guitar . . .'

Vicki shrugged again. 'I'd hoped to move to New York with Hannah, my best friend, after college. I wanted to start a small decorating firm. I had this great idea that I'd hook up rich people with trendy artists. Like, instead of buying people furniture from high-end shops, I'd hire an independent woodworker to make something unique. I'd hire my art school friends to make one-of-a-kind wallpaper. Hannah loved the idea. But Walton's headhunted me. They offered me a ridiculous salary, which is even more ridiculous up in Rochester. I probably save more than I spend. But that's the price. I have to live far from friends and put up with those winters while everyone else is being a twentysomething in a cool place. And no fancy design firm. No cool apartment with Hannah in Brooklyn. Golden handcuffs. That's what they call it, right? When you get paid too much to leave to do what would actually make you happy?'

'I think so,' Joe said, trying to keep his eyes on the road despite his urge to face her. 'At this point, even if I wanted to leave Vegas, I couldn't. I make too much there to start over somewhere else.'

He noticed Vicki turn her head back to the window just then, her expression pensive. Joe tried to change the subject quickly, before her mood soured.

'I dated an interior designer a few years ago,' he offered in an upbeat voice. 'About six years ago, I think. She helped people redecorate their houses before they put them on the market – a stager. She had great taste. I only wish I had asked her to take me furniture shopping before I broke up with her.'

Vicki flashed him a dirty look, but Joe could see that she was suppressing a smile.

They got out of the car and found themselves on the white-gravel parking lot, in between the SUV that had been driving in front of them and a small red sports car with the top down and a license plate that read 'D.C. LAW.' 'Shall we?' Joe asked, with a shrug.

'Do we have a choice?' Vicki responded, walking to his side as they joined the other last-minute guests on a fast pilgrimage to the country club's lawn, where they could see a small altar decorated with purplish-blue hydrangea and striking white calla lilies. As they walked side by side toward the entrance of the country club green, the gap between them shrunk, and their hands accidentally bumped as Vicki sunk into the grass.

A young, tall, acne-scarred boy greeted them as they approached the edge of the ceremony space, where guests were milling about the rows of plastic white chairs arranged like pews.

'Are you here for the bride or groom?' the boy asked.

'We're here for the bride,' Joe said, answering for Vicki, who seemed relieved not to have to speak.

'Uncle Joe?' the boy asked, looking closer.

Joe leaned forward, squinting at the boy.

The boy smiled. 'It's me – Derek. I'm Sandra's son. David's brother. It's great to see you, Uncle Joe. I'm surprised I recognized you. I think I was twelve the last time I saw you.'

'You're probably right,' Joe said, remembering his cousin Sandra's two scrawny kids, whom he'd visited in Philadelphia years ago during a restaurant-industry convention. 'You look great, guy. All grown up.'

'I graduate this year,' Derek said, beaming. 'I'm applying early decision to Cornell.'

Joe almost told the boy that his girlfriend, Sarah, also went to Cornell, but caught himself, remembering Vicki at his side.

Vicki turned to look behind them and bumped Joe's shoulder with her own, hinting to him that there was a line of people waiting to be greeted. 'We should probably find a seat,' Vicki said, pulling Joe's arm by the edge of his brown suit sleeve. Joe looked down at her hand on his arm and smiled with his eyes closed. 'Derek,' he said proudly, 'she's right. We should head in, but we'll catch up at the reception, okay?'

'Sure, Uncle Joe.'

Joe kept his eyes on the ground as they walked, fighting his growing smile as they slid into two adjacent seats. They were surrounded by relatives Joe had been avoiding for years and unrecognizable old people whom Joe presumed to be his brother's coworkers.

There were scattered groups of attractive twenty-somethings, whom Joe assumed were Bee's friends from childhood and college. He wondered which pack Vicki would have been sitting with had he not become her date for the day. He allowed himself to turn and look at her adoringly. She smiled back at him and then suddenly crinkled her nose. 'Do you smell that?' she whispered, leaning into Joe's ear.

'Smell what?' he said, taking the opportunity to place his hand around the back of her chair.

'Something reeks like . . . food. It smells like . . .' She paused, sniffing again. 'Buffalo sauce. That's what it is. It's nauseating.'

Joe chuckled quietly, his face almost touching her hair. He noticed her shoulders relax. She leaned into her seat, which he cradled with his arm.

'It's awful,' she continued. 'It reminds me of the Walton's prepared chicken section.'

'I think I do smell it,' he lied, as he looked at the side of her face and her tiny hands, which gripped the program. Vicki rocked her head from one shoulder to the other, loosening her joints.

Joe noticed an attractive young man with dark wavy hair sitting farther down their row. Not too tall but broad-shouldered. The man leaned forward and waved at Vicki to get her attention.

'I think you have an admirer,' Joe whispered into Vicki's ear. She looked over at the waving man and gave him a robotic wave back. Her face was blank. She didn't smile. Joe felt Vicki's body tense in her seat.

Before he could ask, she turned back to Joe and

whispered, 'That's my friend Hannah's ex-boyfriend Tom and his new girlfriend. We hate him.'

'We do?' Joe asked, grinning wide enough to reveal the dimple in his right cheek.

'Yes,' Vicki said, matching his smile. 'We do. Or, well, more accurately, we resent him and feel abandoned by him. Hannah's a bridesmaid. She's the one we're bringing back to the hotel tonight. You'll meet her later.'

Joe felt his stomach flip. There would be a later.

Vicki artfully turned her head back to Tom, slowly enough so he wouldn't notice, and eyed the woman next to him, a petite blonde who stared forward, oblivious. She was a pretty woman with a freckled face. She wore a tailored black dress with a red belt. She sat up straight and held a matching red bag on her lap.

'She's not that pretty,' Vicki mumbled to herself.

'Oh, come on, now,' Joe said, bringing his head close to her neck. 'Let's not be catty. She looks like a nice young woman.'

'Okay, fine. She's attractive. But she's no Hannah,' Vicki said, defensively, without turning her head from Jaime, the guidance counselor. 'And I don't like her shoes.'

Joe leaned in front of Vicki so he could see the woman's feet. She wore chunky black heels with a strap around the ankle. They were stylish, maybe wrong for the occasion, but not unattractive.

'You're right,' he said playfully. 'The shoes are horribly wrong. She has committed a fashion crime.'

'He broke Hannah's heart,' Vicki said, her voice suddenly quiet, her eyes locking with Joe's, pleading. 'Seeing him with someone else – this woman – it's going to break her.'

'Why?' Joe asked, confused. 'Were they married? Did he cheat on her?'

'No,' Vicki said, defensively. 'They just . . . broke up. Years ago. They lived together in New York, and he decided to move to live near his family in Boston. And she's just not over it.'

'Why not?' Joe asked, still puzzled.

'Because . . .' Vicki shook her head, frustrated. 'Well, I – I don't know. I think she thought Tom was the kind of guy who'd never leave. And then he did. Sometimes it's hard to move on, you know? Especially when you thought you were safe.'

Joe wondered for a moment whether his own girlfriend, Sarah, would describe her situation as safe. It wasn't.

'I get it,' Joe said warmly, patting her back with the hand behind her chair.

Suddenly a woman in a tan pantsuit hurried past their seats, down the aisle, and pointed a strong finger at the string quartet positioned at the front. They began to play an almost somber march, which Joe recognized but couldn't quite place.

From behind the pack of chairs, bridesmaids began to emerge in long black gowns, each woman arm in arm with a man in a matching tuxedo. Hair had been blown straight, eyebrows tweezed. The women wore matching pearl necklaces and tiny pearl earrings.

Joe snickered to himself, remembering the dozens of times he'd served as a groomsman for friends when he was in his twenties. Most of those guys were divorced now. He'd escorted more jealous bridesmaids down aisles than he could remember – women of all shapes and sizes. He'd even slept with a few.

In his peripheral vision, Joe saw Vicki light up with the widest smile he'd seen on her face since meeting her. She was beaming at the pack of bridesmaids, her body almost half-standing as she leaned toward the end of the aisle to see the procession.

'Which one is your friend?' Joe whispered to her, now that bridesmaids and groomsmen were quickly making their way to the flowered altar where Bee's fiancée waited, his hands clasped in front of his waist.

'She's the third one down the line. The shortest one.'

'She's beautiful,' Joe said, now eyeing Hannah. 'You're right – she is better looking than our friend with the bad shoes,' he added, knowing it would make Vicki smile.

Sharing the same instinct, Joe and Vicki snapped their heads to the right to see if they could catch Tom's reaction to Hannah's big entrance. As expected, Tom was staring at Hannah, watching her closely as she continued her timed march. Tom rubbed his forehead and winced as he watched Hannah reach the altar and then turn to face the guests. She stood in the center of the row of bridesmaids, next to the rosy-cheeked matron of honor, who positioned herself just a bit too close to the bride, as if she longed to be the center of attention.

'Did you just see the way Tom looked at Hannah?' Joe asked Vicki, now invested in her friend's drama. He was amused at the way he rattled off the names, like soap opera characters.

'Yes,' Vicki whispered, pleased, her eyes still on Tom. 'That was . . . exactly what I hoped for. That was exactly right. That was the look of someone who is over-whelmed with regret.'

'We'd better get on our feet before we miss Bee,' Joe said, beaming as he spotted the bride, his favorite niece, whom he hadn't seen or called in years.

Joe and Vicki stood up with the rest of the spectators as Bee began her slow march toward matrimony. She nodded at the guests at the ends of the aisles as she walked. Her arm was locked with her father's, who maintained a stoic facial expression. As usual, he revealed nothing.

Joe tried to imagine his own daughter making a similar march with him on her arm. It didn't seem possible, at least not now. When she was younger, Cynthia had eagerly taken Joe's phone calls and been ecstatic about her occasional visits to Las Vegas, which he packed with shows, buffets, and day trips to the desert. But in the past couple of years, she'd barely returned his messages. He could hear her whine when her mother asked him to take his phone calls.

Joe's girlfriend, Sarah, had comforted him by explaining that Cynthia was simply going through puberty, but it went beyond that, Joe thought. After all, he was the one who had given Cynthia the birds-and-bees talk. He was the one she'd called when she had her first crush, and when she got her first period and was too embarrassed to tell her mother. Puberty should have only strengthened their bond, but the last time Cynthia had seen him in Vegas, she'd yelled at him, accusing him of being an apathetic parent. She'd criticized his lifestyle and mocked his relationship.

'She's, like, half your age,' Cynthia had said about Sarah, shortly after they'd met.

'That's actually not true. If she were half my age, she'd be twenty-one. She's thirty-one.'

'She is closer to my age than your age,' Cynthia had countered.

Joe paused for a minute, calculating as fast as he could.

'Not true. Cynthia, I just don't know what's going on here. If you don't like Sarah, fine. She won't come over when you're here. But I never see you, and I just want to spend some time with you.'

'I think,' Cynthia said, her eyes covered in glittery blue eye shadow, 'that if you actually wanted to see me, you'd come to see Mom and me in Maine.'

Joe was shaken out of the memory by Vicki grabbing his arm. Bee was passing their row and gave them a quick wink. Joe's eyes welled with tears. It had always been easier with Bee than with his own daughter. Bee had adored Joe when she was a child and only grew to like him more during her teenage years. It was Uncle Joe who fed her chocolate in private when she was still allergic, giving her an antihistamine as she ate a Snickers bar so that by the time she and Joe returned home from their long walk around the Ellicott City historic district, no one would know the difference. It was Uncle Joe who would take Bee to the mall in Columbia, where he'd buy her the nail polish and the cheap accessories that Donna had determined were a waste of money.

Joe smiled warmly at Bee and then at Vicki. He and Vicki then leaned into each other like proud parents, their shoulders touching.

'She looks perfect,' Vicki said, her eyes suddenly full of sad tears. Her mouth drooped. Her shoulders jerked and she swallowed a sob.

Joe put his arm around her, confused, but felt victory as she leaned into his embrace and placed one of her hands on the front of his brown lapel. 'It's okay,' he whispered, pulling a tissue out of one of his pockets. She composed herself quickly as the guests sat down.

'Are you all right?' Joe asked, whispering in her ear as she sat up too straight, shifting her eyes down the aisle to see if Tom had spotted her brief breakdown.

'I'm fine,' Vicki said, almost inaudibly. 'Actually,' she whispered too loudly, as the pastor started the ceremony, 'I'm fucking depressed.'

Two older women in front of them turned in their seats to flash an angry look at Vicki and Joe. Joe recognized them as Donna's sisters.

Joe tried to suppress laughter at the ladies' school-marmishness, but Vicki was already giggling. Fearing that they would cause a scene, they both hung their heads, looking at their laps, their shoulders jerking wildly as they attempted to keep silent. They leaned into each other, trying to control themselves. In the corner of his eye, Joe saw that Tom was now looking their way, puzzled about what was so amusing. He stared at Vicki, confused, then flashed a weak grin as he made eye contact with Joe.

Joe turned to Vicki, whose head was still down. He could hear the pastor welcoming the guests to the ceremony, but he didn't look up. He offered Vicki his hand, and she grabbed it, squeezing it tight.

Phil

As soon as the bride and groom said, 'I do,' Phil sprung from his folding chair to find the bathroom in the clubhouse's lobby. Once inside, he fished his cell phone out of his pocket and scrolled through it to find the last number he'd dialed, trying not to think about the call from his bookie he'd let go to voice mail. He hit 'send' and saw 'Mom' flash on the screen. She picked up after two rings.

'Hello?' He could hear more sickness in her raspy voice. She sounded muffled, like there was a layer of cotton between the phone and her face.

'Nancy, you sound terrible,' he said, teasing her by calling her by her first name.

'I actually feel better than I did last night, honey. Wait – what time is it? Isn't it time for the wedding? Are you in Annapolis yet?' She ended her question with a cough.

'I'm here. They just said "I do,"' Phil said in a whisper, wondering if anyone on the other side of the bathroom door could hear him.

Nancy continued, firing off questions about the ceremony, which he mostly ignored. 'How does Barb look? What was the bride's dress like? Did Matt look nervous? What are you wearing? Are you wearing something clean?'

'Yes, Mom,' Phil lied, wondering if he should spray himself with the can of air freshener perched on the toilet, to mask the smell of buffalo wings. He quickly decided against it. It would be worse if he wound up smelling like chicken and Lysol.

'Honey, tell me about Barb. She must be so proud. Her youngest son married – she's so lucky.'

'I haven't seen her, Mom,' Phil answered gruffly, acknowledging the jab. 'She was sitting in front, and I was in the back. I didn't want to block anybody's view.'

Nancy wouldn't question that. Phil was always mindful of his height, especially at concerts and movies, where he felt like a giant who stood in the way of everyone else's view. Phil's ex-girlfriend Elizabeth, who was five foot two, had always been impressed by his empathy for short people. On their second real date, he'd taken her to Baltimore's historic Charles Theater, the only place he knew of that showed arty films. Elizabeth had walked ahead of him to one of the middle rows, prepared to snag two of the best seats in the house, but Phil called her name from the back of the theater, explaining that at six foot six he didn't feel comfortable sitting where he'd wind up restricting the view of many normal-sized humans.

'Wow,' Elizabeth had said, surprised. 'That's really . . . considerate.'

'Short people are people too,' Phil had responded to her sarcastically as he slid into one of the back-row seats, making sure that no one was behind him and no one was in front of her.

'No, don't get me wrong. It's nice,' Elizabeth had said. 'I just never knew that tall people were so concerned about short people. It always seems that there's a tall person in front of me who couldn't care less.'

'Well, my mom is only five feet tall,' Phil had explained. 'So I'm used to accommodating short women.'

'That's sweet,' Elizabeth had said, smiling at him warmly.

Of course, a year and a half later, Elizabeth wouldn't consider Phil's concern for his mother to be at all sweet.

'You're in love with your mother!' she'd yelled during one of their last battles, before she stormed out of his apartment, slamming his front door, and then her own. They were next-door neighbors, so it was always a two-door slam, one right after the other.

That fight had started after Phil canceled their trip to Virginia Beach. He'd promised to take Elizabeth down there for a long weekend. It was all set – they'd even negotiated to stay at one of Phil's friend's timeshares – but a day before they were supposed to leave Phil got a call from Nancy. She invited him to dinner and told him that she'd already made his favorite dish, beef Wellington.

'I said I'd go,' Phil explained.

'Why didn't you just tell her we have plans to go away?' Elizabeth asked, already incensed.

'Well, to be honest, she sounded weird. Kind of lonely. She spent six hours making me a beef Wellington, and it's already in the fridge. I don't want her to be by herself this weekend. I just have a bad feeling, like if I leave, something bad will happen. My dad's birthday is next week. My mom is probably dreading it.'

That's when Elizabeth cracked – first literally, nervously pushing her neck back and forth, so the air between her bones let out a loud snap – and then emotionally as she openly targeted Phil's relationship with his mother for the first time. She'd made passive-aggressive jabs in the past about Phil's mother being a grown woman who could take care of herself, but on this day, there was no filter.

'That's funny, Phil, because I kind of thought you were hoping to get laid this weekend. Or maybe that's why you're going to your mom's.'

'Come on, Elizabeth.' He didn't have anything else to say. The silence filled the room as he watched Elizabeth boil.

'Go home, then, Phil. Do whatever you want.'

With that, she left and slammed the doors. After a few seconds, Phil walked to the wall and placed his ear against it. He could always hear her on the phone after their fights, yelling about him to a friend or to her own mother, who lived in California. Usually an hour or so after the battle had ended he could hear male and female voices, which meant she'd turned on the television. He would keep his ear against the one wall they shared until he could figure out what she was watching. Usually it was one of the *Sex and the City* episodes she'd recorded. Elizabeth DVR'd almost every rerun of that series, despite the fact that she owned most of the seasons on DVD.

Phil hated *Sex and the City*, but he appreciated the show's ability to put his girlfriend in a better mood. He'd call her after fights, knowing what she was watching, and she would answer without saying hello. She would breathe into the phone, and he would say something like, 'Carrie Bradshaw is going to look even uglier on my flat screen.' She would laugh, disarmed, and would return to his apartment with one of her DVDs, which they'd watch in silence, cuddling.

That routine worked until there were ultimatums and deadlines for proposals and moving in. Phil didn't meet those deadlines, and she kept her word about moving on. Phone calls weren't returned. Her eyes stayed on the peeling brown carpet when they passed each other in the hallway. Phil couldn't be sure, but he believed that since they'd broken up three months ago Elizabeth had stopped using the television in her living room so he wouldn't know what she was watching.

His mother asked about her a few times after the breakup, advising, 'You should call her,' as if he hadn't. 'She's a good girl, Phil. I'm sure whatever you did will be forgiven.'

But it was what he hadn't done that was the problem. He hadn't asked her to marry him. He refused to consider cohabitation, explaining that he was from a very Catholic family and that living together before marriage just wouldn't fly. Elizabeth reminded him that his brother had lived with his wife for months before marriage, but Phil dismissed the example. 'My mom knew they moved in together before marriage and she was pissed. It was awkward for everybody. I'm not going to do that to her.'

From inside a stall in the clubhouse's bathroom, Phil now listened to his mother, who was rambling off an excited message that he was supposed to pass on to Barb. 'Tell her she's a good mother, and tell her that this doesn't mean that she's old, and Phil, honey, tell her that as soon as I can I'll come visit. Or maybe the next time she's up in Maryland she can see me. I imagine she'll be here more often now that her daughter-in-law's family is here. Tell her that I have so much to talk to her about.'

'Okay, Mom,' Phil said, opening the bathroom door to find three irritable teenagers waiting outside. 'Mom, I've got to go. It's time for the reception.'

'About time, man,' one of the boys grunted as Phil slid by. Phil grimaced, wishing he could kick the kid out of the ballpark.

Suddenly desperate to leave, and to avoid his bookie's next call, Phil considered making a quick exit. 'Mom,' he asked, hopefully, 'what if I bailed on the reception in an hour or so and drove home? I could pick up some

soup for you. We could go to the pub in the morning
for omelets, if you feel well enough. I could take the
dog out so you don't have to.'

'No, honey,' Nancy said quickly, with as much author-
ity as she could muster between coughs. 'You have to
stay at that wedding. Barb needs to see that we're there
for her. And I won't have you driving so many hours in
one day.'

'But Mom,' Phil whined, 'you're all alone down there.
And there are so many people here. Barb would want
me to take care of you. She won't even notice I'm gone.'

'Honey,' Nancy said, 'I'm fine. Now go have a good
time. Go talk to the bridesmaids.'

Phil rolled his eyes. 'Okay, Mom.'

'Good-bye, sweetie.'

The clubhouse was now crowded with packs of guests
moving through it, from cocktails on the patio to the
tent that had just opened for the reception. The clubhouse's foyer was regal and clean, with a few leather
couches next to shelves of yellowed books. There were
two tables in the center of the room, one that held place
cards with every guest's table assignment, the other

dominated by a laptop computer. The computer was cued up to a digital photomontage of scenes from Bee and Matt's coupledom.

Shots of the two of them giggling in the UNC law-school cafeteria morphed into candid photos of them on a boat somewhere tropical. Every now and then an image of a younger Bee or Matt flashed on the screen. There were a few good ones of Matt with a 1980s-inspired mullet, probably from middle school. There were some pictures of Bee from college. One grainy candid showed Bee laughing with a young woman Phil recognized as one of the bridesmaids. The bridesmaid in question was blonde in this photo, artificially so. Her hair was now brown and straight. She was prettier in person. Phil had laughed to himself as he watched her fidget during the service.

Phil frowned as the picture melted away, resurfacing as a new image, this one of Bee and Matt in an apple orchard. Phil recognized the shot from the 'save the date' card on his mother's refrigerator. Phil rolled his eyes and looked at the table with the seating assignments. He figured he would wait until the crowd dispersed to find his place card. It didn't matter to him where he'd been placed; no matter where he sat he'd be among strangers. In the meantime he figured he'd better get to a TV to find out what was going on and whether his bookie was calling with good or terrible news.

He followed a long hallway toward the back of the building, where he was pleased to find the club's lounge. Much to his delight, the television was on above the bar. Three older men who seemed unaffiliated with the wedding sat on leather lounge chairs not far from the TV. They looked to be golfers, country club members who probably spent most of their Saturday afternoons drinking tumblers of bourbon after finishing up on the green, to avoid going home to their wives.

They were seated around a small wooden table, all facing forward, their eyes fixated on the Maryland-Rutgers football game.

Phil stared at the men in the chairs, trying to gauge how opposed they'd be to changing the channel for just a few minutes. On any other day, he'd gladly choose Maryland and Rutgers over socializing at a stranger's wedding, but today he had a ridiculous amount of money on the Oregon-California football game, which was happening at the same time, across the country. The aggressive bet was out of character for Phil, who thought of himself as a conservative, recreational gambler. Phil balled his hands into fists, wondering what he wasn't seeing on CBS as Maryland and Rutgers continued, as expected, to do nothing of note on ESPN.

Phil liked Oregon, enough that he felt good taking a risk, but, to be honest with himself, it was too soon in the season to feel confident that the Ducks could win by more than six points on the road. He'd risked five hundred and fifty dollars to win five hundred on that play, but that wasn't what scared him. It was his second bet, a last-minute decision to try to win fifteen hundred dollars on the over, which frightened him. It was a decision that forced him to root for both teams to score. If Oregon and California didn't combine to go over seventy-one and a half points, and Oregon didn't win by more than six, he'd be out a total of twenty-two hundred bucks. He would have to dip into his savings account for his mortgage money.

He'd made the out-of-character bet three nights ago, after seeing Elizabeth leave her apartment in date makeup. She didn't make eye contact with him; she simply ducked uncomfortably as she walked briskly down the hall to grab the elevator door before it closed.

She was wearing the same outfit she'd worn on their fancier dates, the few outings that involved dinner reservations. As he watched her disappear, as the elevator door closed, he thought about what was on tap for his own evening — a night of television and chips.

He'd made himself comfortable quickly that night, grabbing a beer from the refrigerator and sinking into the couch with his newly purchased, oversized bag of Doritos. Then he tuned in to ESPN just in time to watch a feature about Oregon's offensive coordinator, a hotshot who had been hired from the University of New Hampshire whose career was on a quick rise. Two and a half beers and an hour later, Phil called Hank to place the bet. Hank was Phil's longtime bookie, whom he'd seen more frequently years ago when he was a more aggressive gambler. After Phil requested this new bet, Hank paused before responding.

'Really, Phil?' he finally asked.

'Hank,' Phil said. 'This guy was a crackerjack up at UNH. I like the line.'

Hank was quiet, his silence teeming with judgment.

'Hank, you've never had to chase me down. Aren't you supposed to want me to take some risks?'

'I don't need to chase you down because I'm not a bookie,' Hank blurted into the phone nervously, as if the line were bugged. 'I run an informal gaming community.'

'Yeah, okay. You're a model citizen, Hank,' Phil said. 'Give me Oregon and the over.'

Now Phil was in the heart of Terrapin country, stuck

watching the Maryland-Rutgers game. It was all Eliza-beth's fault, he thought. Elizabeth and her date makeup and her skirt with the flowers on it.

Elizabeth and Elana had rented the condo next to Phil's for three years, but for the first of those years, they did little to acknowledge Phil other than to nod and smile when he passed them in the hall on the way to and from the building's carpeted elevator. Phil knew their first names thanks to the thin walls and the mailbox in the lobby.

Elana was the more outgoing of the two. She had a laugh that sounded like a cartoon witch's cackle and unruly curly hair that Phil believed a more-sophisticated woman would iron straight. She was thin except for her arms, which were usually too big for her shirtsleeves. It seemed to Phil that at any moment Elana's muscles would expand and that her top would rip to pieces, just as if she were the Incredible Hulk.

Elizabeth, the more attractive of the two, was a mystery, at least in the beginning. She kept to herself and rarely made small talk with anyone in the halls. She often left before seven in the morning, and she had not requested a parking space out back because she traveled by bicycle. For that reason – and because of the tiny diamond stud in her nose – Phil assumed that she was some sort of hippie. This theory was supported by Elizabeth's regular uniform: long, flowing skirts and tight tank tops.

For the first year that the women lived next door to Phil, he assumed Elizabeth had a boyfriend, even though there was no evidence to suggest that she did. She always came home alone and there were never any unidentified men lingering in the hallway. It just seemed to Phil that Elizabeth should be attached, maybe to an equally attractive hippie guy, someone with a full beard who played Frisbee.

Phil hoped to talk to her one day and steal her away from this fictional man. He lingered in the hallway to hold doors for Elizabeth, but he couldn't think of a way to start up a conversation.

He was finally given an opportunity, a gift from God, as he told his friends, two years ago, on the Friday after Thanksgiving, when the building was mostly empty. Phil's apartment complex, which wasn't far from the University of Maryland medical buildings, was mostly inhabited by graduate students who left on holidays to be with their out-of-state families.

At about eleven that night, long after Phil had reheated and consumed the salty turkey leftovers sent home with him by his mother the night before, he heard a soft tapping on his door. He opened it to find a pale and clammy Elizabeth leaning against the hallway wall, trying to smile politely as she clutched her stomach and winced.

'I'm Elizabeth from next door,' she said, her eyes red and dry. 'There's something wrong. I think I'm sick. I need you to call somebody.'

Quickly Phil took Elizabeth's hands and walked her to his couch, where she lay down, her legs knocking over a small stack of sports magazines that had been collecting dust on his coffee table.

'Do you want some water?' Phil had asked without moving. He was frozen next to the couch, looking down at his patient, who, based on her facial expression, was in an immeasurable amount of pain. 'Do you know what's wrong?'

'What does it feel like when you need your appendix out?' Elizabeth asked. 'I think my back is exploding.'

Phil kept quiet, taking a moment to enjoy the adrenaline rush. He felt panicked because he feared Elizabeth might die on his couch. But he was buoyantly giddy, suddenly light on his usually heavy feet, because this was the best thing to happen to him in at least six months, which was the last time a girl had been horizontal on his couch.

And this wasn't just any girl; it was Elizabeth, the mystery neighbor he'd imagined kissing every time he spotted her locking her bike to the pole in the lobby.

He adored her size, her petite stature. She couldn't have been more than 105 pounds. He liked to imagine being naked with her, with her curled up on top of him like a baby bear. In this fantasy, when he took the time to have it, he imagined that he did not have any chest hair and that he had a prominent six-pack as opposed to his real-life four-pack that was threatening to become a two-pack every time he ate a second peanut butter sandwich.

That was all just a dream, but here she was, on his couch, stretched out on her back with her eyes closed, shaking with fear and needing him – the baby bear come to life.

'I think I have to go to the hospital,' Elizabeth said, jarring Phil back to reality.

Slowly, she stood up on her own, using the arm of the couch for balance. She walked to the door, nodding to Phil as a signal that he should follow. He obeyed, grabbing the keys to his Durango and moving out to the hallway, where he waited for her to go into her apartment to grab her wallet and jacket.

The ride to the hospital was a short one; the emergency room was just down the street. Elizabeth kept her eyes closed and her hands on her stomach as they drove the short distance. When they arrived, Elizabeth was wheeled away, and Phil was comforted by nurses who assumed he was her boyfriend. He took on the responsibility proudly, answering as many questions as he could, pretending he knew more about Elizabeth than he did.

He read magazines in the waiting area until a nurse took him aside and explained that Elizabeth had developed a serious kidney infection that should have been treated days ago. It could be cured with antibiotics, but she would spend the rest of the night in the hospital. He would be able to pick her up in the morning. The nurse asked that he clear his Saturday to watch over her.

The request delighted Phil. He stopped into Elizabeth's room that night, just before he left the hospital, and told her he'd be back for her in the morning. Elizabeth opened her eyes and smiled. She asked softly, 'Phil, do you mind calling Elana tonight? Will you tell her I need her to come back early from her parents' to help me tomorrow? I'll give you her cell phone number.'

Phil frowned, angry that Elana might take his place during the recovery process. 'Yeah – I'll call her,' he said, programming the digits into his phone just before patting Elizabeth's hand and making his way to the door.

When he arrived back at the building, he followed Elizabeth's instructions and called Elana with the news.

Elana's reacted to Elizabeth's health problem so loudly that Phil moved the phone receiver away from his ear.

'Oh! My! God!' she yelled. 'Is she okaaay?'

'She's fine. She just wants you to know. If you're stuck at home for Thanksgiving, don't worry. I can watch out for her tomorrow. I'm not going anywhere.'

'That is sooo nice of you,' Elana had said. 'And here I always thought you were an asshole,' she continued, before letting out one of her signature menacing giggles. 'You sure you can watch her until Sunday? I won't be home until Sunday night.'

'Of course,' Phil said confidently, pleased that Elana didn't put up a fight.

The following twenty-four hours made up what was probably the best day Phil had experienced in a number of years. He picked Elizabeth up from the emergency room and brought her back to their building, where he bundled her up on his couch. She seemed effortlessly comfortable there, despite the fact that they barely knew each other. He ordered wraps from the Middle Eastern place down the street and told her they could watch anything she wanted on television, which turned out to be repeats of *Sex and the City*. That destroyed Phil a bit. He hated that show, especially the way the characters always said 'meanwhile.'

'They say that word, like, fifty times an episode,' Phil told Elizabeth.

'They do not,' Elizabeth responded, smiling as she dug a spoon into the frozen yogurt she'd ordered with her hummus wrap.

'They do so,' Phil said. 'That's all they say on this show. "Meanwhile, while Samantha was going uptown, I was going downtown,"' he said, in his best female voice. '"Meanwhile,"' he continued, accentuating the word, '"while Miranda was being a lawyer, Carrie slept with, like, a hundred guys."'

'Shut up,' Elizabeth barked playfully, throwing a pillow at his face.

Later on Phil put Elizabeth to bed in his room, and he happily slept on the couch, fighting all urges to go in and join her. By the time Elana returned the next day, it was clear that he and Elizabeth were on the precipice of coupledom. A week after Phil returned Elizabeth to her apartment, she treated him to a thank-you dinner. After the meal they both leaned in for a kiss, in front of her door and then his, and then she followed him inside.

They spent much of the rest of the cold season traveling in socks between their fourth-floor apartments, sometimes allowing Elana to hang out as a third wheel, sometimes shutting her out by hiding in Phil's apartment.

When baseball season began in May, Phil gave Elizabeth and Elana free tickets in the grandstand and asked his vendor friends to slip them kettle corn and sodas. He took Elizabeth home to his mother's and showed her where he used to play basketball in high school. He was secretly thrilled when she seemed impressed that there was a photo of him in the trophy case, from his senior year, just before he went off to play college ball. They had sleepovers three times a week, giving Phil enough space to feel as though he had a nice girlfriend but that it wasn't too serious.

It was blissful until the following March, just six months ago, when Elizabeth began asking all the big questions. It was a preseason Sunday. Elizabeth had woken up hours before Phil had any intention of starting his day.

'Are you up?' she asked loudly, waking him.

'Are you?' he muttered, smiling into his pillow.

He could hear her cracking her knuckles. He turned

to her, but she stared ahead, her eyes glassy, her lips hardened into a line.

'What's up?' he asked, his stomach suddenly burning with a bad feeling. She turned to him. She was sitting up straight so she looked down onto his face, her eyes sad and tired as if she'd spent the morning rehearsing a conversation that she expected to end poorly.

'Phil,' she said, taking a long pause.

'Yes,' he responded, sitting up next to her. There was at least a foot between them.

'I have this nagging feeling that this is it.'

'That what is it?' Phil said, his tone giving away that he understood what she meant all too well.

'What I mean is, is this it? Are we going to move in with each other at some point? Are you thinking marriage or kids? I mean, I'm not. Not right now. But I'm going to be done with school next year, and we've been together for a year and a half, and I've just had this weird feeling for a while that this is it.'

Phil was silent. He waited for her to continue.

'You're not going to say anything?'

'I don't know what you want me to say.' He kept his eyes on the television at the foot of the bed, which was off. He could feel her eyes on his cheek.

She began to cry.

'I've always told myself I didn't want to be one of those nagging girlfriends. But you're always at the ballpark in the summer. And I thought we'd get more serious this winter, but you were at your mother's half the time. Like, every other day.'

'She's all alone down there, Elizabeth,' Phil responded harshly.

'She's in her sixties. She can fend for herself. And that's not my point. I think it's great that you spend so much time with your mother. It's just weird that you rarely ever invite me. We live a half hour away from the house you grew up in, and I think I've been there twice.'

'That's because you spend holidays with your family in California,' Phil said.

'And every time I go to California, I invite you,' Elizabeth continued. 'You've never come to visit my family. There's something weird with your mom, Phil. It's like she likes me, but you don't want her to. It's like . . . It's like you don't want to share her.'

Phil was silent again. His stomach let out a loud growl.

'What do you want me to do?' Phil asked in his most annoyed voice.

Elizabeth sniffled and took a deep breath. More

confidently she said, slowly, 'I think we should move in together.'

Phil turned his eyes back to the dark television, avoiding her stare. His face was red. 'Absolutely not. It's not happening.'

'Why?' she demanded, the tears falling again.

'First of all, we haven't been together that long. Second of all, and I've told you this, my family is traditionally religious. I'm not moving in with anybody before marriage.'

'Are you kidding me?' Elizabeth said. 'This is really about God?'

Elizabeth crossed her legs on the bed and put a pillow over her lap. She took another deep breath, trying to calm herself. 'Didn't you tell me that your brother moved in with his wife before they got married?'

'Yeah,' Phil said, biting his lip, irritated with himself that he'd shared that detail about his brother's relationship. 'But we all pretended it wasn't happening. We lied to my mom. I'm sure she knew they were living together, but I can assure you that she didn't like it.'

'So, are you telling me we're not going to move in together, or that we eventually will move in together but we'll have to lie to your mom, or that we should get married first?'

Phil was quiet again. He wasn't quite sure what he'd meant to imply. He'd assumed that Elizabeth would eventually move back to California without him. He was sad about their ill-fated relationship, and had even wallowed in some alcohol-induced self-pity about the impending breakup with friends from the ballpark, but he'd never considered how the separation would play itself out. He'd convinced himself that Elizabeth knew her fate, that their time together had an expiration date. She wasn't from Baltimore. There was no reason for her to stay. And in the end, Phil didn't see himself with a woman like Elizabeth, who shopped for vegan cookies and talked about buying an electric car. They were from different worlds.

Phil spoke softly now, hoping to keep her calm. 'I think I like things . . . like they are now. Can't we do this for a while and see how we're feeling when you graduate?'

Elizabeth broke into a sob so heavy the bed shook.

'Jesus,' Phil said under his breath, 'what did I say?'

She tossed the pillow from her lap and pulled Phil's navy sheets off her legs. She stood up from the bed and frantically paced around the room, grabbing the few things that belonged to her. A hairbrush. A DVD.

'Elana's right,' Elizabeth said, stopping to glare at him.

'She says you're just biding your time until I'm done with school. She says you're a serial monogamist who is in love with his mother.'

Phil's eyes were wide. 'Are you fucking kidding me?' he barked. 'You're going to listen to Elana? Because she's had so much luck with men? Jesus. In love with my mother? That's classic, Elizabeth. Just because I don't want to marry you, I'm some sort of Norman Bates character. That's perfect.'

Elizabeth's froze. The hairbrush fell to the floor.

'So that's it. You don't want to marry me.'

Phil looked down and instinctively placed his hands on his stomach. It burned uncomfortably. He needed some milk. 'That's not what I said,' he whispered, wincing from the pain.

'Yes, it is,' Elizabeth responded, her voice calmer than it had been. She walked out of his bedroom and shut the door behind her softly. He could hear her gently close his front door and then her own. He was frightened by her sudden composure.

After a few moments of silence, Phil took a deep breath and left his room, tiptoeing to the kitchen so that Elizabeth wouldn't hear any movement from next door. He poured himself a glass of milk and chugged it, picturing the cold, thick liquid coating his tender insides.

He wanted desperately to turn on his television – not to play *Sex and the City* to lure Elizabeth back, but to watch ESPN. He just wanted to zone out and forget about everything. But he remained frozen in the center of his living-room sofa, with the television off, too paranoid that Elizabeth might hear him through their shared wall if he turned it on. It seemed insensitive to watch *SportsCenter* after what had just transpired. Instead he flipped through old copies of *Sports Illustrated* until he could no longer stand the silence and then retired to his room, where he watched ESPN in bed, with the volume so low that he could only make out every few words.

His seclusion didn't end for quite some time. For weeks, Phil lived as quietly as he could, fearful of dropping a dish or speaking too loud while he was on the phone, petrified that Elizabeth would be reminded that he was alive. When he used the elevator, he found himself repeatedly pushing the buttons, as if his manic movements would make the old car travel faster. On game nights he sprinted from the front of the building to his car, worried he would catch her on her way home from class. He managed not to see her at all.

Twice he saw Elana. Once by the mailboxes, just days after the breakup. She gave Phil a knowing frown and said, 'She's getting by,' as if he'd asked. He responded with an earnest nod.

The second time was about three weeks after the breakup. Elana had stopped to talk to Phil in front of his apartment door. She asked him if he'd ever met Nick Markakis, the Baltimore ballplayer who women always seemed to want to sleep with, and of course Phil had. He saw the guy almost every night. When Phil told her this, Elana licked her lips and bobbed her head from left to right, not quite listening to the rest of his answer. She was flirting with him. What an asshole, Phil thought. He imagined that her curls were hissing snakes. For a moment, he considered calling Elizabeth to inform her that her so-called friend was trying to get into his pants.

It was about six weeks after the breakup that the Orioles ended an eleven-game home stretch and took a road trip to the West Coast, leaving Phil with his nights free.

On that first free Thursday, Phil spent much of the night on the couch, flipping between several cable stations until he settled on a repeat of the medical show *House*, a program that had become a favorite of his mother's. After watching the show for about twenty minutes, Phil decided that the young female doctor on the program reminded him of Elizabeth. She was much taller than Elizabeth and, in fact, didn't look much like Elizabeth, but this doctor on *House* was female, and Phil was lonely, and she made Phil think of Elizabeth's breasts and Elizabeth's smile and Elizabeth's nose ring and the time Elizabeth gave him oral sex even though she had a head cold and both of them laughed every time she paused to sneeze.

Before Phil could stop himself, he was standing up, suddenly determined to go next door and win her back.

Then, with as much intensity, Phil sat back down, wondering if Elizabeth was even there, if she would want to see him, and what seeing her would mean. Then he had another troubling thought: what if Elizabeth was already dating someone else?

'Fucking piece of shit,' Phil said out loud, referring to his imaginary rival.

At that moment Phil devised a safe plan. He would go next door and ask Elizabeth if she still had his Emilio's take-out menu, which he knew she did. Once he retrieved the menu, he would suggest they order food together, to save the delivery guy a trip. If there was a man in Elizabeth's apartment, or if she looked apathetic about seeing him, he would take the menu and retreat.

Flawless, Phil thought, as he hurried into his bathroom to make sure his hair was in place.

Elizabeth answered the door looking even smaller than Phil remembered her. He didn't even get the chance to ask for the menu. He barely even registered what she was wearing, which was, in fact, his old Loyola sweatshirt. Before he could say anything about Emilio's, Elizabeth pulled him into her apartment by his shirt, took his hands, and walked him straight to her bedroom.

On her full-size bed, which had always been too small for both of them, she straddled his stomach and kissed him with her mouth open wide so he couldn't breathe.

Had Phil been able to speak, he would have said, 'Thank you.'

She allowed him to enter her without a condom, which had only happened twice before, once when they first said 'I love you' and once toward the end of the relationship when they were both very drunk. As Phil watched Elizabeth move up and down on top of him, he decided they would get married and have a baby girl. Maybe he would move to California. He liked Dodger Stadium.

But none of that happened. Not long after their reconciliation, early in July, Elizabeth told Phil she'd changed her mind about a second chance.

'I thought this was what I wanted, but I just keep wondering when it's going to blow up again,' Elizabeth explained calmly. 'You were right. I'm eventually going back to California, and you're always going to be here.'

'Sure,' Phil said, because there wasn't anything else to say. He thought of what so many coaches said after lost games, when they spoke to fill the silence at press conferences. 'It is what it is,' he muttered.

Elizabeth continued, justifying her departure without the tears he'd grown accustomed to during their previous relationship talks. 'There's nothing to suggest that anything is different here. You haven't asked me to move in, and let's face it, you're not going to. People don't change. You haven't, and I certainly haven't. I love you, but I have to move on. We both do.'

She waited then in anticipation of his response, but he froze, not knowing what else to say to her. Was he supposed to ask her to move in – right that second? Was he supposed to tell her he wanted to marry her?

Before he could decide on an appropriate statement, Elizabeth hunched forward, kissed Phil on his forehead, got up from the couch, wiped her eyes with her pointer fingers as if she'd cried, and walked through his door, closing it politely behind her.

Once school started again, Phil began tracking Elizabeth's comings and goings so he could catch her in the elevator, anything to remind her that he was still next door, just a few feet away. He found himself leaving the apartment when he didn't need to, running fake errands to increase the odds of a sighting.

Then, last Wednesday, Phil got his wish. He saw Elizabeth walking down the hall in her date-night best, her knee-length floral skirt and a light blue shirt that he believed was the only thing she owned with a collar. In that moment he knew it was really over.

Less than two hours later, Phil used his Doritos-stained fingers to call Hank and bet more than two grand on Oregon.

Rob

Rob answered the phone. 'Who is it?' he asked in a facetious singsong falsetto. He was lying in bed, reading a two-month-old *New Yorker* that he'd swiped from the periodical room at work the day before. He'd been drifting into sleep when the phone began to buzz. Hannah panted through the phone, skipping the greeting.

'Vicki says she's ugly, but I think she's pretty,' Hannah shout-whispered, hyperventilating into the receiver, her voice shaky.

She followed the statement by giving herself a quick fix from her inhaler. Anyone besides Rob might have thought the sharp burst of air was simply the sound of Hannah's heavy breathing, but he recognized it as her albuterol routine. It was the familiar exhale, puff, and inhale that he'd hear in the middle of the night years ago when he'd knocked on Hannah's door and slept over. Her dependence on the puffer reminded him of the geeky kids in elementary school who had allergic reactions to bee stings, except for the fact that Hannah was a grown woman who had always looked strangely unnatural using the inhaler in sexy pajamas, with her cleavage spilling over her silk tank top as she took two puffs and then fell asleep next to him.

'Don't abuse that thing,' Rob responded smugly. 'It'll stop working.'

Hannah let out an exasperated sigh that ended with a croaky cough. 'Between the stress and the pollen and the fact that everyone at this wedding smokes, I haven't been able to stop using my inhaler.

'That said, the rest of me feels fantastic,' she continued, her voice higher. 'The maid of honor gave me some magic pills.'

Rob set the magazine down next to him and sat up straight. Pills would explain why Hannah sounded so manic. She'd always been high strung, but today her voice was uncharacteristically tense, as if she might laugh or cry at the end of each sentence.

'Hannah, what kind of pills did you take?' Rob asked, slowly, in his most parental tone. 'Were they allergy pills? Can you tell me what the pills looked like?'

Rob sprung out of bed and shuffled into the living room, where he'd left his own bag of medicine, Lucy's assorted mix of uppers and downers.

'I think it was white,' Hannah said. 'And round. And then there was a white one that was more like a square. Why?'

Rob wiped his forehead. Now he was worried about Hannah, who could barely stomach a glass of wine on top of all her allergy medications, let alone a Xanax or Valium.

'You shouldn't be taking pills that aren't prescribed to you,' Rob said, shaking his head at his own hypocrisy.

'You're telling me what to do?' Hannah laughed, just as surprised that Rob was the one giving the lecture about drug use. 'Listen,' she continued, 'don't worry about me. The pills are making everything better. It's like I'm seeing this whole thing from outside my body. I don't care that Tom has moved on. I don't care that the top of this bra is ripping a hole in my neck. I feel – impenetrable.'

Rob held his own bag of pills in front of his face to inspect each white round and square pill, wondering which one Hannah might have taken.

'Look, that's great. I'm glad no one can penetrate you right now, but I want you to promise me that whatever you do you'll stay away from alcohol. The pills are enough for a lightweight like you. Keep drinking water.'

'I already had some wine while we were taking pictures. Prosciutto. It tasted like apple juice.'

'Wine and ham?'

'I didn't have any ham. I had wine. Like champagne.'

Rob stifled a laugh. 'You mean you had prosecco? Not prosciutto, prosecco, Hannah.'

'Whatever,' Hannah responded, suddenly distracted. 'You know, Rob, I could never cast you. I've tried, but I think you'd have to play yourself in a movie. I actually think you're good-looking enough to play yourself, you know?'

'Hannah,' Rob continued, dropping the bag of pills on his kitchen table so he could pull nervously at his hair. A tuft of his bangs stuck up straight from all his nervous raking. 'I want you to listen to me. No more wine. No more pills. I want you to find a friend, find Vicki or one of the bridesmaids, and tell them to watch you. Make sure someone gets you to bed safely. Make sure –'

Rob stopped short at the sound of a repetitive thud coming from his bathroom. It sounded like someone was kicking the cabinet under the sink from the inside, a muffled, hollow banging that shook the bathroom door.

'Hannah, I have to go. Please, take care, all right? No drinking. You'll be okay.' Rob quickly hung up and ran toward the noise.

As he put his hand on the bathroom doorknob, he heard another loud thud followed by a squeal. He threw open the door and saw Liz, or more accurately, the end of Liz's tail. Her head was stuck behind the toilet, between the back end of the porcelain base and the tiled wall behind it. Her midsection was trapped under the medicine cabinet, which appeared to have fallen from where it usually hung above the toilet. Her tail was slapping furiously against the wall and the side of the bathtub to her right. Liz was trying to convulse – Rob could see her body jerk in the familiar epileptic rhythm – but she was ensnared by the toilet and the broken medicine cabinet. As Rob focused, his knees locked, he saw that Liz was bleeding. The cabinet had punctured her midsection.

'Jesus Christ!' he shouted. His voice echoed.

He pulled at his hair for a few seconds, in shock. 'Jesus!' he yelled again.

Rob finally took three big lunges, to close the distance between him and Liz, and carefully lifted the medicine cabinet off her torso. He hurled the heavy wooden box, which was filled with his toiletries, into the tub with so much force that its mirrored door shattered.

With the weight off her stomach, Liz began to twitch more feverishly. Rob got on his knees and leaned around the other side of the toilet to see her face. Her eyes were wide with panic. She looked at Rob confused, desperate. Her seizure was dying down, but now she appeared to be thrashing from pain, her movements steadier than the involuntary convulsions that accompanied her epileptic fits.

'Hold on, baby,' he told her, responding to her whimper.

Rob moved to the other side of the toilet to see how badly the cabinet had sliced her stomach. There was too much blood to see the size of the wound. He stroked her legs and leaned into her, placing his left hand on the source of the bleeding, like he'd seen doctors do for gunshot victims on hospital shows.

'We're going to fix it. We're going to fix it, babe.'

He took his hand off the wound and placed both of his forearms under Liz's still-shaking torso so he could pull her body from behind the toilet and carry her through the house and out the front door. He made a quick stop in the living room to grab his keys and wallet from the coffee table. He kicked the front door closed with his foot, neglecting to lock it, and kissed the top of Liz's head.

He held her against his chest like a baby as he opened the backseat of his old Audi with his free hand. Then he placed her down gently, her stomach bleeding onto his vinyl seats.

'It's okay, babe,' he repeated as he hopped into the front seat and revved the engine.

The moment reminded him of all the movies he'd seen in which a man brings a panting woman in labor to the hospital. The radio had popped on loud, still tuned to the college station that on Saturday nights played a block of old-school hip-hop. Liz's whimpering was suddenly drowned out by 'Return of the Mack,' which played so loud that the car vibrated. 'Fuck!' Rob yelled and quickly shut the stereo off. But then he turned it back on, lowering the volume, hoping that the music would calm Liz down. She always loved music. In her healthier days, she'd jumped around – almost galloping – whenever Bob Dylan's 'Hurricane' came up on his CD player.

With that thought, he shut the radio off again and started singing the song, hoping she'd recognize it.

'Pistol shots ring out in the barroom night. Enter Patty Valentine from the upper hall.'

Not hearing much of a response from the backseat, Rob moved on to 'Ballad of a Thin Man' and then 'Are You Ready?' the song on Dylan's born-again Christian album that always seemed to make Liz pant with extra enthusiasm, as if she were experiencing her own religious awakening.

'Are you ready to meet Jesus? Are you where you ought to be?'

Rob was not religious, but singing the lyrics caused his eyes to well up with big tears. It was all too ominous. He wondered if Liz felt the same way. He continued to sing, wiping the tears from his cheeks with the back of his wrist.

In the rearview mirror he could see that Liz's eyes were closed. The tiny movements in her chest told him that she was still breathing. Maybe she was sleeping. Or maybe she was listening to him. Rob decided to switch back to her favorite, 'Hurricane,' and slurred the words like Dylan. He tried to match Dylan's nasal tone.

By verse three, Rob had pulled his car into a handicapped spot directly in front of the animal hospital. It only took seconds for him to get out of the Audi and grab Liz, who was still breathing, albeit shallowly, her eyes now open. She looked almost amused as Rob raced through the waiting room, somewhat unsure of where he was going.

The place was surprisingly packed for a Saturday night. Families with whimpering mutts and newborn puppies stared at him, horrified, as he walked briskly with the bleeding dog in his arms.

A vet he'd never seen before, a slender young woman with dark hair, cut him off at the door to an operating room. 'Can I help you, sir?'

'She's bleeding. A medicine cabinet fell on her. And she has canine epilepsy.'

Before Rob could continue, the woman calmly placed her arms under Liz's legs and removed her from his embrace. Rob followed her as she brought Liz down a narrow hallway to an empty room with green checkered wallpaper. She placed Liz on a table that looked similar to what Rob might see in his own doctor's office, a narrow bench with a green plastic cover and thin white paper rolled out on top.

The pretty vet ran her hands up and down Liz's stomach, stopping at the wound. Rob watched as another woman in scrubs came into the room and put gloves on.

'Sir, it might be best for you to wait outside,' the second woman said, giving Rob a sympathetic look.

'Is she going to be okay?' Rob asked.

'I don't know yet,' the vet said distractedly, as the other woman ushered him out of the room, the doors between him and Liz swinging closed behind him.

Hannah

'Don't leave me,' Hannah said, pouting at Vicki, whose new gray-haired friend was waiting just a few feet away.

Hannah couldn't figure out when and why Vicki had become so chummy with this older man, whom Vicki had introduced briefly as Bee's uncle. It wasn't like the new, postcollege Vicki to talk to strangers. It certainly wasn't like the new Vicki to warm up to a man who quite obviously wanted to sleep with her.

'We'll be two tables away if you need anything,' Vicki responded reassuringly. 'If you go crazy, just come over and pull up a chair.'

'*We?*' Hannah whispered, throwing a sharp glance at Bee's uncle, who stood a few feet away from them with two glasses of red wine in his hands, presumably one for him and one for Vicki. He was staring blankly at the table in front of him, shifting his weight between his feet. Hannah scowled and looked back at Vicki, who was still smiling at the uncle.

'Are you two a "we" now? You and Bee's uncle? What is he, sixty?'

'He's, like, forty-two,' Vicki said, flashing an angry glance at Hannah, and adding in a loud whisper, 'He's a lot younger than Bee's dad. And by the way, it's not like that.'

Hannah eyes softened with regret. Vicki was in a good mood, which was rare these days.

Hannah rubbed the back of her neck as she considered for a moment that she was, if anything, jealous that she hadn't found her own partner at the wedding, aside from Dawn, who was more of a taskmaster than an actual friend.

Rob certainly hadn't made good on his promise to be Hannah's security blanket during the weekend. Not only had he been a no-show, he was now rushing her off the phone.

Hannah glanced over at Bee's uncle and gave him a closer look. In his tailored brown suit, with his wavy salt-and-pepper hair, he could be a celebrity. He was fit and had a strong chin. He had good posture. He wasn't quite George Clooney. But Treat Williams?

'You're casting him. Stop it,' Vicki said, recognizing Hannah's focused eyes.

'Fine.'

'Well,' Vicki said, giving up a small smile, 'at least tell me who you picked.'

'Treat Williams.'

'Who is Treat Williams?'

'He was the dad on *Everwood*. And he was in the movie adaptation of *Hair*.'

'No way,' Vicki said, leaning into Hannah so Joe remained out of earshot. 'That's not good enough. At least give me Robert Downey Jr.'

'No way,' Hannah mimicked back. 'That's too good. Wishful thinking. Your guy's too old.'

'He's in his forties!' Vicki snapped too loud, prompting both women to look down and suppress laughter. Joe flashed Vicki a questioning look, his cheeks flushed.

Hannah shot him a sheepish smile in return. He tentatively grinned back in her direction, took a sip from one of the wineglasses, and looked away.

'How about Scott Bakula?' Hannah asked, thoughtfully.

'I don't know who he is either.'

'You know, from *Quantum Leap*.'

Vicki's eyes narrowed. 'What's *Quantum Leap*?'

Hannah put her hand to her forehead. 'Are you kidding me? How do you not know what *Quantum Leap* is? How are we even friends?'

Vicki rolled her eyes. 'Not everybody watches movies and television for a living, Hannah. Some of us have grown-up jobs.'

'So,' Hannah said, ignoring the jab from her monumentally depressed friend who, at the moment, appeared to be almost giddy. 'If it's not "like that," as you put it, then what is it like? Because I'm pretty sure that Uncle Joe wants to make out with you. And if I were you, I'd go for it. Maybe he can work his way to Robert Downey Jr. status by the end of the night. He's on the right track with that suit.'

Vicki's eyes narrowed. 'Can you not make this creepy?'

'I didn't say it was creepy,' Hannah said, her voice dripping with implication. 'I just said that there's an attractive older man who wants to see you naked. It's only creepy if you think it's creepy.'

'No, Hannah, I mean, it's not like that. He's just a nice guy. He has a daughter. A teenage daughter. He loves her. And he adores Bee. He works in the restaurant industry, so he understands what I do for a living. He's cool.'

'Whatever makes you happy,' Hannah said, trying to

stay focused despite the fact that her heart suddenly seemed to be racing. Her arms felt numb and her fingers tingled. Her armpits had gone from slightly moist to uncomfortably wet in a matter of seconds, and as she tried to focus on Vicki's mouth and the words coming out of it, Hannah felt her stomach lurch. She only caught the end of Vicki's thoughts on Uncle Joe.

'. . . just nice to be around him,' Vicki continued, as Hannah closed her eyes. 'I don't know, maybe it's just good to be around someone who thinks my job is interesting even if I don't . . .'

Vicki took a closer look at Hannah, now eyeing her with uncertainty.

'Hannah? Are you okay?'

'Yes,' Hannah said, pressing her hands into her cramping stomach to temporarily dull the strange pain. 'I'm fine. I think . . . I think I might be having a reaction to a pill.'

'What pill?' Vicki said in a motherly tone.

'It's fine,' Hannah said, breathing heavily, with her hands on her hips like she'd just finished a marathon. 'Go sit down. I'll come over if I need anything.'

'Okay,' Vicki said tentatively. 'Listen, just in case you lose me later, we're in room 140. I forgot my key, so we'll have to get one from the front desk. Where's your bag of clothes for later, by the way?'

'It's up in the tower with the rest of the bridesmaids' stuff. Make sure I grab it before we leave.'

Hannah glanced over at the table where she was supposed to be sitting. She'd be the ninth guest at a table for eight, crammed between the other bridesmaids and their significant others. Dawn was already seated there with her husband, a stocky thirty-something man who seemed overly focused on buttering a roll.

'I don't get it,' Hannah said, finally giving in to her jealousy with a whine. 'How are you and Bee's uncle even sitting together? Were you assigned to the same table?' Hannah pouted as Vicki held up her index finger to Joe to signal that she'd be joining him in just a minute.

'We're breaking the rules,' Vicki whispered, smirking. 'Joe's actually supposed to be sitting with Bee's dad's law partners, but I'm saving him. Rob didn't show up, so Joe's going to take his seat. Thank you, Rob.'

Hannah frowned. If there was an empty seat next to Vicki, shouldn't she be the one to make use of it? She watched Vicki make eye contact again with Joe, who held up one of the glasses of wine, beckoning her to join him. Hannah sighed, realizing that there was no good reason for her to steal Rob's seat from a man Vicki obviously wanted close by.

'Okay, then,' Hannah said, defeated. 'I'm going to go

sit with the young lawyers and the beauty queen. Have fun with Scott Bakula. Who else is at your table, by the way? You're not sitting with Tom, are you?' Hannah's eyes narrowed, panicked.

'No, Bee knows better than to put me anywhere near Tom. I'm with the groom's brothers and some of his cousins.'

'Wait – are you sitting with the hot brother?' Hannah asked, moving her hands from her stomach to her chest and clasping them over her cleavage. 'Are you sitting with Jimmy Fee?'

'I don't know,' Vicki said. 'Why? Who's Jimmy Fee?'

'The groom's brother,' Hannah said, jealous again. 'I met him when I got here. He's gorgeous, and so is his girlfriend. He'd be played by Justin Timberlake, I swear. Please, take mental notes for me.'

'Will do,' Vicki promised, just before giving Hannah one last look of concern. 'Hannah, are you sure you're okay? You look . . . warm. What kind of pill did you take?'

'Just a Benadryl. I'm fine. I'll visit you at the table in a few. Go have fun.'

'Okay,' Vicki agreed tentatively. 'Come get me if you don't feel well.'

Hannah winked and turned around so she could find

her place at the bridesmaids' table. She walked to the empty seat between Dawn and the nice bridesmaid, Lisa, with whom she'd spooned at the bachelorette party months before. Next to Lisa was Lisa's fiancé, a pale redhead with a spotty rash on his very thick neck. Cory Monteith from *Glee*, Hannah thought. Lisa's fiancé scratched the skin around his collar, grimacing as it turned dark red. 'He gets heat rash,' Lisa whispered to Hannah, noticing that Hannah was staring. 'It's so humid today and his suit is suffocating.'

'Honey,' Cory Monteith snapped, embarrassed as he heard his betrothed diagnose him as if he were a child.

'I'm sorry,' Lisa responded meekly. 'I just wanted to explain . . .'

Hannah looked away to avoid the conflict.

On the other side of the hydrangea centerpiece was Jackie the abandoner, who picked at her salad in silence. She looked up, her eyes meeting Hannah's.

Jackie's mouth puckered as she raised her eyebrows.

'What's wrong with you?' Jackie snapped at Hannah. 'You look like you're about to pass out.'

'Nothing,' Hannah responded, confused. She didn't understand what Jackie was talking about. She was sweaty but awake, wired and excited.

Hannah tapped her right toe under the table, trying

to release some of the energy she felt welling up inside her, but it wasn't enough. She felt trapped, too static in her chair, desperate to get up and run instead of waiting patiently as country club servers continued to place plates of salad in front of each guest. Hannah had the sudden urge to kick something or to yell. Her arms, which were at her sides clutching the chair beneath her, had a mind of their own. They longed to reach for the ceiling. She imagined how good it would feel to hop on an elliptical machine at her gym back in New York.

'So, Hannah, you work in movies?'

Hannah wiped her sweating forehead and looked over in the direction of the voice, which echoed in her ears. It was Jackie's new boyfriend, Will, the ear, nose, and throat doctor. He looked to be about thirty-five. He was balding and had a nice smile. Christopher Meloni from *Law & Order: Special Victims Unit*, she decided. Will's teeth were bright white. Hannah found herself counting them in her head. There were at least ten visible teeth. She squinted, trying to get a look at his incisors.

Will's smile vanished.

'Are you okay?' he asked, Jackie still watching Hannah with uneasy eyes.

'What?' Hannah responded, suddenly twisting in her

chair to see if she could relieve some of the tension in her back.

'I just asked if you were okay,' Jackie's boyfriend said tentatively. 'I had asked about your job. I heard you work in movies and theater – in New York City. Sounds very exciting.'

'Yes!' Hannah responded, suddenly aware that she'd shouted. 'Yes,' she repeated, more subtly, her eyes shifting.

'What exactly do you do? Are you a director? A producer?'

'Jesus, no,' Hannah answered, perhaps too aggressively. She took another sip of the white wine that had been placed in front of her. 'I'm a casting director,' she continued. 'I cast plays and commercials. And I recently started casting some films.'

'That's fascinating,' the ear, nose, and throat doctor responded enthusiastically, suddenly leaning forward and firing off questions at a speed that made Hannah nauseated. 'Have you cast anything I've seen? Do you do Broadway? How do you know who to cast? Have you met a lot of famous people? God, it must be so much fun. I mean, you must love your job, right?'

Hannah closed her eyes. His words suffocated her. He didn't stop.

'When I first got to college, there was a part of me that wondered if I should go into theater, but it just didn't seem stable,' the doctor continued. 'But I think I would have loved it. Maybe someday. I always wonder how doctors get jobs advising medical shows. I think I'd be great at that. Do you know how people get those jobs?'

Jackie's boyfriend had hunched forward, his elbows on the table in front of him. He stared at Hannah, awaiting her response. She felt her eyes well up with tears. She grabbed her stomach and closed her eyes as fresh sweat beaded above her lip.

She blinked away the moisture and fought a sudden urge to flip the table. She imagined the wineglass in front of her shattering into little pieces. She imagined the inquisitive doctor's perfect teeth falling out of his mouth. She could feel her heartbeat in her fingertips. She curled her toes and closed her eyes. She wiped her nose and mouth with her napkin.

'Jesus, Hannah. What the hell is wrong?' Jackie asked, her voice soft and concerned.

'I don't know,' Hannah murmured, her eyes still closed.

Just minutes ago Hannah had been so calm. She'd seen Tom from across the room and had felt nothing.

More accurately, she'd felt pain, confusion, and excitement, but it was as if those emotions had been tamed by a greater force. Intellectually she knew she was upset, but she was incapable of actually feeling her emotions. Hannah assumed it was the pills that had dulled her senses and dispelled whatever negative emotions would have otherwise taken over her brain.

She was fine with that, thankful that Dawn had been thoughtful enough to drug her. But now she felt like Cinderella at midnight. Her body, which had behaved like a stretch limo all night, threatened to turn back into a pumpkin. It was as if she wore a corset that was quickly unraveling.

She tried to refocus and maintain eye contact with Jackie's boyfriend.

'Are you sure you're okay?' he asked, now glancing at Dawn, whose eyes were on her husband as he buttered his third roll of the night. Jason Segel, Hannah thought.

'Stop it!' Dawn snapped in her husband's ear. 'No more bread or no cake for you.'

Hannah let out a sharp 'Ha!' prompting Dawn to flash her an angry glance. For a moment, Hannah felt normal again. She inhaled deeply, let it out, and allowed herself to talk. She turned her attention back to Jackie's doctor boyfriend.

'My background is in theater,' she told him, speaking clearly. 'I started right after college, interned with a bunch of small theaters and the New York Shakespeare Festival. Then I did some touring musicals and more-corporate, industrial projects. Then commercials. I've just started with independent films. No blockbusters. Most of those are cast out of LA.

'And as far as doctor shows and consultants go,' Hannah continued, proud of her sudden ability to be articulate, 'I don't know how it works. But I could ask around. I know –'

Hannah placed her hands on top of the table in front of her. She hadn't touched her salad, but a server was already removing it and replacing it with an entrée. 'Here's your crab, miss,' the waiter said. 'Unless you asked for the vegetarian meal?'

'Crab is fine,' Hannah said, thankful for the interruption.

'The movies,' Jackie's boyfriend continued, his eyes on Hannah's hands, which were now pulling at both ends of her cloth napkin as if she hoped to rip it in two. 'What are some of the movies you've cast? You sure I haven't heard of them?'

Hannah couldn't say any more. The calmness had passed and now it felt as if a balloon were expanding inside her chest, pressing against her organs. She dabbed the napkin on the most recent layer of sweat that had formed on her lip. She closed her eyes and was suddenly pleased to hear the shrill sound of microphone feedback, a piercing shriek that caused all the guests to turn their attention to the front of the tent, near the band.

Bonnie Hunt, the wedding planner, stood at the center of it all. She spoke softly into a microphone, sounding more like a preschool teacher than an event coordinator.

'And now, Ladies and Gentlemen, it's time to hear from the matron of honor.'

Hannah saw that Dawn had already made her way to the front of the tent. She was standing right beside the wedding planner, her arm extended to grab the microphone as quickly as she could. As soon as Bonnie Hunt surrendered it, Dawn clutched it with both hands and walked forward so that she was in the center of the dance floor. She smiled at the guests, waiting for all talking to cease before beginning her speech.

Hannah found herself stunned by how beautiful Dawn looked under the sparkling tent lights. It was now almost dark outside, and in the twilight Dawn's face was illuminated by the strings of white bulbs that lined the tent. Up until this moment, Hannah hadn't noticed

Dawn's eyeliner. Or was it eye shadow? Regardless, the matron of honor looked like a princess. Dawn's eyes did, in fact, pop. She was stunning. She was a fairy godmother or, better yet, a Good Witch who could help her get home. She should have wings, Hannah thought.

There was no sound now besides the hum of the portable refrigerators and the bustling of the servers who traveled from table to table clearing dishes, so Dawn started in with her first line, her southern Reese Witherspoon voice ringing through the tent.

'Webster's dictionary defines "sisterhood" as "the state of being a sister." It also defines "sisterhood" as "the solidarity of women based on shared conditions, experiences, or concerns."' Dawn paused for a long, dramatic breath. 'That's all true,' she said, her face serious. 'but I define sisterhood as Bee, my best friend.'

With that, Dawn reached over to the nearby podium and grabbed a stack of index cards that appeared to contain the rest of her speech. There had to be about fifty cards in the stack. Hannah could hear a few of the younger guests groan from a few tables away.

Hannah put her hand over her mouth to hide her grin. She suppressed a laugh as Dawn continued to talk, saying just a few words at a time between long, dramatic pauses. Hannah looked over to Dawn's husband, who was taking advantage of his wife's position at the front of the room by quickly buttering a fourth roll and shoving it his mouth, swallowing after only a few chews. He smiled devilishly at his unchaperoned behavior.

'Last year I got into a car accident,' Dawn continued, her voice echoing like chimes. 'I was flat on my back. The doctors told me I'd need to wear a neck brace. Who was there for me, at my side?'

Dawn stopped before answering her own question and leaned forward.

'I don't have a sister,' Dawn continued, ignoring her own question altogether, her voice low and somber for dramatic effect. 'But I do have a sister now.'

Hannah felt her arms shaking. She was laughing, still silently but now conspicuously. Without thought, her eyes darted to Tom, who sat several tables to her right, to see if he was enjoying the moment as much as she was. She hadn't known where he was sitting – she hadn't allowed herself to scan the room for his face – but she found it now within seconds, almost as if she sensed his presence. Much to Hannah's surprise, Tom was already staring back at her, his eyes wide as he found her smile. Hannah's expression turned into a pained smirk. Tom, who was also laughing silently, bit his lip.

Their eyes remained locked as Dawn continued the

seemingly endless story of her back surgery – about how Bee would bring her dinners during her long recovery. It was the most nonsensical, self-absorbed wedding toast Hannah had ever heard. It failed to acknowledge Bee's new husband. It ignored the topic of marriage altogether. And as the speech, now in its sixth minute, continued, Dawn became more and more histrionic, the breaths between her sentences sounding like gasps.

Tom's girlfriend, Jaime, the guidance counselor, stared forward, straight faced, while Tom and Hannah shared the moment, their eyes fixed on each other as they reacted in tandem to Dawn's proclamations and hypothetical questions that went awkwardly unanswered. Hannah and Tom were still gazing at each other when Dawn reluctantly handed the microphone back to Bonnie Hunt, who seemed desperate to move things along after the maid of honor's extended monologue. Hannah's smile flatlined. It was over. Tom acknowledged her now-anxious expression with a sad grin and a long blink. His eyes shifted to his girlfriend, who was digging for something in her purse.

Hannah no longer wanted to flip the table. She wanted to run to Tom and jump into his lap. She didn't even need him to turn into Paul Rudd. She imagined Tom whispering in her ear that he still loved her.

The fantasy was cut short by another shriek from the microphone.

'And now the best man,' Bonnie Hunt said, handing the microphone over to the good-looking brother of the groom, Jimmy Fee. Hannah gazed at the stage. Even with Tom's eyes on her from across the room, she couldn't stop herself from staring at Jimmy Fee, who was, without exaggeration, one of the most attractive people she'd ever seen in her life, better looking than her actor friends in New York. He was the kind of guy who could pull off a fedora, Hannah thought, which is why Justin Timberlake would be a perfect casting choice. But now, looking at him under the spotlight, on the dance floor, Hannah didn't think Justin would do him justice. Jimmy had dark hair that seemed to be sticking up without the help of any product. He had a chin dimple and full, almost feminine, lips. In his wedding tux, he looked like a less-motivated James Bond. 'Maybe James Franco,' Hannah whispered to herself.

She shifted in her chair and looked over to Vicki, who met her gaze with a knowing smirk. Vicki's grin made her feel warm all over. Hannah then noticed Joe eyeing them both with some confusion, wanting desperately to be in on the joke. Poor Scott Bakula, Hannah thought.

Jimmy, who held the microphone so low that it was almost at his waist, had already loosened his bowtie and had unbuttoned the top of his tuxedo shirt. He smiled with his eyes closed, swaying enough to suggest mild intoxication. Before he could open his mouth for what would no doubt be a crowd-wooing toast no matter what he planned to say, he was greeted by his fan club, the younger men in the Fee family who were sitting at Vicki and Joe's table. They whispered in a bass rumble, almost in unison, 'The Feeeever.' One of the Fees, presumably the drunkest of the bunch, shouted, 'Jimmy Fever!'

Hannah watched Vicki and Joe giggle as their table-mates hooted.

The rest of the guests laughed at the response to Jimmy Fee, some more than others. Even Bee's mother, Donna, appeared to be charmed, despite the rudeness of the interruption.

'Thank you, folks,' Jimmy said, already raising his champagne glass with his left hand and bringing the microphone close to his face with his right. 'I'm gonna keep this short and sweet because I don't think any of you want to hear any more chitchat.'

Dawn, still visible in the distance, scowled at the insult.

'To my baby brother and his wife, the beautiful Bee – may all your ups and downs be between the sheets.'

'Hear! Hear!' barked one of the young men at Vicki's table. 'To Jimmy Feever!'

There was some wild laughter, and Bee began a round of applause. Hannah glanced back at Tom, suddenly remembering that she'd been having a moment with him, but he was no longer looking at her. He was whispering something in Jaime the guidance counselor's ear. She was laughing. He had his arm around her.

'You gotta love those Fees,' proclaimed Jackie's boyfriend. 'What a fun family.'

Hannah nodded and stood up, making a quick decision to walk over to the bar for another drink. She felt a spreading dread that she could only assume had something to do with the pills combined with the allergy medication she'd taken earlier in the day and the three glasses of wine she'd consumed since she'd walked down the aisle. Her moment with Tom probably hadn't helped. She and Tom still shared the same sense of humor. They still looked to each other to be in on the same joke. Yet she didn't know him anymore. He was living with someone else. He had a new life that didn't include her in any way.

'Another white, please,' Hannah ordered, handing her

glass to a bartender, who reached for the generic white wine and began to pour. Hannah turned back to the guests again, looking at Tom's table. This time she saw Tom's girlfriend talking to one of Hannah's acquaintances from college, a guy named Bill Cohen, whom Hannah hadn't spoken to since she and Tom had parted ways. Hannah had told Tom during the breakup that she would take possession of their New York friends – including Vicki – and that he could have everyone in New England, which was basically just Bill Cohen, who was an accountant in Manchester, New Hampshire. Hannah was never very attached to Bill anyway.

Hannah turned back to the bartender and reclaimed her drink.

The wedding planner's voice suddenly bellowed through the tent. 'Ladies and gentlemen, if everyone could take their seats and turn their eyes to the dance floor for the traditional father-daughter dance. Presenting Mrs Bee Fee and her father, Richard.'

Hannah winced and muttered to herself, 'Beefy.' She wondered if Bee was also cringing at the sound of her new name.

'Hey.'

The voice, which came from behind Hannah, startled her, causing her to whip around and almost spill her drink on her dress. She clutched the wineglass with two hands, trying to stop the chardonnay blend from splashing over the top.

Hannah looked up to see Tom. Her lips felt dry. She didn't respond and instead looked him over, examining his face for changes. Her eyes went up to his hairline, to see if he'd lost any more of it. Balding had been one of his persistent fears when they were together.

'Are you looking at my hairline?' he asked incredulously.

'No,' Hannah barked defensively, trying to bring her eyes back to his face. 'I'm just – no.'

'I haven't lost any more hair,' Tom said, now in the voice he used to save for their arguments about whose turn it was to clean the bathroom or who had left the oven on after dinner.

'I didn't say you did. Jesus, Tom.'

They both paused, staring each other down, and then dropped their defenses.

'Look, I just wanted to say hello,' Tom said. 'This is awkward, obviously, and I wanted to make it easier. And I wanted to talk to you and see how you are . . .' He trailed off.

Hannah frowned. She didn't want any of this to be

easy. She wanted this to be as painful as possible so that Tom realized his terrible mistake.

'I don't know what you want me to say,' Hannah said, her hands trembling.

'Hannah, I don't know what we're supposed to say. I guess — I just don't want you to be angry. I'm not exactly sure why you're so angry, to be honest. I think I should be angrier than I am —'

Hannah stopped him. 'I can't do this,' she interrupted, leaving him silent and with his mouth agape. She felt herself tearing up and wanted to get out of his sight line before she cried like a child. She stepped around him and looked for an exit. She could hear Tom saying something behind her, but she couldn't make out the words. She felt overheated and wobbly. She wondered for a second how long it had been since she'd consumed food.

She considered finding Vicki, to make an escape, and began marching to the table where she and Uncle Joe were making small talk with Jimmy Fee and Matt's cousins, but Hannah changed directions once she got halfway there, realizing how much she suddenly needed space. She decided she'd go exploring instead and walked out of the tent and into the clubhouse, where guests had lined up to use the bathrooms. She passed the line, opting to make her way down a narrow hallway that eventually led into a bar. It was a cozy room with dark leather furniture and low tables.

Three white-haired men in preppy golf uniforms sat on the lounge chairs. They were watching the large flat-screen television that hung over the bar. They sipped something from tumblers. Hannah assumed they were club members who just happened to be on the grounds that day. She smiled at the one man who had noticed her. He gave her a nod.

She looked over at the bar. There was a younger man, maybe in his late thirties, sitting on one of the stools, a beer bottle in his hand. He was also watching television, his eyes on whatever game was on the big screen. Even slouching, the man's body looked too big for the bar. He had to be well over six feet tall.

Hannah stepped to the side of the man so she could see his face. He was good-looking, traditionally masculine in a way she wasn't used to. Most actors who played masculine men in movies and on stage weren't very masculine in person. She actually didn't know many actors who were taller than five foot nine. Hannah instinctively began scrolling through her mental Rolodex of movie stars who might be able to play this man in a film. 'Matthew McConaughey,' she muttered to herself. No. That was wrong. This man's forehead was creased with rows of squiggly lines, like he might be a constant worrier. She needed someone more serious. 'Clive Owen,' Hannah muttered this time, following the name with another negative head shake. Too serious, she thought. This man was pensive and mature but also strangely boyish. He was the kind of guy who'd look young even when he was old.

The man at the bar was dressed in a rumpled suit with an orange stain on the elbow. He was definitely a wedding guest, not a golfer. His lips moved, but he didn't make a sound. He was mouthing numbers, doing some sort of math equation in his head. Hannah was parched and warm. She took a seat on one of the stools next to the man, set her wine down on the bar, and asked for a glass of water.

'David Boreanaz,' she whispered to herself almost inaudibly as he turned to notice her. 'Definitely David Boreanaz.'

Phil

*I*n a panic Phil turned his head to the left so the score on the television screen was out of his sight line. He bit his bottom lip hard, puncturing it, and then brought his beer bottle to his mouth to soften the sting. Unless Oregon and California could make miracles in the next five minutes, he was going to lose an unreasonable amount of money, and he wasn't sure he wanted to watch it happen. He had no interest in watching fans in blue and gold cheering in the stands.

Not only that, Phil knew that the old men sitting at the other end of the stuffy country club bar had been watching him watch the game ever since he'd asked for their permission to change the channel. In his peripheral vision, he'd seen them monitor his reactions to fumbles and first downs. He'd even overheard one of them, an older man who most likely had a hearing problem, shout, 'Want to bet on how much he's about to lose?' The man had been shushed by his friends, who chuckled and stared at Phil, probably hoping he'd turn to them and reveal the amount.

Phil took the bottle away from his lips and set it back on the bar. Much to his surprise, he noticed a woman sitting two stools away. She hadn't been there a few seconds before, but he certainly recognized her. It was one of the bridesmaids, the bustiest and shortest of the bunch, the one he'd seen in the photomontage on the computer in the lobby.

It was impossible not to notice cleavage in a V-neck dress, Phil thought defensively, as if he could hear Elizabeth chastising him for objectifying this bridesmaid. Really it wasn't his fault. The bridesmaids' dresses, while classy, long, and black, dipped strangely low in the front and were quite revealing, unless the woman was built like an ironing board.

The bridesmaid smiled at him. Her eyes were glassy. She was double fisting – a wineglass in one hand and what looked to be a pint glass full of water in the other.

'Tell me that's a big glass of gin and not water,' Phil said to the bridesmaid, her smile making him confident. He looked closer at her face. She was perspiring, mostly over her lip. She dabbed her face with a cocktail napkin and asked the bartender for a Diet Coke before turning back to him with an embarrassed smile.

'Triple fisting?' Phil asked nervously, suddenly concerned that she might get sick right in front of him. 'You okay?'

The bridesmaid's smile turned sheepish, her eyes revealing panic.

'I look terrible, don't I?' she asked pleadingly. 'I look crazy, right? How terrible do I look?'

Phil didn't know what she meant exactly, because he had no basis for comparison. He'd only seen this woman in person once before, earlier that night, as she walked down the aisle during the wedding ceremony. Despite the perspiration, he thought she was very attractive.

'You look a little flustered, I guess. You look like you might be coming down with something – or like you had too much to drink.'

'I've just had too much wine and an allergy pill and some other pills,' she explained almost apologetically. 'I should probably head back to the hotel and pass out.'

'But you'd miss the cake,' Phil said, suddenly not wanting his new companion to leave.

The bridesmaid's eyes widened, her smile childlike. 'You're right. I want cake.'

'Me too,' Phil said. 'That's why I'm still here.'

'I'm Hannah,' the bridesmaid said. 'You're a friend of the groom, I presume?'

Phil shook his head, grinning. 'Not really.'

'The bride, then? You're related to Bee?'

'Never met the bride,' Phil said, enjoying his temporary mysteriousness.

'Crashing, then?'

Hannah put her hands around her tall glass of Diet Coke as she swung her legs back and forth. Phil decided to stop giving her a hard time. 'My mom is an old friend of the groom's mom. It was actually my mom who was supposed to come today, but she got sick, so she asked me to come in her place.'

'That's odd,' Hannah said, her head cocked to the side.

'My mom didn't want to waste the food,' Phil explained, realizing how strange it all sounded as soon as he said it. 'She wanted someone to represent the family. I guess it is sort of weird. She just really loves the Fees, so she wanted someone to be here for them. Not like they need it. There are, like, five hundred Fees at this wedding.'

Hannah took a sip of soda. 'It's actually nice that your mom made you go.' She suddenly shot him an accusing look. 'Actually, it would be nicer if you were representing your family at the wedding – instead of watching football in the bar.'

'Fair enough,' Phil said, his body now turned to face Hannah, his back to the old men, who, Phil figured, were probably now discussing his powers of seduction. 'But you're hiding here too.' Phil flashed his eyes nervously at the television. 'And if it makes you feel any better, I'm about to lose a bet on this game. So it's not like I'm having any fun back here.'

Hannah was puzzled. 'What do you mean? Like, you put money on this game? The one that's on right now?' She glanced at the television.

'Yeah. In about two minutes I'll lose more than two thousand dollars,' Phil said, suddenly finding it harder to force a smile.

'You mean you gambled on a football game?' Hannah's eyes grew wide. 'Like . . . a real bet?'

'Well, I placed a bet with this bookie, a friend of my brother. Later this week, depending on how I do today, I'll either get an envelope of cash or give an envelope of cash.'

Phil didn't know why he was telling her any of this. He felt ridiculous.

'You have a *bookie*?' Hannah asked. She was grinning now, and riveted.

'He's not a real bookie,' Phil said. 'Like I said, he's a friend of my brother.'

'That's kind of exciting,' Hannah said, staring at the television.

She brought her bloodshot eyes back to his face. She

seemed to be waiting for him to say something, so he continued.

'It's really more like a game than anything else. It's just something to do.'

'And if you don't have money for the bookie . . . is it like the mafia? Will he kill you?'

Phil liked her, he decided, although he couldn't tell if she was making fun of him.

'I do have the money, and if I didn't, I'd just owe him and pay him later. He's a nice guy.'

'And you're going to lose? For sure?'

Phil glanced at the television screen. He saw the California Golden Bears on the sidelines with their helmets off, embracing. He shook his head. This was bad, but thankfully he was distracted.

'For sure,' he said with a half smile. 'It just happened. Thank you, Oregon, for not doing a goddamned thing for me today.'

'What are you going to do?' Hannah asked sympathetically, after taking a sip of water.

'Nothing,' Phil said, shrugging. 'I'll take the hit. I'll give an envelope to Hank. It's either that or I bet on the Rainbows and go to bed.'

Hannah tilted her head and raised her eyebrows. 'Is that a gay joke? Betting on rainbows?'

'It's what people say,' Phil responded, turning away from the television as the bartender changed the channel back to ESPN. 'It's something we gamblers say.' He put emphasis on the word 'gamblers,' mocking her initial shock at the word 'bookie.'

'The Rainbows,' Phil explained, 'are the football team at the University of Hawaii. The guys who gamble on college sports have this saying, that if you're in the hole for the week and you want to make one last bet to try to cover your losses, the Hawaii game is the last college game you can bet on because of the time difference. So people who gamble — my brother, Mickey, and his friends, at least — they always say that if you're in big trouble, you may as well just put all your money on the Rainbows on a Saturday night and just go to bed. You sleep it off and hope you wake up to a win.'

'Or you wake up further in the hole,' Hannah said. 'If the Rainbows lose.'

'Well, yeah,' Phil said. 'It's just a saying. I've never bet on the Rainbows, at least not to get out of a hole.'

'Bet on the Rainbows,' Hannah said slowly, her eyes even glassier than they'd been a few minutes ago. 'I like it. It sounds like an old country song.'

Phil smiled, watching Hannah take a napkin from the

bar and wipe another layer of sweat off her face without embarrassment.

'So now that we're buddies,' Phil said, 'I've got to say, you look a little panicked. Are you really all right? You're sweating bullets. I would have thought you had money on a game too.'

Hannah frowned and clutched her stomach.

'Yikes,' Phil said, seeing her face. 'I'm sorry. I shouldn't have asked. It's none of my business.'

'No no,' Hannah said. 'I'm not mad at you. I was just happier talking about the Rainbows.'

'It's okay. Someone has to be miserable at every wedding,' Phil said. 'Usually it's one of the brides-maids, right? Every wedding I've ever been to, there's always some woman who runs into the bathroom in tears.'

Hannah nodded, amused. 'It has been a long week-end, I guess. And there are people here I'd rather not have to see. And I've had too much to drink, and I've taken medication that wasn't prescribed to me. Maybe I should just bet on the Rainbows and go to sleep.'

'Maybe you should,' Phil said, in a voice so flirtatious he was instantly ashamed of himself.

He cleared his throat, anxious to move on to a new topic so the conversation wouldn't end. 'So I assume you're a big-shot lawyer like the bride and groom?' Phil asked matter-of-factly.

'Me? No way. I went to Syracuse with Bee. For undergrad.'

'Big East,' Phil said, nodding approvingly.

'I guess,' Hannah said, not understanding the reference. 'I met Bee in the dorms during freshman year. She went to law school, and I'm a casting director in New York.'

'Casting? Like for movies?' Phil asked, his eyes now as wide as Hannah's had been when he'd talked about his bookie.

'Yeah. Well, little movies right now. But good movies. Tiny independent films. And commercials. Lots of commercials.'

'Commercials?' Phil asked, almost shouting with surprise, as if casting commercials was a more impressive feat than finding talent for the big screen. 'Have you done any commercials I've seen? Have you done beer commercials?'

'No beer,' Hannah said, giddy that this man was wowed by the part of her casting résumé that Tom had found objectionable. 'But – I once cast a Tripledog Steak House commercial.'

Phil tried to remember commercials for Tripledog's. There were two Tripledog locations within ten minutes of his hometown. He sometimes ate there with his mother, if she looked too tired to cook. He closed his eyes, humming the theme song to himself.

'I remember a Tripledog commercial with a cowboy. Some gay cowboy who lassos a pig that some family winds up eating at a picnic table.'

'I cast that gay cowboy,' Hannah said, leaning back on her stool, her elbow on the bar. 'He wasn't supposed to be a gay cowboy, by the way. Just a cowboy. I'm not sure his sexual orientation is relevant to the commercial.'

'Well, I assumed he was gay. All my friends used to make fun of that commercial.'

'Well,' Hannah said, slouching on her stool, 'I suppose he was gay in real life. Actually, if I remember correctly, all the guys who showed up for the Tripledog auditions were pretty effeminate. He might have been the straightest cowboy I could find in Manhattan on that day.'

'Wow,' Phil said, kicking Hannah's legs softly with one of his own. 'I'm sitting with the woman who cast the Tripledog gay-cowboy commercial. I should get your autograph.'

Hannah kicked his legs with one of hers, smiling. 'You're easily impressed.'

Phil grinned. 'No, really, that's a big deal. I remember a few years ago, on this fishing trip I take every year with my brother and his friends, we saw that commercial, and we all did impressions of it. My brother tried to lasso a Bud Light. He kept swinging his hips around as he did it. Who wants to cast a movie when you can cast the Tripledog Steak House commercial?'

'Well,' Hannah responded, suddenly wondering about her BlackBerry, 'that's what I want to do, cast movies that have a real audience. And I'm so close. I might be casting a movie with Natalie Portman. In fact, what time is it on the West Coast?'

'God, that sounds like a sweet job,' Phil replied, ignoring the question. He eyed their touching legs as he took the last swig of his beer.

'I guess it is pretty fun when it's not competitive and stressful,' Hannah agreed. 'Try it now.'

'What do you mean?' Phil asked, puzzled.

'Cast us. Cast this room. I do this all day. It keeps my skills strong. Cast us. Cast those guys over there.' Hannah not-so-subtly pointed to the old men across the room, who were now leaning forward in silence, trying to hear as much of the conversation as they could.

Phil smirked and glanced at the threesome. 'You want me to cast them? Like, pick actors who would play those guys in a movie?'

'Exactly.'

Phil thought for a minute. 'Who's the guy in those old oatmeal commercials?'

'Wilford Brimley?'

'Right. That guy. He'd play all of them.'

'That's cheating,' Hannah said. 'He can only play one of them. Pick another actor.'

'Fine – who's the guy who plays the butler in *Batman*? The British guy.'

'You mean Alfred?' Hannah asked, amused.

'Sure. The old guy.'

'Depends on which *Batman*. In Tim Burton's *Batman*, Alfred is Michael Gough, who I'm pretty sure is dead. In the more recent *Batman*, Alfred is Michael Caine. If I were you, I'd go for Michael Caine, assuming you have the budget to afford him, Mr Casting Director.'

'Fine,' Phil said. 'I've run out of old guys. I think that's all I can do.'

'What about us?' Hannah asked.

'What do you mean?' Phil responded, mimicking her sinister smile with one of his own.

'Cast us. Who would play us in this movie?'

Phil let a chuckle escape. 'Had I known I was going to be in a movie today, I would have dry-cleaned my suit.'

'Come on,' Hannah said. 'Play the game. Everything

is a movie. Wilford Brimley, Michael Caine . . . maybe Ed Asner for the guy on the left. And now, tell me, who would play us?'

'It's weird,' Phil said, almost to himself. 'All the action stars I like, the actors who are in my favorite movies, they're all way too short to play me. Why do only short guys play action heroes?'

'Because everyone's short in Hollywood – little bodies, big heads, and under five foot nine,' Hannah answered. 'I think it's rather revealing that you'd want to be played by an action hero. Are you an FBI agent or something? A Secret Service man – one who has a bookie?'

Phil thought of himself in his Camden Yards security gear. 'Something like that,' he laughed. 'I do provide a secret service.'

Phil gave Hannah a closer look as he considered what actresses might play her in their fake movie. The famous women he thought of late at night – Winona Ryder; the actress from *House* who reminded him of Elizabeth; and, for whatever reason, Heather Locklear – they just weren't right.

Phil examined Hannah's blue eyes, her top-heavy but athletic stature, and her pale skin. Her lips looked puffy. There were tiny lines around her eyes, the faint beginnings of the aging process, but he liked the look of them. The small crevices became more pronounced when she smiled.

'I got it,' Phil said, suddenly leaning into Hannah, who was accepting a new glass of white wine from the bartender. 'You're the girl from *Titanic*, and I'm Larry Bird.' Phil grinned.

'Larry Bird?'

'Boston Celtics. Larry Bird. He'd play me in the movie. I played basketball in college, and I want to be played by a basketball player. I want to be played by Larry Bird – but Larry Bird from 1984.'

'Wait,' Hannah said, switching from her wine to the Diet Coke again. 'That's cheating. You can't cast from back in time. The movie happens now. If Larry Bird plays you in the movie, it's the present-day Larry Bird. Can he act? Is he even still alive?'

'I can't believe you just asked that,' Phil said. 'Of course he's alive. Jesus Christ.'

'Fine. Then you're played by an old basketball player, and I'm Kate Winslet,' Hannah said. 'That's ridiculous, by the way. Can you imagine a sex scene with those two people? Disgusting.'

Phil flashed a victorious smile. 'So in the movie about us, about tonight, we have sex?'

Hannah put her glass down, embarrassed. 'I – I just

meant there's always a sex scene. Larry Bird can have sex with whomever he wants.'

Phil felt himself blush. Before he could think of what to say, Hannah spoke again. She took swigs of wine and Diet Coke in rapid succession and then asked, pointedly, 'Since we're getting personal, who would you cast as the love of your life? In the movie of your life. Who plays your soul mate?'

'What? Like, the actress I most want to sleep with?'

'No. More than that. You can pick any actress in the world to play Mrs Larry Bird. Who would it be?'

'You go first,' Phil said. 'Who's Mr Kate Winslet?'

'Paul Rudd,' Hannah said, almost too quickly. 'For me, it is and will always be Paul Rudd.'

Phil rolled his eyes. 'Another short guy.'

'To each her own,' Hannah quipped. 'Now your turn.'

'Well,' Phil said, trying to keep his voice light, 'if we're talking soul mates, I guess I'd have to say the woman from that show *House*. You know, the one about the doctor with the limp? The nice woman doctor could play Mrs Bird. She reminds me of my ex-girlfriend.'

Hannah shot him a curious smile. Phil froze, realizing what he just said. The actress who reminded him of Elizabeth is who he'd want to play his wife in a movie. As if she'd read his mind, Hannah lifted herself from the bar stool and found her footing. She picked up her wineglass, leaving the Diet Coke and the water half-empty, the glasses sweating onto the wood.

'Break's over. I think I have to go back in there,' she said casually.

Phil couldn't hide his disappointment. He stood up next to her and took a step toward her. 'You don't have to go back in there. No one will know. Everyone's drunk by now.'

Hannah tilted her head and looked up at him. On their feet, there was at least a foot between them. 'I'm a bridesmaid. It's my duty. I'm sorry Oregon and California let you down, Mr Bird.'

'It's okay. It happens,' Phil said.

She started to walk away, and he surprised himself by yelling after her.

'Maybe I'll see you back in there,' he shouted. Phil looked down, suddenly mortified by the volume of his own voice. When he looked back up, she was staring at him, her eyes dazed.

'We could talk some more about the Rainbows,' she responded, her voice sedate.

'Fair enough,' Phil muttered.

'Good-bye, Larry.' He watched her disappear into the hallway. Behind him, Wilford Brimley, Michael Caine, and Ed Asner started a slow round of applause.

Rob

The vet came out of the swinging white double doors and stood in front of Rob, who was slouching on the linoleum floor, his back against a row of vending machines.

Rob took a deep breath and found the courage to make eye contact with her. He was prepared to beg, to plead with this woman until she gave him the news he wanted to hear. With shaky hands he pulled his worn leather wallet from his back pocket. Three receipts and a dollar bill fell out. He tried to find his silver credit card in the pack of plastic but his fingers fumbled.

'I'll spend anything,' he said assertively before the vet could even speak. He would not let them convince him to put Liz down. 'I have a credit card, and we'll just charge it. I mean, surgery can't be over what, a grand? I can do that.'

'Sir, she's gone,' the vet said softly.

Rob's head snapped up.

'What? What do you mean?'

The vet then squatted next to Rob and placed her hand on his shoulder.

'Mr Nutley, I'm very, very sorry.'

'I don't understand. Are you saying I have to put her to sleep?'

'Mr Nutley,' the woman continued, now closing her eyes for a long blink. 'She's already gone. It was her time.'

Rob felt himself begin to cry. It had been years since he'd let out tears and this was the second time tonight. The dampness on his face felt alien. He used the collar of his T-shirt to wipe the moisture from his cheeks.

'It wasn't her time,' he said angrily. 'She got crushed by a medicine cabinet. That's not natural causes.'

Rob noticed a middle-aged man and his daughter staring at him from the other side of the waiting room. The girl held a sleeping rabbit in her lap. Her eyes were red, as if she was preparing herself for similar news.

'Sir,' the vet said, shifting her body so they were facing each other. 'It wasn't just the accident. She was a very sick dog. Even if a cabinet hadn't fallen on top of her, she wouldn't have had long. You did all you could. I see in her file that you helped her live much longer than another owner might have. You have to let her go now.'

'The fucking IKEA medicine chest,' Rob said, tears now rolling down his cheeks, his shoulders jerking. 'I put it up with, like, one goddamn screw. It's got to be about forty pounds. I don't know what I was thinking.'

'Many owners would have put her down months ago. You took very good care of her. There is no blame here. She's no longer in pain now. She's with God.'

Rob peeked at the shiny gold cross hanging from the vet's neck. He'd never been religious, but he was comforted by the veterinarian's assumption that Liz was in heaven. He didn't believe in heaven for people, but when Liz first got sick, he liked to imagine that she'd eventually experience a better afterlife where she could eat chocolate without vomiting and live a life without seizures.

'Do you know exactly how long she would have lasted if this hadn't happened?' Rob asked the vet quietly. 'When would she have just died, you know, naturally?'

'There's no way of knowing. Months maybe. Maybe a year. Maybe weeks. There's no way of predicting these things. Mr Nutley, is there someone we can call? Some-one who can meet you here and help you make some decisions about what to do with the body? Is there someone who can help you get home?'

Rob thought of Lucy, but she was long gone. And even if she was still around, she wouldn't have been much help. Lucy Barber had no empathy for the weak.

Then Rob thought of Hannah, who by now, he figured, was probably drowning in self-pity, or perhaps prosecco that she was calling prosciutto. He suddenly longed for her, remembering how he used to feel when he lounged next to her in bed, how she'd shower after her walk home from the bars on Marshall Street and would come out smelling like vanilla and baby powder. 'A cake made of linen,' he'd tell her, sniffing her armpits as she giggled. He remembered how they talked so effortlessly, how he sometimes avoided drinking on their sleepover nights so he could better enjoy their conversations. He also remembered the cold mornings, how the boundaries were immediately reset when the sun rose.

Rob never knew if he'd denied his feelings for her back then because he was afraid of hurting Bee or because he feared rejection, that Hannah would give him a definite no, flashing him the same frigid look she gave him every time he woke up in her house.

Even if Hannah had wanted more back then, Rob wasn't convinced that the twenty-year-old version of him would have considered it. He was difficult in Syracuse, sometimes mean. He hadn't liked himself very much back then. He would have never told her that he looked forward to those nights, and that he went through an unexpected withdrawal after he stopped visiting Hannah's apartment in an effort to ease out of his life at school.

Rob knew that if Hannah were here now, she would say nice things about all he'd done for Liz. She would say the right things, just as he could save her from the pity party she was probably having in Annapolis. But she was miles away and a decade removed from their history together.

'I'm all alone on this one,' Rob said to the vet, more dramatically than he would have liked. He reluctantly accepted a tissue from a middle-aged female nurse who approached him with a box of Kleenex.

'What happens with the body?' Rob said in a business-like tone, trying to overcompensate for his tears with unnatural composure.

'Well, sir,' the vet said, still sitting on the floor. 'Some families have burial plans for their dogs. We have partnerships with two pet cemeteries in the area. I can give you a catalog with their fees, if you'd like to look. If you decide to go in that direction, you'll leave Liz here and they'll come for the body.'

Rob shook his head at the thought of a stranger taking the dog and putting her in the ground.

'I'll do it myself,' Rob said. 'I'm going to bury her in the backyard.'

Back at home, the ground was harder to break than Rob imagined it would be. Movies had led him to believe that backyards crumbled easily to make holes for burying mob men and murdered spouses. In reality it had been an unusually cold month in Austin and the ground was hard and dry. It didn't help that his shovel was plastic and probably meant for light gardening.

It took an hour for Rob to dig three feet down. He paused to examine the ditch and tried to convince himself that it was deep enough for a burial, but he knew better and shook his head. The expression 'six feet under' existed for a reason, he thought. He imagined a flood pulling Liz's remains out onto the lawn. He kept digging.

It was another hour before he felt confident about the depth of the hole. Liz's body was still in a dark sheet just a few feet from the opening. Rob sat down next to her and lit a cigarette. He spaced out the drags, trying to make the most of the moment. He kept his left hand on Liz's stomach while he puffed, wishing her body

didn't feel so cold through the sheet. He tried to memo-
rize the contour of her torso, the tender hub where he
would scratch her belly before they both fell asleep.

Refilling the hole was too easy. In under a half hour,
the ditch was gone and Liz's body was blanketed in dry
bits of earth that Rob patted down and smoothed with
his hands. He felt as though he should say something,
even though he was the only one there.

'I loved you, girl . . .' he started, and then stopped.

Rob realized that he didn't need to tell Liz he loved
her; there was no need for silly proclamations of his
loyalty and affection. Even if she were still alive, there
was nothing Liz ever needed to hear from him. She'd
understood his intense devotion. He might owe explana-
tions, apologies, and clarifications to many of the
humans in his life, but Liz had never been confused
about his intentions. They'd always been pure. He'd
always made her needs a priority.

Instead of continuing a funereal speech, he thought
about the Liz Phair song that was on the radio when he
first found her, and which inspired her name.

For the second time that night, he sang, doing his
best to remember the lyrics to 'Supernova,' a song he
barely liked. It made him feel a little better, so when he
was done with Liz Phair, he moved on to all the songs

that had made Liz jump around the apartment – not just
'Hurricane,' but Bruce Springsteen's 'Rosalita' and 'Born
to Run.'

Eventually Rob's teeth were chattering, so he stood
up and went inside, allowing his last song to be Dylan's
'Love Sick.'

Rob's phone, which he'd left in the house during the
trip to the animal hospital, was blinking on the table by
the front door. There were four missed calls from
Hannah. He smiled weakly at the sight of her name and
wrapped his arms around his chest.

He was tempted to dial her back and tell her what
had happened, but the thought of it was overwhelming.
He looked around the living room. A pile of magazines
had fallen off the couch and onto the floor. Somehow
one of his teetering bookshelves had collapsed, probably from the force with which he slammed the door
on his way to the hospital. The mess of books made a
small mountain. Two plastic IKEA screws had rolled
out into the center of the room.

Rob didn't have the strength to clean the room. He
thought about taking a hot shower, to clean himself, but
he remembered that his tub was full of broken glass and
dog blood.

The small house was too quiet. Without Liz, there

were no footsteps on the wooden floors and no heavy breathing coming from the bedroom. Rob walked into the kitchen and looked down at the half-eaten bowl of dry dog food that Liz had pushed into her water dish. Bloated pieces of the kibble floated on top of the liquid. He closed his eyes and considered his options. Sleeping wasn't one of them. He was exhausted but wired. He knew what he wanted to do. He walked purposefully to his laptop and turned it on.

Vicki

*J*oe was looking at her so intently, his eyes so focused. Not sexually, Vicki thought as she listened to Joe's excited ramblings about his weekend getaways to the Mojave Desert.

'You should come see it,' he said, a glass of wine still in his hand. 'For East Coasters like us, it's a shock to the system. It's just such different terrain. Suddenly you're in the wilderness. It's like being in some old western.'

Vicki leaned in as he went on about a restaurant near his apartment that serves cactus. She took a bite of her crab cake, which was rife with Old Bay Seasoning. A breeze blew through the tent, brushing her long bangs over her eyes. She smelled salt water.

'Do you smell that air?' she interrupted. 'It smells like a beach in here.'

Joe smiled sheepishly. He placed his hands flat on the

table so her pinky finger touched his. She didn't pull away.

This attention from Joe, while not romantic, Vicki thought, wasn't paternal either. Joe was a friend, a flirtatious one, the kind she would have had back in college. He was the kind of guy who gave her enough attention to make her nervously tuck her hair behind her ears. Their conversation was teeming with potential, but that's all it was, the excited energy that comes with meeting someone who understands you.

Back in college, when they were all single, healthy, attractive people with no commitments, everyone talked to each other like this – intensely and full of confidence and hope. They laughed uncontrollably and never got bored of each other, not even on freezing nights when they were prisoners in their secluded dorm rooms, sometimes not leaving for forty-eight hours straight. Vicki's college friends had been drawn to one another as eighteen-year-olds, and even though they'd coupled off by twenty – Hannah, in secret, with Rob and eventually Tom, and Vicki with the musician-environmentalist Rich, who was now living in Nova Scotia after spending three years with the Peace Corps – it always felt as though the twosomes were just a part of a greater whole. Like it was all just one big romance, no matter who shared the same bed when they all went to sleep.

Back then there were few boundaries and everyone was permitted to have his or her own private friendships and secrets. Once Tom had joined the group, he and Vicki developed their own inside jokes without upsetting Hannah. They watched movies together while Hannah was at the theater, flipping a coin to determine who would drive through the snow, down the slippery hill, to Syracuse Stage, where Hannah would be waiting in her puffy coat on the corner. And while Rob never pursued Bee physically, he'd loved her, staying up all night to edit her papers even though he should have been writing his own. Bee and Tom also became close by taking Wine Tasting 101 during their last semester. They'd tease Hannah during dinner at her apartment, telling her that that her six-dollar bottles of chardonnay tasted oaky and buttery.

Even Vicki and Rob had shared private moments. Vicki had never been drawn to Rob like the others — he was always borrowing money from Rich and the band, and his secret, late-night relationship with Hannah had forced Vicki to keep secrets from Bee — but still they maintained a quiet friendship. During their sophomore year, they would take off together at least once a month to procure alcohol for much of their underage dorm. They'd make CD mixes for the drive to Canada, where they were of age, and do impressions of Rob's band leader, Jared Novak, in the car. They'd come up with lists of fake business names for Vicki's dream company, the design firm she hoped to open after graduating.

'On the Inside,' Rob had said to her during one of their Saturday-afternoon trips over the border.

'I don't get it,' Vicki said.

'It's like when people say someone's pretty on the inside. That's what you'll do. Make a building pretty on the inside. Your design company should be called On the Inside.'

'On . . . the . . . Inside,' Vicki said slowly, considering each word as they pulled out their passports in preparation for the checkpoint. 'That could work.'

'How about just . . . Vicki Clifford Interiors?' she offered.

'Nope. Boring. You'll get more business if it's a pun or something,' Rob said. 'It's like my haircutting place back at home. I go there because it's called From Hair to Eternity. I love that shit.'

Vicki remembered that it was Joe in front of her and shot him a sad smile. It was the first time during the night that she wished Rob had come to the wedding.

Of course, Joe had turned out to be a suitable replacement. He was just like the friends she'd been missing for so long – funny and intuitive.

The people at Vicki's company in Rochester weren't like this. There was no banter, no pause-free conversation. Yet here she'd formed a connection with Joe in a matter of minutes. Maybe it was because he was related to Bee. Or maybe it was because Vicki could be her real self around her college friends.

'I should visit you out there in Vegas,' Vicki said suddenly, meaning every word. She imagined herself in Nevada with Hannah, Bee, and Joe, hiking over hills in the desert heat, backpacks on and water bottles in tow. She hadn't traveled for fun in years.

Vicki was startled by a cigarette-soaked grunt from across the table. It was Jimmy Fee. She'd been trying to avoid direct eye contact with the best man since she sat down at the table, mainly because she thought she might laugh if she did. He was a caricature of the hot guy at the wedding, smoldering with a five o'clock shadow. She felt safer with him in her peripheral vision.

Jimmy Fee had been high-fiving relatives and talking about college football ever since he'd returned to the table after making his best man's speech. Now he was focused on Vicki and Joe, his eyebrows raised.

'You live in Las Vegas?' Jimmy Fee asked Joe longingly.

'Yes, sir,' Joe responded with pride. Vicki considered kicking Joe under the table, but only Hannah or Bee would be able to decode her message. She tapped her right foot under the table and tried to focus.

'Don't be too impressed,' Joe told Jimmy Fee. 'Living in Vegas isn't like visiting Vegas. What happens in Vegas doesn't just stay in Vegas, it's your life. I pay bills there. I do laundry there.'

'But, dude, the women there – they must be just out of control. I mean, even the married ones.' Jimmy let out a loud snort as he laughed.

Vicki's eyes darted to the empty chair next to Jimmy Fee, where his silent but striking girlfriend had been sitting.

'She's in the can,' Jimmy said, answering Vicki's unspoken question. 'It's like the fifth time she's gone tonight. I swear, every time she drinks she spends the whole night in the bathroom.'

'She's gorgeous,' Vicki said, swallowing a gulp, to which Joe could only nod in agreement. Jimmy Fee's girlfriend was unarguably as pretty as him.

'Let me tell you something,' Jimmy said, smirking and leaning across the table. 'It's like they all say. You show me a woman everybody wants to fuck, and I'll show you a guy who's sick of fucking her.'

Vicki covered her mouth with her hand and barked a short laugh. She felt Joe kick her under the table. She kicked him back.

Hannah

Hannah knew there was a problem when she saw a table move or, more accurately, bend – its flat top suddenly turning to liquid like the watches in that Dalí painting that had cluttered so many Syracuse dorm rooms. She'd been spinning wildly to the wedding band's rendition of 'Brick House' when she felt a sudden need to steady herself.

She placed her palms flat and face down in front of her as if she were leaning against an imaginary piece of furniture. She felt temporarily stable, but when she looked up, the table closest to the dance floor appeared to be moving to the left, the top of it dripping in a way that could only mean Hannah was hallucinating. She closed her eyes, hoping to get her bearings, but the darkness behind her lids intensified the feeling.

'Vicki is in room 140,' she whispered to herself.

'She's going to fall,' Hannah heard a male voice say. She scowled, realizing it was a voice she recognized.

'Get away,' she whispered, as she felt Tom come up from behind her to put his hand on her shoulders.

'Easy there. Steady,' he responded quietly, barely audible over the band. She'd always loved his low voice. She instinctively leaned into him, desperate for any support to help her stay on her feet, but then backed away as soon as she found her footing. 'Get away from me,' she barked. She turned her back to him.

'Let's get some air,' Tom said, moving around her swiftly so he could face her again. 'I think we should talk.'

Hannah nodded dizzily and blinked, defeated. Her left eye felt dry. The right one was tearing up. When she looked up to find a way off the dance floor, she spotted the guidance counselor, Jaime, who glared at her and Tom from the back of the tent.

'Wait,' Hannah said, angrily snapping around to face Tom again. 'I don't need air. *You* do.'

She swayed as she continued, her ankles wobbling. Tom stood frozen in front of her, his eyes shifting from side to side to see who might be watching. She continued confidently, batting Tom's arms away as he tried to help her, and pointing at him with her right index finger.

'You want to talk to me? Fine. But don't pretend I need your help.'

The band was getting louder, but the volume wasn't enough to prevent Bee from overhearing the arc of Hannah's rant. The bride broke off from a dance circle she'd formed with her mother and two aunts and did a brisk sashay toward Hannah, who kicked off one of her heels as she barked at Tom. The shoe flew behind her.

'You fucking abandoner!' Hannah said loudly, as Tom tried to grab her shoulder again. 'Go find your girlfriend. Go find your *guidance counselor*.'

Tom froze, his face flushed.

'Go find her,' Hannah continued. 'I'm sure she's looking for you.'

This time, when Tom reached out, he caught her shoulders angrily, stabilizing her.

'You have to stop this,' Tom yelled. Hannah tried to wriggle away, but Tom held on tight. She avoided eye contact like a child, shifting her head around so her eyes were on anything but his face.

'Stop this,' he repeated sternly.

Hannah obeyed and let her eyes drift to his. She stayed silent, temporarily disarmed.

'You – you're acting like I did this,' Tom rambled,

losing his composure, his voice cracking. 'You call *me* an abandoner? Really?'

The band drifted into a draggy version of 'Alone Together,' which allowed Tom to lower the volume of his voice. He let go of Hannah's shoulders, more confident that she wasn't going to run away. Bee now stood a step behind Tom, listening closely.

Hannah stood awkwardly, unbalanced with one shoe on and one off.

'We – we both did this,' Tom said, his voice shaky. 'I left New York, but you could have come with me. I *asked* you to come with me. I told you for an entire year that I wanted to live closer to my family, that I needed to go back to Boston, and you never said a word. I left . . . I left for *me*, because I wanted something different, a lifestyle that was more about *my* needs. I didn't leave because I wanted to leave *you*. I wanted to leave New York. I was in love with you. I assumed that you stayed in New York because it was the life you wanted, with or without me.'

Hannah stayed silent. She raked her palm across her forehead, pushing her wet hair out of her eyes. She shook her head as the lead singer of the band wailed about weathering the great unknown.

'You can be upset that it didn't work out,' Tom

continued, 'but you can't blame me for it. I didn't dump you, Hannah. You chose to stay where you were.'

Bee took a step forward, her eyes incredulous.

'You asked her to come with you? You – you asked her to move to Boston?' She looked at Tom for confirmation, and then to Hannah.

Tom let out an exasperated sigh. 'Of course. I wanted her with me. I –'

'You told me you couldn't see me as anyone's wife,' Hannah snapped, kicking off her other shoe, which landed about two feet away. A young boy on the dance floor, one of Matt's nephews, picked up the satin heel, held it over his head, and danced with it victoriously.

'I couldn't see you as anyone's wife, that's true. Hannah, you seemed so uninterested in us by the time I left. So independent. You had all these new friends. I was hoping you might disagree with me and tell me you would come . . . that you would live my life for just a few years after I'd lived yours in New York.'

Hannah couldn't hear any more of it. As soon as the band began playing 'Superstition,' she staggered away to resume dancing, this time grinding the air, her waist humping an invisible partner. Bee and Tom looked on, their mouths agape, as Hannah turned her back to them and began approaching guests, playfully bumping them with her hips. In her peripheral vision, Hannah saw Bee break her pose and stomp off the dance floor toward the dinner tables. In response, Hannah danced more wildly and mugged for the wedding photographer, who happily took pictures as she stuck out her tongue and lifted her shoeless feet.

Once the cameraman grew tired of her, Hannah slowed her movements and looked back at Tom, who had been rejoined by Jaime the guidance counselor. Hannah identified Jaime's expression as something other than jealousy. Jaime watched Hannah with a mask of concern — her eyes horrified, as if she were witnessing a small child playing in an intersection. Hannah turned away furiously and looked for a suitable dance partner.

Joe

*J*oe was oblivious to Hannah's show on the dance floor until Bee came striding in his direction, the train of her dress fishtailing behind her.

'Uncle Joe,' Bee pleaded, leaning into him, 'I need you. Now.'

'If it isn't my gorgeous, married niece,' he responded, his body still turned toward Vicki. 'Are you looking for a dance partner?'

'I'm looking for a ride. Right now.'

Joe looked up and realized Bee's urgency. Up close and under the glow of the tent lights, he could see that her tan makeup was beginning to collect in the lines on her troubled forehead. Dark circles had emerged from underneath the bride's evaporating concealer.

'Whatever you want, kid,' Joe said tenderly. 'What do you need?'

'I need you to get Hannah back to the hotel,' Bee said, pointing to Hannah, who now had a circle around her on the dance floor. Her body was pressed against Bee's brother, Eric, who appeared to be as drunk as she was. He'd fused his twenty-five-year-old palms to the small of Hannah's back as if he were trying to hold on to a mechanical bull. Hannah kept one hand on the back of his neck and used the other to clutch her inhaler, which Bee knew she'd tucked into the control-top rim of her tights.

Based on the expressions of shock and thrill on the faces of Matt's cousins, who clapped wildly as Hannah and Eric danced in front of them, it was possible that there had been a public kiss or worse.

Vicki stood up quickly, her eyes horrified. She grabbed her clutch from under her chair as Bee tugged at Joe's elbow. 'We have to get her out of here. Can you help me get her back to the room?'

'Let me just run and get her stuff,' Vicki offered. 'Her bag with her wallet is in the tower. I'll get it, and then we'll take her straight back to the inn.'

Joe beamed with pride at Vicki's organized response, the way she took charge of the situation. In that moment she reminded him of Sarah, his girlfriend, who often kept playing concierge long after she was home from work.

'Joe, I'll be right back,' Vicki said. 'Bee, can you pull Hannah off your brother and get her ready to go?'

Joe and Bee nodded. Joe squeezed Vicki's forearm, reassuring her that it would all be okay, and then dipped into his pocket for his keys, wondering how long it would take to put Hannah to bed so he and Vicki could return to his room together.

Vicki

Vicki was galloping as quickly as she could in heels, which wasn't much faster than she could walk. She escaped, past Tom, through the back of the tent, avoiding eye contact with him as he attempted to flag her down, most likely to discuss the flailing Hannah and what should be done with her. Once outside, Vicki let her eyes adjust to the dark so she could find the tower from which Bee and her bridesmaids had emerged hours earlier.

She'd promised Hannah that no matter how much either of them had to drink during the night, she'd make sure to grab the small suitcase and purse that held Hannah's change of clothes, driver's license, cell phone, and wallet. Hannah wouldn't have time before her morning train to New York to return to Tower Gardens for anything she'd left behind.

The cylindrical staircase leading up to the tower's top room was scarily narrow and empty enough to remind Vicki of a horror film or, more appropriately, the setting of a V. C. Andrews book. She paused after reaching the top of the steps and surveyed the empty penthouse, a two-room space with big velvety couches surrounded by suitcases, which presumably belonged to the brides-maids. It wasn't exactly reminiscent of *Flowers in the Attic* up there, despite the fact that it was an attic. Vicki had always imagined Cathy and Chris living in tighter quarters than the tower's top floor, which was larger than most studio apartments in New York.

The tower's penthouse was more in line with how Vicki had imagined the boarding house in *Secrets of the Morning*, the second book in V. C. Andrews's series about a dancer who finds out that her grandfather is actually her father. Vicki shivered remembering the sex scene with Dawn and the handsome Michael Sutton. Before she could start dwelling on his fire hydrant, she shook her head and remembered her mission. Hannah's bags. Taking Hannah back to the hotel with Joe.

Vicki rushed into the suite where, like any good V. C. Andrews heroine, she spotted the strapping silhouette of a man waiting for her in the dark.

Phil

The wedding band was now playing 'Shout.' Phil could hear it from where he still sat, at the bar, trying to decide what to do next. He couldn't face sitting at his assigned wedding table, where he'd have to discuss things he didn't want to talk about, like Bee and Matt, foreign countries, babies, and where he'd been for the last two hours.

Instead he decided to call his mother.

Nancy had told him not to check in again tonight, that she'd most likely be asleep by eight, and that Phil could see her sometime tomorrow. But he figured he could leave a message, just so she wouldn't have to feel alone when she woke up.

He stepped out the back door of the bar, through which the three old men – Phil's audience for much of the night – had exited just a few minutes earlier. That put him on the opposite side of the clubhouse from the reception tent, closer to the parking lot and a maze of small shrubs and out-of-bloom rosebushes.

He paced around the building as the phone rang, until a voice stopped him.

'Hello?' the voice answered.

Phil quickly pressed 'end,' terminating the call before saying a word. It was a man who had answered, so Phil must have dialed the wrong number. He looked at his phone and inspected the name of the contact he'd just called. It said 'Mom.' He paused to think, staring at the cars in the lot, confused.

His hands shaking, he looked back at the phone and pressed 'send' again. This time the man picked up on the second ring.

'Hello,' the man said, irritated, as if he suspected the caller was about to hang up again.

'Hello?' Phil asked, confused.

'Who is this?' the man asked. 'Phil? Is that you?'

'Hand me the phone,' Phil heard his mother shout hoarsely in the background.

Phil pressed 'end' again. Panicked, he scrolled through his contacts until he landed on 'Mickey cell.' He pressed 'send' again.

'Freak show!' Phil's brother yelled into the phone, using his favorite term of endearment for his much-taller younger brother.

'Mickey, mom's in trouble,' Phil rambled into the phone too quickly, his voice unsteady. As he spoke he took long strides toward the parking lot, his car keys out in his free hand. He was almost running.

'Jesus,' Phil's brother said. 'What happened? Did she fall down? Are you with her now? Should I drive over there?'

'There's a guy there,' Phil said, now in front of his Durango. 'Someone's in the house.'

'Who's in the house?' Mickey asked, his voice now panicked like Phil's. 'Like a burglar?'

'I don't know,' Phil said angrily, opening the driver's side door. 'I just called her and a guy answered the phone. And he knew my name. He said Phil.'

'He knew you?' Mickey was calmer now. He let out a small laugh. 'If he knew your name, it was probably just Captain Mulcahy.'

Phil stopped short, his feet digging into the gravel parking lot, and slammed the car door closed again before getting inside.

'Why would Captain Mulcahy be at Mom's?' Phil asked angrily.

'Come on, Philly, you know. Don't make me say it. It's gross. It's Mom.'

'What do you mean? I don't — I don't get it.' Phil stammered, his stomach aching just as it had when he'd seen the text message from Hank after the Cal-Oregon game, the one that said, 'I told you so.'

'He and Mom are dating, Phil. It's a Saturday night. Why wouldn't he be there? He practically lives there.'

Phil leaned over and rested his forehead against the cold window of his SUV. He stared at his steering wheel until his breath made the glass opaque.

'No,' Phil whispered. 'They're just friends, Mickey. She — she hasn't dated anyone since Dad. She calls Captain Mulcahy her "good friend," like they're old people keeping each other company. They're companions.'

'Come on, Phil,' Mickey responded, aggravated. 'I don't have time for this. I have to help put the kids to bed. Angela gave them candy, and I can't get them to sleep.'

'How long have you known?' Phil asked, standing upright again, his free hand on his forehead. 'Did Mom tell you this herself?'

'Phil . . .' Mickey continued.

Phil could hear his brother's children screaming in the background. 'Come on, kids, I'm on with Uncle Phil!' Mickey shouted. He lowered his voice, speaking again into the receiver. 'Phil, Captain Mulcahy spent Christmas with us last year. And then Easter. And he came to Joey's christening in August. What did you think was going on?'

'I don't know, Mickey,' Phil admitted, shrugging as he paced around the front of his car. 'I thought he was coming over to do odd jobs for her, like changing her lightbulbs and fixing her plumbing. I thought he felt bad for her, which is why he stuck around a lot.'

'He's fixing her plumbing all right,' Mickey teased. 'Look, buddy, I've got to go.' Mickey was now using the soothing voice he usually saved for his children. 'We can talk about it tomorrow if you're still upset. But we should be happy for Mom. It's lonely for her down there. Captain Mulcahy is a great guy.'

'Okay,' Phil said, just before pressing 'end.'

Phil slipped the phone into his pocket and walked slowly from the parking lot toward the clubhouse. He stopped in front of a large dogwood tree just outside the entrance. The lights from the reception seeped out of the billowing nylon that circled the party. As the band finished 'We Are Family' and started a rendition of 'I Think We're Alone Now,' Phil punched the tree so hard that he immediately drew blood. He felt like an idiot. He sank to the ground and put his head between his knees.

Vicki

'Sorry. I can't find the lights,' the faceless man said through the dark. 'I hope I didn't scare you.'

'You didn't,' Vicki said, surprising herself by the way she overarticulated her *t*'s, as if she'd developed a slight British accent as soon as she'd entered the magic tower. 'I don't easily scare.'

She smiled in the dark, amused by her contribution to the dialogue. She'd identified the man in the dark almost instantly by the shape and smell of him. They'd been a few seats away from one another at the wedding table, separated only by Joe.

'It's me, Jimmy Fee, from your table. You're Bee's friend, right? The one with the old guy?'

Vicki grimaced in the dark.

'He's not old, and I'm not with him – or, not romantically at least. He's Bee's uncle. We're friends.'

'Hmm,' Jimmy purred from the shadows. He took a step toward her. 'So you're here alone?'

'Yes,' Vicki said, instinctively taking a step back, suddenly aware of the stairs right behind her. She saw him come toward her, and she felt herself take shallow breaths. She thought of the line in *Flowers in the Attic* she'd memorized: 'I had the strong dancer's legs; he had the biceps.' She'd reread that scene so many times that she'd almost detached the page from the binding.

Jimmy grabbed her hand in the dark. 'Be careful,' he said. 'Don't take a tumble.'

She wasn't sure how they started kissing, but it was quick, within seconds of him taking her hand. Up close Jimmy Fee wasn't much taller than she was, thanks to her formal shoes, which boosted her an extra three inches. With their mouths at the same height, all Jimmy had to do was lean forward.

'Don't you have a girlfriend?' Vicki murmured against Jimmy's neck as he began to lift the bottom of her dress, implying that they might do whatever they were going to do standing up, without removing much of their formal wear.

'That's not going to work,' Vicki instructed once she

realized that he wasn't going to answer her concerns about his girlfriend. 'I have tights on.'

There was a massive couch in the center of the room, one large enough to sleep a tall person rather comfortably, but both Vicki and Jimmy knew that this type of sex wasn't for furniture. It was meant to occur on the floor. That's where V. C. Andrews would put it. They bent down so they could lie on the wood in front of the couch and removed just enough of their clothing – her shoes, tights, and underwear, and his pants and boxer shorts – to start the process. He had a condom in his wallet. Of course, she thought to herself, imagining that a guy like Jimmy Fee was always prepared for sex because it probably happened often enough, in attics, at bus stops, in bathrooms, and maybe on planes.

As it started, Vicki stared at the ceiling, wondering how she'd allowed this to happen. The last time she'd been in this position with someone she wasn't dating seriously, she was a senior in college at a group house off campus. She'd been taking advantage of a temporary break from Rich by sleeping with an illustration major in her graphic design class, a guy she would never speak to again. Mike Chadwick. Or was it Steve Chadwick? She couldn't remember the guy's name, but he had a tattoo of Tigger from *Winnie-the-Pooh* on his shoulder.

'Dude,' Jimmy muttered to himself, as Vicki compared her last one-night stand to this one. That one had been messy and unsatisfying. She and Rich were technically broken up, but she'd still felt guilty. It had felt unnatural. But in this country club tower, the sex felt right. Vicki didn't feel like her old college self or even the new depressive western New York self who spent much of the year watching cable in chain hotels. She didn't feel like a woman who needed to stare at a lamp to save her sanity. Tangled up with Jimmy Fee on the floor of a tower by the water, Vicki felt like one of her favorite V. C. Andrews heroines.

She moaned dramatically, almost making herself laugh as Jimmy Fee bounced on top of her, his body propped up by his hands, which remained flat on the floor next to her ears. With his dark hair flopping over his eyes and his lean, muscular arms, which were just about all Vicki could see in the dark, Jimmy was the embodiment of a V. C. Andrews hero or villain — attractive, overconfident, and cheating on a woman who was just downstairs. 'What's so funny?' he asked, panting.

'Nothing,' she said, also out of breath.

'Excuse this,' Vicki said, and then lived her dream by digging her nails into Jimmy Fee's back. 'Goddamn it!' he exclaimed, sounding stunned but pleased.

She was stunned just a few seconds later by a vicious, almost blinding fluorescent light.

Joe

J oe was embarrassed by the volume of his inhalations and exhalations.

He wasn't out of shape – in fact he was more athletic in his forties than he'd been at twenty or thirty – but the run up the spiral staircase had winded him. And the sight of the intercourse on the floor in front of him now made him feel as though his lungs were filling up with fluid.

He'd started his sprint to the tower when, after twenty minutes, Vicki had failed to return to the reception tent. She'd gone on what was supposed to be a quick run to retrieve Hannah's belongings, a task that should only have taken her five or ten minutes at the most, even if she'd stopped to use the bathroom. Joe and Bee began to worry that there had been an accident. Perhaps Vicki had stumbled in her heels or had fallen down the spiral staircase while struggling with Hannah's bags. It was almost pitch dark outside of the tent near the tower, the moon blanketed by a thick layer of fog. It was entirely possible that Vicki was injured and was waiting for someone to help her. He shouldn't have let Vicki make the trip alone, Joe thought as he ran out of the tent with Bee to find her.

Joe had imagined discovering Vicki in the grass, her ankle twisted. He'd fantasized that he would carry her to his car and back to his room in the historic inn. They'd make love under that horrendous print of the Naval Academy chapel that hung just a few feet above the pillows.

Joe and Bee had left Hannah with the matron of honor, Dawn, who upon seeing Hannah's display on the dance floor, had run to assist with the spectacle. She'd been the one to successfully force Hannah off the dance floor and into a chair out of Tom's sight line. She'd squatted in front of Hannah, instructing her to maintain her poise until she'd made it off the country club's grounds. Bee and Joe had rolled their eyes together upon hearing Dawn's advice to the drooling bridesmaid. 'You must rally!' Dawn yelled at her just before Bee and Joe took off toward the tower to find Vicki.

Bee had asked Joe to hold the train of her dress so she didn't trip as they hurried across the grounds. Joe felt strangely proud as he assisted his niece, her dress in his hands as she moved across the grass. His heart pounded.

He was supporting Bee, the one relative who still liked him, and was on his way to rescue Vicki, the woman he really wanted to sleep with.

But about five steps up the spiral stairs, Joe's stomach sank. He and Bee stopped short to listen in terror when they heard a pounding sound from the top floor, where Vicki was supposedly looking for Hannah's bags. Something terrible was happening up there. Joe jumped to the conclusion that one of the country club's staffers was murdering Vicki with an ice pick. Or worse, raping her. Bee apparently had the same thought.

'Hurry,' Bee said, panicked, as she sprung herself from one step to the next, almost losing her white shoes under the bottom of her gown. Joe dropped the train of Bee's dress, bouncing up the steps behind her.

When they made it to the top, they were overwhelmed by loud grunts and thuds coming from the center of the room. 'Find the light,' Bee screamed, as she tried to focus in the dark. Joe frantically ran his fingers along the wall until he felt the plastic switch.

He flipped it, causing rows of fluorescent bulbs to illuminate the space.

Closer to him than he would have imagined was the source of the noise. There was Jimmy Fee, Bee's brother-in-law, on top of Vicki, whose black tights and cotton underwear were in a pile on the floor next to her. Based on Vicki's position – her legs hooked around Jimmy's ankles and her hands clutching his shoulders – Joe knew that whatever was happening in front of him was consensual.

Vicki slapped the back of Jimmy's head, responding to the lights. 'Someone's here,' she said, incapable of ending her sentence without letting out a small, euphoric moan. 'Stop!' she ordered.

'What?' Jimmy responded casually, still pumping away, seemingly unaware of their new visibility.

'Jimmy, there's someone here,' Vicki said again, to which Jimmy replied, 'What?'

'The lights are on!' Vicki snapped, pushing against his chest. Jimmy stopped suddenly and twisted his torso so he could see behind him, and then smiled wide at his audience. He was still inside Vicki, who smiled weakly at Bee.

'Vicki?' Bee muttered, in disbelief. Vicki's dark hair was matted to her forehead. Her cheeks were flushed. 'Jimmy?' Bee continued. 'You guys, what are you doing up here?'

'I told Jennifer I'd grab her pocketbook from the tower before we went back to the hotel,' Jimmy said, removing himself from Vicki, who, once freed, grabbed her underwear and tights and began the clumsy process of putting them back on without exposing more of her bottom half. Jimmy rolled over, so he was sitting face up next to Vicki, and shamelessly removed the condom from the tip of his penis as he talked about his girl-friend's belongings. 'We'd stashed Jennifer's purse up here, at the start of the reception, so she could dance,' Jimmy continued. 'And then I ran into Vicki when I came to get it.'

Joe licked his lips, his mouth suddenly parched. He kept his eyes on Jimmy to avoid looking at Vicki, who was still moving like a worm on the floor, trying to get the top of her tights over her stomach. 'I . . .' Joe started, almost audibly. 'I'm just going to take Hannah back to the inn now, Vicki,' he said softly, as if Vicki hadn't helped come up with the plan less than a half hour ago.

'Thank you. That sounds good,' Vicki responded, in a businesslike voice, as Jimmy stood up and zipped his pants. He walked over to the nearby trash can and tossed the used condom toward it, but it fell to the floor, glis-tening under the harsh fluorescent light. Vicki continued to speak formally, pretending not to see it. 'Hannah's two bags are right over there. The black purse and the blue duffel bag.'

'Will you be needing a ride back to the hotel, as well?' Joe asked, matching her tone and letting out a cough as he walked toward Hannah's bags. He made a wide circle around Vicki, ensuring that he was at least a few feet away from the spot where she and Jimmy Fee had performed their act. Bee stood paralyzed, still evaluating the scene.

'I – I think I can find my own ride,' Vicki responded, her eyes shifting to Bee, who looked away.

'I'll drive Vicki back,' Jimmy said, jumping up, unfazed by the small, wet circle of latex that was now about an inch away from his left shoe. 'It's no biggie. I've got a rental in the lot. It's a Sebring. I asked for an economy, and they bumped me straight up to a convertible. Sweet, right?'

Jimmy grinned proudly and wiped his chin. Vicki smiled nervously at Jimmy and shot an apologetic look to Joe, who coughed again, walked past Bee, and began the descent down the staircase. 'Okay, then,' Vicki could hear Joe grumble as he made it to the third step with Hannah's bags in his hands. Bee waited another moment before lifting her train and starting down the stairs behind him. As soon as they were gone, Jimmy Fee muttered, 'Holy balls. Can you believe that?' He bent over to pick up the condom and threw it straight into the wastebasket as Vicki stood up and adjusted her dress.

Bee and Joe were silent as they walked back across the lawn in the direction of the tent. Joe was a few feet ahead of her with Hannah's bags in his trembling hands. 'I'm sorry,' Bee yelled from behind him. She sprinted a few feet forward and grabbed the back of his jacket to slow him down. 'Joe?' Bee asked, finding his eyes.

'Yeah?' he responded, looking back at her, trying to smile.

She put her hands over her red face.

'Don't mess up your makeup,' Joe said, pulling her fingers from her eyes.

'It's okay,' he continued without waiting for her response.

Bee gave him the shamed look he remembered from her childhood. It was the same face she made as an eight-year-old when she finished multiple candy bars in less than a minute under his watch during his Maryland stays.

'Really,' Joe said, softening. 'There's no need to apologize.'

'I've seen people have sex before,' he continued. 'I live in Las Vegas. No one's going to know about it but us. Now let's go find Hannah so I can get her to the hotel before she vomits all over your reception.'

Bee laughed as Joe circled behind her, taking both of Hannah's bags in one hand so he could place the other on Bee's back for support. They found Hannah where they'd left her, with Dawn, who was now clapping her hands in front of Hannah's face to keep her awake. 'This is unacceptable,' Dawn told her in a sharp tone. 'Tom can see you. You need to rally.'

'I don't care,' Hannah responded, slurring her words, her eyes closed. 'I just want to go to bed.'

'Dawn, she's half-asleep,' Bee sighed. 'Let's just get her out of here.'

Dawn used her thumbs to open Hannah's eyelids manually. The bridesmaid groaned. 'For the love of God,' Dawn said, letting the lids close again. 'I gave her an Adderall. How can she be asleep?'

Joe shot Dawn a look of disbelief and pulled her hands away from Hannah's face.

'What possessed you to give her an amphetamine?'

'I gave her Xanax to even it out,' Dawn said.

Joe looked down at Hannah, whose head rolled back on her neck.

'Well, if you want her, she's all yours,' Dawn responded sharply to Joe, just before walking back to the dance floor. Hannah opened her eyes just long enough to see who the new voices belonged to. 'Joe's going to take you back to the hotel,' Bee said, yelling each word as if Hannah was hard of hearing. Hannah reached out for Joe like a child, allowing him to take both of her hands in his. 'I need my purse,' she murmured.

'Got it,' Joe said, nodding toward Hannah's leather bag and small suitcase, which hung over his shoulder.

'Do you need help walking her out?' Bee asked Joe.

'I'm fine, Bee,' he said. 'Go back to Matt and enjoy your night. You've got a few more songs left.'

Bee's eyes searched for Matt, whom she spotted on the other side of the tent, devouring slices of wedding cake with his mother, Barb, the two of them laughing about something. Bee's shoulders relaxed.

'I'll walk you out first,' Bee told Joe, smiling warmly at her uncle, who kept his arms around Hannah's waist as they took slow steps toward the tent's exit.

Phil

*P*hil hadn't expected anyone to leave the wedding just yet, or at least he hadn't thought about what would happen if the bride herself walked outside to find him sitting on the lawn, his shirt soaked with the blood that had poured from his knuckles after he'd punched the tree.

But the bride was in front of him now, in her long white gown, horrified and suppressing the scream she'd almost let out when she found Phil sitting in the dirt, with his bloody hand in his lap and his oversized frame slumped in front of a patch of shrubbery.

'Oh, God!' Bee said, quickly backing up, as if he might attack.

Even worse, the cute bridesmaid was there. She was being led out of the tent by one of the older men at the party, who held her around her waist as she tried to walk.

'Perfect,' Phil muttered to himself, realizing that the one positive moment of the whole horrible night would be ruined as soon as the bridesmaid, Hannah, noticed that he was bleeding in the mud.

But when Hannah lifted her head and opened her eyes to see what had caused Bee's scream, she smiled warmly, as if she'd run into a friend she hadn't seen in years.

'Larry Bird!' Hannah squealed, pulling away from Joe and running to Phil. She took two steps, fell into his lap, and wrapped her arms around his neck.

'Watch out, Kate Winslet,' Phil whispered in her ear. 'I'm bloody.'

'No, you're not,' she whispered back, hiccuping. 'You're Larry Bird.'

'You're not going to remember this,' he told her, wrapping his cleaner arm around her back and kissing her forehead softly. Her skin was warm. He rocked her from side to side.

'Hmm,' she purred. 'You smell like yummy chicken.'

When it was clear, seconds later, that she was already falling asleep against his chest, Phil looked up to the older man, whom Bee referred to as Uncle Joe, and nodded to him for help.

Joe bent down and took Hannah by the waist, ignoring

her as she whimpered and resisted being pulled from Phil's lap. Frustrated, Joe placed his arms under Hannah's thighs and lifted her over his shoulder. Phil could hear her muttering angrily as Joe walked her to the parking lot.

Still standing in front of the reception tent, Bee winced and asked, 'I don't mean to be rude, but who are you?'

'I'm Nancy MacGowan's son,' Phil replied from the dirt, shrugging. 'She couldn't come so she sent me in her place.'

Bee's face softened. She smiled. 'Nancy was one of my singles.'

Phil stared back at her, puzzled.

'Your mom was supposed to come alone . . . and I didn't know where she'd want to sit . . .' Bee trailed off, frustrated by her own explanation. She paused and then asked, 'How do you know Hannah?'

'We're in the same movie,' Phil said, grinning as he lifted himself from the ground and wiped his bloody hands on his pants. 'Listen, give Matt's mom a hug from my mom, okay? Barb was really good to my mom when we needed her. She's a great lady.'

'Sure,' said Bee, bewildered. 'Is your mom okay, by the way?' she asked politely.

'She's got a cold tonight, but otherwise she's great. She still lives in Matt's old neighborhood, and she has a nice boyfriend now. A police captain.' Phil took a deep breath. 'I guess she's doing really great,' he finished emphatically.

Pleased with himself, he smiled at Bee again and started toward the parking lot before she could respond. 'Congrats, by the way,' he called to her just before swinging his car door closed and starting the engine.

Vicki

'So, is Rochester, like, in Buffalo?' Jimmy Fee's girlfriend, Jennifer, asked from the front passenger seat of the Sebring.

Jennifer was possibly better looking than Jimmy Fee. She had auburn hair that reached halfway down her back. She was skinny but curvy and wore a tight green dress and glittery eye makeup. She walked effortlessly in shoes that were taller than Vicki's.

Vicki wanted to play Hannah's casting game and choose an actress to play the beautiful Jennifer, but in Vicki's dazed state she couldn't think of any actresses' names. This woman should be a model, Vicki thought. Jennifer was perfection, her nipples poking through her dress, their round tips pointing toward the sky.

Jennifer had befriended Vicki shortly after Vicki and

Jimmy Fee returned from the tower, fully dressed, with Jennifer's purse in hand.

'This is Vicki. She's gonna ride back to the hotel with us,' Jimmy had said, taking Jennifer's hands in his and kissing her cheek. Vicki nervously wiped her mouth as Jimmy placed one hand on Jennifer's rear and said, 'Let's dance, baby.'

Jennifer had turned to Vicki and shouted, 'Come with!' As Vicki tried to say, 'No thanks,' Jennifer then grabbed her hand and one of Jimmy's and pulled them both onto the dance floor. They'd made a triangle as they started a tired dance to the wedding band's cover of the Usher song 'Yeah.'

'Can you hear me?' Jennifer now shouted from the front seat of the car.

Vicki shook her head, finally responding to Jennifer's question. 'Rochester isn't very far from Buffalo, but Buffalo is a different city. It gets more snow.'

Vicki put her hand up to her forehead as she looked out the backseat window and considered her situation.

Joe hadn't even looked at Vicki or said good-bye after he'd discovered her midintercourse. He'd simply retrieved Hannah's bags and hurried back to the reception. Vicki felt a pain in her chest, acknowledging to herself that the man with whom she'd spent much of her evening probably thought she was irresponsible and promiscuous. She'd caught him eyeing the dirty condom at Jimmy Fee's feet. She'd been mortified.

Vicki couldn't determine whether she was in trouble with the bride. Bee had caught her having sloppy, partially clothed intercourse with her new brother-in-law during the wedding reception, when she was supposed to be helping Hannah. But, Vicki argued with herself, nervously placing her hands in her lap, Bee had given her reason to believe that she might have condoned the wild behavior. After all, as Vicki left the tent to share a ride back to the historic inns with Jimmy Fee and his girlfriend, Bee had given her a quick hug and whispered in her ear, 'Nice to have you back.'

Now Vicki was in the backseat of a rented convertible, making small talk with the woman whose boyfriend she'd just clawed during an unfinished sex act. Her life in Rochester picking paint colors for grocery stores seemed galaxies away.

'What do you do for work up there?' the girlfriend asked. Jennifer had already volunteered that she ran a boutique down in Raleigh. It sold 'unique gifts,' which she defined as, 'You know, like, funny magnets, coffee table books, and those ice-cube trays in the shape of fruit.'

Vicki considered how she might explain what she did for a living, that the color palette of the walls of Walton's supermarkets across New York, New Jersey, and New England were carefully inspected by her designer's eyes. No matter how Vicki phrased the job description in her head, it sounded awful.

'I run my own interior design firm,' Vicki said, surprising herself with the impromptu lie. 'And,' she continued slowly, shifting forward in her seat, 'I'm moving to New York to launch my own business there. I want to bring art to people's homes, to act as a liaison between struggling artists and people who are redecorating their apartments.'

'Cool,' responded the girlfriend, who was almost instantly drowned out by the car radio.

Jimmy Fee had scanned through the stations until he settled on 100.7, which played 'Why Can't This Be Love?' Vicki dipped her hand in her purse and stroked the V. C. Andrews paperback that barely fit in it. She'd brought it along with her today, assuming she'd be bored enough to read during the reception. Vicki smiled, took the novel out of her purse, and dropped it on the floor of the car.

Joe

*J*oe put her in the backseat of the car, although he wasn't sure why. It's wasn't as though she needed to lie down. In fact, he'd told her not to. His experience with drunks in cars had taught him that going horizontal was a bad idea.

He gave her some chewing gum from his jacket pocket and told her to roll down the window. Air was important, he advised. She responded with a soft whimper.

They were mostly silent during the ride back to the hotel. He heard her moan a few times. In the rearview mirror, he saw her snap her bra angrily. 'You're an asshole,' she said, talking to the bra like it was a person. A few times, when he checked the mirror and saw her eyes closed, Joe yelled, 'All right back there?' She would respond by nodding.

'Please don't throw up,' he'd muttered to himself a few times during the trip. 'Rental car. Rental car. Rental car,' he repeated.

Once they made it to the parking lot, Hannah very willingly accepted his help out of the car and kept her hand in his so he could lead her inside.

'You're not so bad, Scott Bakula,' Hannah slurred as she followed him through the lobby. Joe shook his head, his mood sour. This wasn't how his night was supposed to end. He thought of Vicki and wondered for a moment where she might be. Then he pushed the thought out of his mind. He didn't want to know. Instead he remembered Sarah, his girlfriend. She had plans to see a show at the Cosmopolitan tonight – the Strokes. She'd been giddy when her friend had bought the tickets, which had made it even easier for him to go to the wedding without worrying about hurting her feelings. Sarah would be home late tonight and would probably fall asleep in front of the television. Joe's shoulders relaxed at the thought of her covered in the thin knitted blanket she kept on her couch.

It was an easy walk to Hannah's room, which was on the first floor of the hotel. The front desk clerk had given him an extra key too easily, Joe thought. There he was, a sober older man holding an incapacitated, drunk twentysomething in his arms, and the man at the front desk hadn't questioned his motives or his identity when he demanded a key for a room that wasn't his own.

When he got to room 140, Joe feared that Vicki might already be there. He didn't know what he'd do if he had to face her again after the incident in the tower. He was still furious about her betrayal even though he knew she owed him nothing. He was relieved, when he entered the room, to find it quiet, the sheets still untouched. Vicki's luggage was on the floor near the second bed, her small suitcase open next to her guitar case, which was closed and locked. Joe looked away from Vicki's personal items and walked Hannah to the bed closer to the door, allowing her to lean back and rest her head against a pillow. But within seconds, she moaned and scrambled off the bed and into the bathroom. Joe followed.

He marveled at Hannah's efficiency. She held her hair back in a perfect ponytail with her left hand as she heaved straight into the toilet, not allowing one drop of vomit to fall onto the seat or the floor. 'You're a pro,' Joe told her, wincing and grinning as she threw up mostly clear liquid.

He reached out to help her when she tried to stand up, but she pushed him away, shaking her head wildly.

With the bathroom door still open, Hannah gathered her dress around her waist, pulled her underwear to her knees, and sat down on the toilet seat. She faced Joe, unashamed.

Joe backed up to the doorway and kept his eyes on the floor as he heard the sounds of gas and urine hitting the toilet bowl. 'Ugh,' Hannah groaned. 'I'm sorry. It's coming out of every orifice.'

'Indeed,' Joe whispered, his hands at his sides.

When she was done and had flushed, she washed her hands and walked back to the bed. She propped herself up again with three pillows and asked Joe to fetch a wet washcloth for her forehead.

'You want me to go back in there?' Joe asked, pointing to the bathroom.

'Please,' Hannah groaned. 'Just hold your breath.'

Joe followed her instructions and kept his mouth shut as he wet the first washcloth he saw and ran back out of the bathroom. He met Hannah on the bed and pressed the cool rag to her hot skin. Just then he heard a knock at the door. Joe froze, assuming that Vicki had finally returned without her key. But when he opened the door, he found Bee.

'Is she okay?' the bride asked.

Bee's makeup had faded, and curls had escaped from

her tightly wound hairdo, probably from dancing. Joe thought she looked prettier now than she had when pinned so tightly for the ceremony.

'You're back?' Joe asked Bee, quickly checking his watch to see how long it had taken him to get Hannah to bed.

'I'm just running to my room to change into jeans. A bunch of us are going to a bar somewhere downtown, and I don't want to ruin my dress. I figured I'd check on Hannah before I left. Did she throw up?'

'She's fine,' Joe assured her. 'Go have fun.'

'Beeee! Is that Bee?' Hannah was yelling from the bed.

Hearing her name, Bee entered the room. She sat down on the bed next to Hannah, who removed the washcloth from her forehead and looked up at her sheepishly.

'I'm sorry,' Hannah said softly, placing her hand over Bee's.

'For what?'

Joe took a seat on Vicki's bed and watched them.

'For getting drunk and embarrassing you.' Hannah took a deep breath. 'And for Tom. I feel bad that everyone thought . . . I just feel bad. He probably isn't as horrible as I think he is.'

'I know,' Bee said, squeezing Hannah's fingers tight. 'I thought it would be easier for you tonight. I thought you'd have Rob here to distract you. I thought that with Rob here, next to Tom, you'd get some perspective. I'm – I'm so sorry Rob didn't show.'

Hannah sat up, the tower of pillows collapsing behind her. Joe stayed silent and tried to remember if anyone – namely Vicki – had mentioned the name Rob before now. Who was Rob?

'Bee,' Hannah pleaded, her voice sober. 'I need to tell you something about Rob and me. I need to tell you that Rob and I used to –'

'I know,' Bee said again, calmly cutting Hannah off. She winked and let go of Hannah's hand. 'I mean, I don't know all the details, but I knew how he felt about you as soon we got to the Cape that one summer. I saw him . . . I saw him standing in front of your door, Hannah.'

'What?' Hannah asked, fighting a yawn. 'I don't understand.'

'It was the first night we were at Tom's parents' house on the Cape. Everyone had gone to sleep. You were in one of the guest rooms by yourself. I was down the hall. Anyway, in the middle of the night I got up to go to the bathroom, and I saw Rob just standing in front of your door. He was just staring at it and scowling, like he was angry with himself. Eventually he just walked back to his own room and shut the door behind him. I guess I knew then, and it all made sense. But by then it was too late. He was back in Austin the next week.'

'But,' Bee continued, 'I thought maybe he'd wind up knocking on your door this weekend. I mean, that was my hope, that he'd find the courage.'

Hannah kept her eyes on Bee as she stood up from the bed, Joe following her lead. Hannah started to speak but silenced herself. She simply stared at the bride, her eyes wide. She let out a long yawn.

'Sleep,' Bee said. Joe reached down and straightened Bee's dress, which had shifted awkwardly while she was sitting.

'Thanks, Bee,' Hannah said, clumsily getting under the covers, her formal dress hanging out from under the bed sheet.

'Oh, wait!' Hannah called out as Joe and Bee walked toward the door. 'Can one of you grab my BlackBerry from my bag? I just need to check one thing.'

Joe leaned over and fished through Hannah's personal belongings to find the shiny silver BlackBerry with the red leather cover. He placed the apparatus in front of her.

Hannah grabbed it and began pushing buttons until she found what she was looking for, a text sent at ten o'clock from a 310 area code.

Hannah read it, leaned back, and placed the phone next to her on the bed. She closed her eyes and bit her bottom lip. 'She said yes,' Hannah finally mumbled, almost too quietly for Joe and Bee to hear. 'She's in.'

'Who?' Joe asked.

'Natalie,' Hannah barely responded, her breathing already slow and heavy.

'Who's Natalie?' Bee and Joe asked in unison.

But Hannah was already asleep, her mouth closed and curving up at the edges.

Rob

*R*ob was dirty. He didn't smell — at least not like body odor, as far as he could tell — but he was filthy, his clothes marked with dark stains, his face covered in mud, dirt, and blood.

By the time he'd booked his last-minute red-eye to BWI, from which he would take a 6:00 a.m. shuttle to Annapolis, Rob only had a half hour to get to the airport. There had been no time to shower and, anyway, his bathroom still looked like a crime scene. It would have taken him hours to mop up Liz's blood and to remove the glass shards from the tub so it was safe to step into, so he skipped bathing altogether.

He was still wearing the outfit he'd worn during Liz's burial — his favorite jeans and gray University of Texas T-shirt. He could have changed into fresh clothes but he opted not to. He wanted his entrance into Hannah's hotel room to be dramatic. And his wardrobe matched his mood; he felt as if he'd survived a great battle.

Rob grabbed a small duffel bag and a backpack for the trip. In them, he packed a week's worth of outfits and a paperback book that had been sitting untouched on his coffee table. It was a novel told from the perspective of a child with autism. His coworkers at the library had raved about it, and it was next on his list. He decided to bring it, despite his misgivings about the dog on its cover.

The flight cost about six hundred dollars, which Rob had put on his one credit card. It would have been more affordable to buy a round-trip, but he wasn't sure when he wanted to return so he'd left it open-ended. He planned to call his boss at the library and explain that there had been a death in the family. The women at work knew Liz and would allow him to take bereavement leave. And he wouldn't be missing much at the library. Late September was slow in acquisitions. The students had bought their textbooks for class and were not yet interested in pleasure reading.

Rob arrived at the airport just in time, making a flat-out run to the gate just seconds before it closed.

He was able to get a good three hours' sleep on the plane and even read a quarter of the autism book. By the time his plane landed at BWI, the sun had started to rise. Rob was disoriented from the lack of sleep. The shuttle ride didn't help. The inside of the white van had a weird odor that made Rob carsick. It was a blend of artificial vanilla and cinnamon that made him cover his nose and mouth with his T-shirt until he was dropped at the tip of Annapolis's shopping district, just past the main rotary.

'The Robert Johnson House is right up on State Circle,' the driver said. Had Rob not been close to gagging he would have asked for walking directions, but instead he nodded and slammed the door, taking a big gasp of fresh air as soon as the vehicle pulled away.

He soon found himself wandering down what looked like the city's main retail drag, a line of tiny shops with Naval Academy sweatshirts in the windows. The store directly to the right of him displayed a red apron with brown mallets painted on the chest. The front of it read, 'I got crabs in Maryland.' Rob smiled.

At the end of the cobblestone strip, Rob found the water. The calm waves of the Atlantic lapped against the white sailboats anchored not far from the shoreline. Rob was motionless, his hair barely shifting in the light ocean breeze. He'd forgotten what it was like to be this close to the shore.

Rob closed his eyes and smelled the salt in the air. The scent reminded him of his final weekend on the East Coast, when Tom had offered to take him, Hannah, Vicki, Bee, and Rich to his family's summer house on Cape Cod.

Rob had spent much of the weekend sour about the fact that he couldn't sleep in Hannah's room. They'd barely talked since the school year had ended, and they'd ridden in separate cars on the Cape – she with Vicki and Rich, and he with Tom and Bee. A day into the trip, Rob noticed that Hannah had become more comfortable with Tom. They took an early walk together on the beach without the rest of the group. They sat next to each other at dinner.

'Don't you think they're cute?' Bee had asked Rob on the last night of the trip, as Tom, Hannah, Vicki, and Rich examined a mess of seaweed a few feet in front of them.

'Who?' Rob had responded apathetically.

'Tom and Hannah,' Bee had said, grinning. 'It's about time Hannah dated someone.'

Rob had grunted angrily as he'd watched Tom playfully push Hannah toward the water, as if he might throw her into the still-freezing waves. Hannah had screamed wildly, trying to outrun Tom's arms, which eventually grabbed her around her waist.

Rob figured they'd just started dating that weekend. He wondered now how much time Hannah later spent in Yarmouth Port with Tom's family, whether she summered with the Keatings, sharing a room with Tom in that classic white Cape house a mile from the water.

Rob staggered back suddenly, a loud squeaking noise and a thud jolting him from his memory. He turned to face the street and saw a young man opening the nearby coffee shop. Two customers were already waiting outside.

Rob pulled his cell phone out of his pocket and checked the time. It was eight. If businesses were already opening, it was late enough to wake her up.

Joe

*J*oe tapped his foot under the table as he picked
at his breakfast. Ordinarily he avoided carbohy-
drates, but the muffins on the buffet at the Governor
Calvert House beckoned to him, and he believed that
he deserved a crusty, sugary treat before the long ride
that awaited him.

He sat next to Donna, his sister-in-law who despised
him. She was silent this morning, her face pale. She
focused on her plate, deep in thought. Uncharacteristic behavior for Bee's mother, as far as Joe knew.
Usually she'd take a moment like this to pick at his
outfit or ask loaded questions about the Vegas crime
rate.

Instead she looked forlorn, and Joe found himself
experiencing unfamiliar empathy. He assumed this was
some sort of mother-of-the-bride letdown. Donna

tapped her fingers slowly against her coffee cup as her eyes closed for long blinks.

'Donna,' Joe whispered, interrupting her meditation.

'Yes?'

'Are you all right?'

'Yes. Of course. Just tired.'

'It was a beautiful wedding,' he said, leaning toward her so he could bump her shoulder with his own.

'Thank you, Joe,' Donna said almost defensively, her body relaxing once she decided he wasn't kidding.

Joe figured it was his plan for the rest of the day that empowered him to speak kindly to Donna. After he'd kissed Bee good night and returned to his room down the hall at the Robert Johnson House, he'd made a quick decision to extend his East Coast trip for at least another week. He'd used his iPhone to send an e-mail to his ex, Rachel, warning her that he'd be making an unexpected voyage to see Cynthia in Maine. Then he booked a room for himself at a hotel in Portland. He'd left a voice mail for his business partner, who, luckily, was also his best friend and wouldn't stand in the way of his seeing his daughter. He also called Sarah to tell her about his plans.

She'd just returned from the concert. Her voice was raspy, as if she'd been yelling all night.

'It was weird. They didn't play "Last Night,"' Sarah

told him. 'I guess they're sick of it, but I still like that one.'

'That's lame,' Joe had said, stealing one of Sarah's favorite words. 'Listen, Sarah, I'm going to stay out here a few more days and drive up to see Cynthia. I mean, I'm on the East Coast, right?'

'That's such a good idea, Joe,' Sarah told him, her tired voice cracking. 'I mean, I miss you, but Cynthia's going to be thrilled.'

'I don't know about that,' Joe responded, as he climbed into his hotel bed alone, shaking his head as he remembered that he'd hoped to have Vicki with him.

'She will,' Sarah had assured him. 'Cynthia's a teenager. She's not allowed to let you know when she's happy.'

Now Joe was at breakfast with the adults, and he didn't hate the company. He peered to his left. A few tables away, Bee stabbed at her hash browns with her fork and popped some into her mouth. Across from her, her new husband, Matt, slowly sipped from a glass of orange juice.

Joe eyed Jimmy Fee, who sat next to Bee. Across from Jimmy was his girlfriend, a beautiful albeit trashy-looking woman who still wore her eye makeup from the night before. She was covered in a tank top and an off-the-shoulder gray sweatshirt that reminded Joe of the

cover of his old *Flashdance* record. He accidentally made
eye contact with Jimmy, who gave him a gentleman's
nod. Not knowing what else to do, Joe nodded back and
looked back down at the remnants of blueberry muffin
on his plate.

'How long will it take you to get to Maine?' Donna
asked, causing Bee's father, Richard, to look up, surprised.

'You're heading up to see Cynthia?' Richard asked.

'I'm banking on ten hours,' Joe said, not giving his
brother the satisfaction of hearing an explanation for
his change of plans. 'No matter when I leave, I'll get
stuck around New York.'

Ignored, Richard went back to his eggs.

When Joe was finished with his coffee, he walked over
to Bee to say good-bye. He thanked her for a memorable evening. His niece giggled into his chest as they
hugged tightly. 'It was memorable for me too.'

Richard then walked over to shake Joe's hand, and
Donna, who still sat at the table, smiled at him. Joe
considered that a victory.

It was a partially misty morning, making Annapolis look
like the nautical paintings that hung around the country

club's lobby. This was Joe's favorite weather for a long drive, no glare from the sun, no rain to make it slippery. He kept the windows open before he got onto the highway so he could enjoy the breeze for at least a few minutes. Las Vegas was rarely cool enough for open windows. He was seldom exposed to real outdoor air. In the windowless buildings where he spent most of his days, he breathed the frigid hotel air-conditioning that pumped through the casinos twenty-four hours a day.

Joe sighed and turned up the radio as he merged onto Route 50, a light breeze ruffling the collar of his jacket.

He turned the dial to the first pop station he could find so he would be moderately schooled in today's Top 40 by the time he saw his daughter. He was convinced that she might like him more if he knew at least a few contemporary songs.

Rob

*R*ob had been waiting at least ten minutes for the couple in front of him to check out. The woman, a petite blonde who wore her hair in a tightly pinned bun, had already yelled at her husband twice, first to reprimand him for waking up late and then about his diet. 'Egg whites!' she'd barked at him. 'Especially after what you ate last night.'

The woman's shrill voice aggravated his dull headache.

Once the couple moved out of the way, Rob said to the young man at the counter, 'I'm looking for Hannah Martin's room.'

The desk clerk eyed Rob suspiciously, his eyes drifting to the blood stains on Rob's shirt. 'Sir,' the clerk responded, his voice short, 'we don't give out the room numbers of our guests.'

'But she is staying here?' Rob asked. 'I wasn't sure I had the right place. All these historic inns look the same.'

This clerk narrowed his eyes and placed his hand on the receiver of a phone on the counter, as if he might be about to call the police.

Rob understood that he probably did look like an abusive boyfriend searching for his girlfriend in hiding. He smiled at the nervous hotel clerk and took a step back, wondering if he should wait for Hannah outside.

'Excuse me,' the woman with the shrill voice interrupted. She stood to the side of him with her husband and luggage. 'Who are you?' she asked Rob, grinning as she continued. 'How do you know Hannah?'

Rob turned around and scanned her from head to sneakers. Her round face was covered in blush and powder. She was probably one of the bridesmaids Hannah had called him about during the weekend. She had a ski-slope nose and pretty, sparkling eyes. Her teeth were a too-perfect bright white.

'I'm Rob, a friend of Hannah's from college,' he said, grinning back at the lady in pink, whose vicious smile grew as she eyed his bloodstains. 'I was supposed to be at Bee's wedding, but my flight was delayed.'

'That's quite a delay,' the lady in pink said, jutting her hip to the side. The woman's husband, a thick-necked man with freckles and wavy hair, was lost in thought, tapping his toe nervously.

'Yes. It was a big delay. I missed some of the festivities, I assume.'

'You missed all of them.' The pink lady was no longer smiling now. She was growing tired of the conversation and noticed that her husband was making his way out the door.

'Would you happen to know Hannah's room number? I want to surprise her.'

The pink lady hesitated, looking him over carefully. 'Hannah's friend Rob, huh?' She gave in. 'She should be in 140. Her room was next to mine.'

Rob almost ran down the hallway. After the long journey, he was desperate to see Hannah's face. He wondered if they'd have time to take a nap before checkout.

But when he got to the room, it was Vicki who greeted him.

Hannah

Hannah could hear Vicki and a male voice on the other side of the door, but she couldn't make out who it belonged to. At first she assumed it was the hotel's cleaning service, but there was no discussion of towels or checkout times. She could hear the man mumble questions and then Vicki thoughtfully respond. Suddenly Hannah panicked, concerned that the voice might be Tom's. She cracked the bathroom door so she could make out more of the conversation.

'Don't call me Vick. No one calls me Vick,' she could hear Vicki say.

'I always called you that,' the man said.

'I always hated it,' she said playfully.

Hannah knew who it was then and quickly wiped the fog that had collected on the bathroom mirror so she could see how she looked. There were dark circles under her eyes and her face was pale like a vampire's. There were also weird indentations all over her body. She'd fallen asleep in her dress and bra, and her face had been pressed hard against the pillows and a washcloth. Her awkward landing position for the night had left her with diagonal lines across her neck and, more noticeably, her right cheek, which was peppered with little dots. Well, Hannah thought, there was nothing she could do about any of it. Her makeup bag was out by the bed. She was shocked. How was he here?

'So you made it, huh? What are you doing here now? The wedding is over, Rob,' Vicki said in the next room.

'I don't know. I . . . I had . . . I had a death in the family, I guess. I just thought maybe I'd meet up with Hannah and spend a few days in New York. Check out some grad schools in the city. This wasn't exactly a planned excursion. I only got a one-way ticket.'

Hannah listened intently and grabbed her brush to make her hair look sleek and tamed, as if she were in a shampoo commercial.

'I'm going to New York with Hannah too. I'm starting my own business,' Vicki said. Hannah dropped the brush in surprise. It made a thud on the bath mat. She'd been asleep when Vicki had returned to the room, and when Hannah had woken up, Vicki was still under the covers. They hadn't been able to talk since the wedding. With Rob in the room and Vicki discussing New York plans, Hannah wondered to what extent she had blacked out the night before.

'I've already called her fold-out couch,' Vicki continued to Rob, 'so you're on the loveseat. Or the floor.'

'I'm not sleeping on the floor, Vick,' Rob said. Hannah thought he sounded smug. She could imagine Vicki's scowl.

'We'll figure it out,' Vicki responded, more agreeably than Hannah would have expected.

Hannah wrapped a white towel around her torso. It was smaller than she wanted it to be, giving her the option of revealing too much leg or chest. She opted for chest and glanced down to make sure the white terry-cloth covered her nipples.

'So how are we getting to New York?' Rob asked Vicki, whom Hannah could hear zipping her suitcase.

'Hannah has a train ticket, but we might as well just hop in my car. I'm sure I can find a place to park it in Brooklyn, at least for a few days.'

'Do you think I should tell Bee I'm here?' Rob asked more thoughtfully. Hannah pondered the question herself in the bathroom.

'I wouldn't,' Vicki said. 'For a number of reasons that

I'd rather not go into, I think we should all just escape as fast as we can.'

At that Hannah threw open the bathroom door and stepped from the white, wet tile onto the tan carpet. The steam from the shower escaped with her, making her feel as though she were emerging through a fog of dry ice.

Phil

*P*hil was awake earlier than he expected to be. He'd returned to Baltimore from Annapolis fairly early, just before midnight, but had been unable to sleep, reliving the phone call to his mother as he held an ice pack to his swelling hand. He hadn't fallen asleep until after four, and when he woke up at seven, his pillowcase was covered in blood, as was the sweat suit he'd changed into before nodding off in front of the television in the bedroom.

He was supposed to visit his mother today – it had been his idea to bring her food as she recovered from the flu – but he couldn't imagine that she really needed it. He thought she could fare just fine without him this morning.

And now that it was nine and there was movement in the hallways of his condo complex, Phil decided it was time to put in motion the plan he'd devised shortly after 2:00 a.m., when he'd given up on sleep and admitted to himself that what he wanted more than anything else at that moment was not so far away.

He walked to the couch in his living room and sat there until nine thirty, when he heard the sounds of slow shuffling coming from next door. When the noises became louder, he turned on the television and used his remote to scroll through his DVR listings. There was still one *Sex and the City* episode at the bottom of the pack, just after an entire season of *24*, which he'd taped more than a year ago.

Phil brought the DVR cursor to the episode, 'A Woman's Right to Shoes.' Phil hadn't erased it because, secretly, he didn't hate it. It was the one where Carrie Bradshaw is forced to remove her expensive footwear at a baby shower. She winds up losing her high heels and making a big stink about it.

Phil had liked that episode because he also resented having to go around in socks at his friends' houses. It wasn't that he was afraid of his shoes being stolen; it was that he felt like an ogre whenever his feet were exposed. Socks were underwear for the feet, he used to tell Elizabeth. You're not supposed to walk around in them in front of strangers.

Phil had considered erasing 'A Woman's Right to Shoes' after the breakup, and had deleted all of Elizabeth's other programs to make room for more of his own, but he couldn't bear to let this one go, and today it would serve a purpose.

Phil clutched the remote control with his right hand, his thumb hovering unsteadily over the 'play' button. He waited until he heard her footsteps closer to their shared wall before he made a move. When he was sure that she was close, perhaps munching on a bagel on the couch or about to turn on her own television on the other side of the thin drywall barrier, he brought his thumb down and quickly turned up the volume as loud as it would go. He listened to the *Sex and the City* theme song, which played so loud that Phil could feel the marimba melody buzz in his feet. He saw the familiar footage of Carrie Bradshaw walking through New York City in a tutu.

Phil turned to the wall. 'Come on,' he whispered to himself as he waited for her to take the bait.

Hannah

Hannah stopped in front of Rob, her hair still dripping, the towel snug around her body. She took in his sloppy hair first, then his eyes, which seemed darker than the last time she'd seen them, and then his T-shirt, which was covered in dried blood. He smiled wickedly, watching her register the mess.

'Are you going to tell us who you murdered?' she asked, trying to keep her voice flat.

He didn't respond.

Hannah leaned forward. 'I'm not harboring a criminal in New York,' she said, keeping her face a few inches from his. 'I'll turn you in.'

'You wouldn't,' Rob said, his voice low.

Hannah tugged at the bottom of her towel, making sure she was still covered. She and Rob stared at each other silently, frozen. Hannah placed her fingers on a patch of blood on the shoulder of his shirt.

'It's nothing,' he whispered, his eyes glassy.

'Just get your clothes on and let's go,' Vicki barked, snapping Hannah out of her pose. 'You can have a staring contest for the next four hours in the car if you want, but we have to get out of here.'

'So we're all going?' Hannah asked softly. 'Really?'

Vicki nodded.

Hannah moved quickly then, shuffling past Rob toward her suitcase and then back to the bathroom to change. She felt his eyes on her as she emerged yet again, this time dressed, her face covered in a thin coat of makeup. Her wet hair was pulled back, her feet stuffed into flip-flops.

Without asking, Rob picked up one of Hannah's bags and went for the door. Vicki kicked her guitar case under the bed. Hannah watched, confused. 'Leave it. Please. I don't want it,' Vicki said shyly as she grabbed her bag.

They didn't get a chance to say good-bye to the wedding party. Not Bee, who was presumably tied up with family at the optional brunch, nor the other bridesmaids, who were either still in bed with their significant others or had departed on early flights to Raleigh. Hannah thought she saw Jackie in the lobby as she,

Vicki, and Rob ran through the front door, but she couldn't be sure.

Vicki led them behind the inn to the small parking lot, the wheels of their luggage tripping over the cobble-stones.

'I need coffee,' Vicki said sharply just before she threw her suitcase into the trunk and climbed into the driver's seat.

'We can stop down the street,' Hannah offered. 'There are sixteen coffee shops in this town.'

'No,' Vicki responded, as she fished for her sunglasses in the glove compartment. 'We're doing drive-through on 95. I want to get to New York as fast as I can.' Hannah beamed in response.

As Vicki revved the engine, Hannah flipped open the vanity mirror on the visor so she could watch Rob arrange himself in the backseat behind her. His head was down as he reached into his duffel bag and pulled out his sunglasses and a paperback book that he placed on the seat next to him.

Just before Rob put his sunglasses on, he caught Hannah's reflection in the mirror and grinned. He licked his lips and winked at her.

Embarrassed, she quickly readjusted the mirror so she could only see her own reflection. Her eyes were red, but the puckered lines on her neck from the halter bra were beginning to fade.

She leaned down and grabbed the BlackBerry from her purse, suddenly wondering how much of last night was a dream. She found the last text message and reread the three words to make sure she hadn't invented them. 'It's a go!!!' the assistant had written. Hannah stared at the screen in awe.

Then her mind drifted again to the backseat.

She smiled to herself as she gave in and tilted the mirror so that she could see him again. He was already looking at her, his hands fingering the book, which was now in his lap. He leaned back and slid his body forward, placing one of his feet on the arm rest between the front seats. The tip of his sneaker touched Hannah's arm. She leaned into it.

'We're only five miles from the Bay Bridge,' Vicki announced, reading the green sign on the side of the highway. Hannah and Rob flashed matching grins. Hannah kept her eyes on him as she responded softly, 'That means that in two hundred miles we'll be home.'

Acknowledgments

My love, thanks, and awkward hugs go to Pete Thamel, Tina Valinsky, and Shirley Craig, who were bossy; my graceful agent, Katherine Flynn, who became family; my awe-inspiring editor Denise Roy, who makes everything less scary; Bryan Rafanelli, who gave it a name; Sarah Rodman and Devra First, who read the messiest versions; my friends at the *Boston Globe* who keep me in the safest of cocoons; Nancy, Tim, Elana, Ariela, and Sarah Knight for a cool basement; Kathy and Scott Levine; Grandpa Marty Goldstein; Hayley Kaufman for necessary distractions; Stephenie

Meyer for reading material; the Rooney/Russo kingdom; Paul and all Faircloths; Marisa Katz for Annapolis; Jaime Green Roberts and Rachel Cohen; Tom Perrotta; Tito Bottitta and Upstatement; Nicole Lamy and Scott Heller; Julian Benbow and the city of Richmond; Rachel Zarrell; Lauren Iacono; Adam Ezra; Kara Baskin; Sara Faith Alterman; Mark Shanahan, Michelle McGonagle, and Julia and Beckett Shanahan; Elizabeth McQueen, Desaray Smith, and Laura Heffernan; Danielle Kost, Jenn Abelson, and Jessica Douglas Perez; Paige Mudd, Shawn Badgley, Steve Cohen, Bill Ehninger, and Evan Thies, who left an impression; Ed Ryan, who did/does; my sister, Brette Goldstein, who makes miracles; and my mom, Leslie Goldstein, who taught me that the Singles are often the most extraordinary people in the room.

And to everyone who reads or lurks on 'Love Letters,' especially the originals: You are my conscience and the reason I spring out of bed in the morning. I drunkenly kick a shoe – with love – in your general direction.